He kissed her again.

What was one more sin? This time Angelina was so shocked she didn't push him away before Corin could deepen the kiss, could press her against the hard length of his firm body, could run his hands through those soft ringlets. When he did release her, Angelina's eyes were glazed, her lips were tingling, and her knees were threatening to abandon her altogether. She was pale and paralyzed.

"Breathe, Lena," Corin advised, admiring his handiwork with a self-satisfied smile but stepping back a pace from her punishing right arm....

THE PRIMROSE PATH

Barbara Metzger

FAWCETT CREST • NEW YORK

A Fawcett Crest Book
Published by Ballantine Books
Copyright © 1997 by Barbara Metzger

http://www.randomhouse.com

Library of Congress Catalog Card Number: 96-90888

ISBN 0-449-22509-7

Manufactured in the United States of America

First Edition: April 1997

10 9 8 7 6 5 4 3 2 1

There have been a lot of books—twenty—with a lot of dogs in them.
But there is only one Hero.

Chapter One

*P*rimrose Cottage was going to the dogs. Literally.

Corin Knowlton, Viscount Knowle, jumped to his feet. "The devil you say. Not even Aunt Sophie would leave a perfectly good house to a pack of mongrels."

Yes, she would. And did.

The solicitor cleared his throat until Corin resumed his seat. Mr. Spenser was a large man, looking out of place behind Lady Sophie's delicate gilt Florentine desk. Then again, Mr. Spenser looked no more out of place than Corin felt on his spindly chair with the ruffled cushion. Every surface in the room was covered in lace or ribbon or fluttery floral-print fabric. Every surface, that is, that wasn't covered by a dog. A dog that was going to inherit his, Viscount Knowle's, cottage.

"Bloody hell," Corin swore, ignoring the cluster of servants standing at the rear of the study in their shawls and cloaks, "that can't be legal."

"I assure you, my lord, that your late aunt's last will and testament is perfectly legal. The firm of Spenser, Gilroy, and McMartin would not produce an inferior document." Mr. Spenser glared over his spectacles at the younger man, but Lord Knowle wasn't about to be

1

intimidated by any pompous, pettifogging paper shuffler. He'd faced English public schools, French cannon, and the Almack's patronesses. One snuff-stained solicitor couldn't faze him, especially when the man was spouting claptrap about Primrose Cottage having been bequeathed to a motley collection of curs.

"Legal, my arse," Corin said now, setting one of the housemaids to tittering until she was shushed by the housekeeper. "If children cannot hold property, and women cannot hold property, then four-legged, fur-bearing creatures certainly cannot hold property."

Mr. Spenser realigned his papers. "Nor do they in this instance, as I was about to explain. The dogs do not own Primrose Cottage under the terms of your late aunt's will; the house is instead to be maintained for their comfort under the proper trusteeship."

"Ha! I wonder who gets to feather his nest with that tidy little windfall."

Mr. Spenser ignored the viscount's muttered contempt. "Lady Sophie named three administrators: myself, Reverend Benning, and Squire Hardwick."

Three unimpeachable, respected gentlemen, dash it. Corin tapped his fingers on the arm of his chair.

Spenser frowned at him. "Squire Aloysius Hardwick is the local magistrate, my lord."

"I know who Squire Hardwick is, by Jupiter. I don't care if you've wrapped it all in jurisprudence jargon, overseen by a panel of archbishops. The whole thing is crazy. And Aunt Sophie had to be dicked in the nob to think of such a thing. No court will accept that piece of fustian. You do recall that bit about being of sound mind, don't you?"

"Your aunt was crippled in body, my lord, not in her mind. I have here a note from her physician, attesting to Lady Sophie's mental acuity, witnessed by the vicar and the magistrate." Mr. Spenser blew on his fingers, then thumbed through his folders until he found another document. He handed it across the desk to Viscount Knowle. "And another, signed by the chairman of the College of Physicians, who personally interviewed my client the same week the will was drawn up. I myself played whist with the lady not a sennight before her death, my lord, and found her to be eminently rational. I lost ten pounds to her that evening. Oh, and so did Bishop Rushford. I believe General Cathcart was her partner."

So much for impugning the witnesses. Corin was on his feet again, pacing. He was warmer that way, at any rate. Deuce take it, the place was freezing, despite the fire in the hearth that was likely for the comfort of the dogs. The dogs who were hairy heirs to *his* legacy! "I don't care if Aunt Sophie marked the cards! Primrose Cottage was not hers to give. It was supposed to revert back to the Knoll, become part of the Knowlton estate again with her demise."

"Begging your pardon, my lord, but those were not the precise words on the deed." Mr. Spenser blew on his fingers to warm them again, before rifling through another folder. "As you must be aware, Primrose Cottage was originally—and until quite recently as these things are counted—a neighboring estate. It was never part of the Knowle viscountcy holdings, and therefore is not subject to the entailment."

"It's on the corner of the estate, dash it."

"But it is not part of the estate. Your grandfather purchased it himself, with his personal monies."

"Yes, yes, I know. He wanted a private place to bring his mistresses. Everyone knew that. Later my father let Aunt Sophie have the use of it, because it was easier for her to get around in than Knowle Castle." And because Aunt Sophie and Corin's own mother didn't see eye to eye about running the Knoll. That was putting it mildly. Everyone in the county knew the two fought like cats and . . . dogs. Corin ran his hand through his already disordered blond curls, wishing he had his hat. And his gloves. "Aunt Sophie had no issue, no heir, no husband. Nor was she likely to, considering the nature of her infirmities. So Father assumed—no, he intended—that the cottage and its acreage would revert to the estate."

The solicitor found the correct paper. "Here it is. . . . 'Shall be hereby deeded to my sister, Sophronia Rose Knowlton.' You see, there was nothing in your father's will about her lifetime tenancy."

"But that's what he meant! He only included the deed in his will in case Mama tried to—That is, my father thought that if Aunt Sophie did get married or moved or passed on, the land and the house would become part of the Knoll again."

"And so it shall. You can add Primrose Cottage to the entailment as soon as Lady Sophie's last pet goes on to its final reward."

From the look on Lord Knowle's face, that fortunate day would come sooner, rather than later, if he had anything to do with the care of the benighted beasts.

He didn't.

"To reiterate, your aunt left the administration of her estate to myself and the others, but she left the maintenance of the cottage itself and the welfare of her beloved pets to Miss Angelina Armstead."

"Who the deuce is Angelina Armstead?" the viscount demanded, moving closer to the mantel and what little warmth the hearth beneath it gave. He tried to nudge a sleeping bulldog aside with his toe, but the old dog just showed its worn teeth and growled. When one of the servants called out, "No, Windy," the bulldog begrudged Corin an inch nearer the fire, as if it owned the place, by Jupiter!

Mr. Spenser cleared his throat again. "Miss Armstead was your aunt's companion, my lord. I believe you know her as Lena." The older man nodded his head toward a dark-clad figure seated at the back of the room, near the door.

Corin had thought she was just another of the servants, avidly listening to hear the word "pension." He vaguely recalled his aunt's most recent companion, a somber shadow pushing the Bath chair. Yes, there was the gray shawl and the mousy brown bun at the back of her head, under a wide black mobcap. According to the terms Spenser was enumerating, the companion could buy herself a new bonnet or two—or the whole blasted milliner's shop if she wanted. Five thousand pounds outright, plus five thousand pounds per annum for each year she stayed with the cursed canines.

"Hell and damnation," he swore, "I see what happened. A pension wasn't enough for the grasping harpy, so the jade played on my aunt's tender sensibilities. The companion couldn't get the house and fortune from Aunt Sophie outright, so she cozened her into this faradiddle fund for the fleabags."

The figure in back sat up straighter, clutching a small dog to her flat chest, but it was Mr. Spenser who answered the viscount's charges. "If I may read from the will, my lord: 'The above remuneration and recompense I gladly bequeath to my loyal companion and dear friend, Miss Angelina Armstead, unbeknownst to her. My hope is that when all my beloved pets have found good homes or are reunited with me in heaven, my dear Lena can make a good life for herself, for all the joy she has brought me.' Did you say something, my lord?"

Nothing repeatable in polite company. "No, no, go on." While the solicitor droned on about the generous retirements Aunt Sophie left to the rest of her servants, with even more handsome benefits if they stayed on to help care for her dogs, the viscount resumed his pacing. Thinking to look out, or to let more light into the room so he could better see the female who would be living on his property, he parted the heavy damask drapes at one window. Well, it was no wonder they were all shivering despite the fireplace. It might be April, but the day was still too cold for the windows to be open. He slammed it shut.

"Oh, my lord, you don't want to be aclosing—" a servant said.

But Mr. Spenser frowned the speaker into silence. He repeated the last bequest, then dismissed the servants.

Corin stepped closer to the desk. "That's it, then? I get the rest? My aunt was more than generous with her retainers, but I know her fortune far exceeded the amounts you mentioned, even including the exorbitant sums set aside for the upkeep of this palace for pugs."

Spenser coughed. "Ah, not quite, my lord. As you say, Lady Sophie was a wealthy woman. Her mother's fortune, don't you know, was not an allowance or annuity from the Knowle estate," he hurriedly reminded the viscount, lest there be any confusion over the source of Lady Sophie's income.

Corin nodded his understanding, having advised his aunt about some of her investments. "Go on, tell me what harebrained scheme she had for the rest of her fortune. What is it? Buying coats for London's hackney horses?"

The solicitor removed his spectacles to wipe them. Then he used the same handkerchief to wipe his suddenly damp brow. "She, ah, set aside the remainder of her capital, and the income therefrom, to purchase, maintain, and endow a, ah, home for unwanted dogs in the village of Knowlton Heights."

"A what?" Corin shouted. "A home for unmarried mothers, for injured veterans, or penniless orphans—those I can see. Even a home for retired lady's maids. But a home for dogs?" He pounded on the mantel. The bulldog rolled over. Mr. Spenser coughed. Corin ran to open the window.

"Your aunt sincerely believed that we are all God's creatures, my lord, from the highest to the lowest. She did support many worthy charities in her lifetime, but

6

this is what she wished to do after her death, create a shelter or hospital or home for neglected beasts. She hadn't decided precisely what to call the foundation." Noting the scowl on the viscount's face, Mr. Spenser tried to inject a more cheerful note by explaining, "It shouldn't take the full amount of Lady Sophie's resources, my lord. Once the house, kennel, or whatever is built and the endowment is established to provide continued funding, you will inherit the rest."

"If I live so long!"

"Oh, no, my lord, a parcel has already been selected for the site, and an architect has been consulted. Your aunt had hoped to see the project completed before she— But one never knows, does one? Nevertheless, you'll eventually come into a tidy bit of capital, along with the cottage, of course. And it's not as if Lady Sophie forgot to mention you altogether, my lord. Here, this paragraph." The lawyer readjusted his spectacles. " 'Henceforth, due issue, predecease . . .' Ah, here. '. . . Entire remaining assets and accounts shall then devolve upon my nephew, my next of kin and sole heir, Corin James Alexander Knowlton, seventh Viscount Knowle, Baron of Darleigh, Lord Rotterdean—' "

"You don't have to read them all, man. I do know my own titles and dignities."

"Quite. 'Upon my nephew, my next of kin and sole heir, et cetera, et cetera, who presently needs nothing but to learn to appreciate what he already has.' "

Corin snorted. "That sounds just like the old bat. Well, don't expect me to appreciate being cheated of my own property, sir. I'll find a way to overturn that blasted will if I have to petition St. Peter himself. I'm sure *he* doesn't want a bunch of malodorous mutts littering up his place any more than I do mine. Good day, sir." Corin turned to go but paused near the door, where Miss Armstead sat with the rat-size terrier in her lap. Two others yipped at the viscount from under her chair, but the companion kept her head lowered. All he could see of her was the untidy brownish bun at the back of her neck, tied with a black ribbon. The dogs all had black ribbons in their topknots, too. Corin shuddered. "My congratulations to you, ma'am," he said. "For now."

Chapter Two

$\mathscr{A}$ngelina was numb. She hadn't thought she could cry one more tear, not after the past two weeks. Why, all of her handkerchiefs were so sodden, she'd taken to wiping her eyes on the little dogs in her lap. When Lucy got damp she switched to Lucky, then Lacy. They didn't even mind, sharing her grief.

Five years Angelina had been with Lady Sophie, five of the best years of her twenty-one. Certainly they'd been the happiest since her parents died when she was a young child. Her childhood had ended then, too, for she was sent to live with her paternal grandparents. Reverend Armstead and his wife were fervent Reformers, zealous proselytizers, devout believers—in everything except love, kindness, and joy. Singing, dancing, laughing, idle conversation—all were the Devil's devices. Work and prayer, prayer and work, those made a proper upbringing for an unwanted ward from an unsanctioned marriage.

Thankfully Angelina's grandparents were called to become missionaries. At least Angelina was thankful, for she was placed in a school for girls. Although it was a rigid, moralistic type of institution, she was with other young people. The heathen savages must not have been quite so grateful, for they promptly dispatched the Armsteads to their Maker.

The tiny pittance from the missionary fund went to pay Angelina's tuition, and she was able to exchange chores for her room and board. Of course then she was no more than the servant girl Lena, beneath the notice of the other students, neglected by the instructors, abused by the rest of the staff.

There Angelina stayed until she was ten and six, when Lady Sophie Knowlton's housekeeper came, looking to hire a companion for her mistress. Lady Sophie wanted someone young, the woman said, to help exercise her dogs. Angelina would have exercised tigers in Timbuktu for the chance to leave the prison of school.

After a long carriage ride, Lena was left waiting in a vast marble-floored foyer, where she was joined by three dogs that came to inspect the intruder. Already nervous about the coming interview, Lena was quaking in her shabby boots at the sight of the unknown animals. She tried to hide behind an umbrella stand. She'd never had a pet of her own, never even been near enough a dog to touch it that she could remember. All she could think of now, seeing three open mouths and three sets of sharp teeth, was her grandparents and the cannibals. No one had ever said, of course, but she'd always wondered. Well, at least her grandparents had died for their beliefs.

Angelina believed she'd like very much to live in a house such as this, where even the animals looked well fed. She came out from behind the umbrella stand and let the dogs sniff her, lick her hands, and lean against her. Soon enough she was sitting on the floor, laughing and playing and getting her face washed. By the time Lady Sophie was wheeled into the foyer in her Bath chair, Angelina was covered in dog hairs and smiles. She got the position.

It was like having a home and a family—romping with the dogs, reading to Lady Sophie, pushing her chair through the gardens or the halls of Primrose Cottage. Lady Sophie's friends accepted Lena once she learned to play whist, and the servants spoiled her because she made their mistress so happy. And the dogs, well, everyone knew there was no more loyal, undemanding affection to be found. Angelina thrived.

Then Lady Sophie was gone, and with her the life that Angelina had come to love as much as she loved her sweet mistress. Tears wouldn't bring Lady Sophie back, nor the security and warmth that Angelina had found for the first time since her parents' deaths. She'd be alone again, cast off from everything she cherished. She grieved for her friend and grieved for herself. Tears didn't help, but she cried anyway.

Now Angelina wept tears of relief and gratitude that she wouldn't have to leave Primrose Cottage and the dogs, that she'd have enough funds to purchase a small house of her own someday, that dear Lady Sophie had cared enough to remember her in her will. Angelina had known, of course, that Lady Sophie would make provisions for her pets, but she never expected such generosity for herself, such kindness, such care for her future. Tears fell on Lucky, who squirmed in her lap. Lucy and Lacy were barking, so Angelina looked up—to find her ladyship's nephew staring at her.

"You have her eyes, you know."

His brow lowered. "Pardon me?"

"Lady Sophie's eyes, my lord. They were the same blue-gray as yours." They weren't quite, though, Angelina could see now. The viscount's eyes didn't have his aunt's twinkle, nor the tiny laugh lines at the corner. In fact, Lord Knowle's eyes were narrowed and harsh. "You're angry," she said.

Angry? The frumpy female with her eyes all red and puffy and her nose swollen and dripping thought that he might be angry? His aunt wasn't the one dicked in the nob, this shabby spinster was. "Yes, Miss, ah, Armstead, I am angry that my aunt chose to leave part of my family's property to her pets."

"But they were *her* family, my lord. What would you have had her do with them?" She stroked the one in her lap with work-roughened hands, he noted.

"I don't give a da—That is, some provision could have been made if Aunt Sophie had only consulted me."

"But you never came to call, my lord. Last summer, was it, when you visited last? You didn't even spend the Christmas holidays at the Knoll this year."

"I'm a busy man, Miss Armstead, with many obligations and calls on my time, such as Parliament, my investments—" Deuce take it, why was he making excuses to a paid companion? "Furthermore, Aunt Sophie did not precisely welcome my visits. To be precise, when I called last summer, she told me in no uncertain terms to get out and never bother her again."

"You shouted at Caesar," she said, as though that explained his aunt's unwarranted behavior.

"The blasted mutt lifted his leg on my new boots," he shouted again, sending the three little mop dogs into a frenzy of high-pitched yipping.

"Caesar doesn't like men."

From the looks of Miss Armstead—straggly hair, shapeless clothes, mottled complexion—Corin decided his aunt's companion didn't care much for men, either, but she wouldn't—

"We think he'd been beaten by his former owner. A man, of course."

"Of course," he repeated dryly, as though all men brutalized innocent animals. Miss Armstead's opinion of the male gender—human species—was becoming more clear by the moment.

Angelina didn't know any men. That is, she knew Lady Sophie's elderly gentlemen friends and the male servants, naturally, but young men, handsome, muscular, virile aristocrats, simply hadn't come her way. She'd retired when Viscount Knowle visited with his aunt, respecting their privacy, and never left Lady Sophie's side when they were at social functions. Females without looks or dowry or connections were not exactly sought after at the local assemblies. Now Angelina was glad, if they were all as arrogant as his lordship. Haughty, he was, and greedy, to be resentful of the poor dogs with no-where else to go. Still, she owed it to her benefactress to be courteous to her nephew, so she told him, "She went peacefully, you know."

"Excuse me?"

"Your aunt, she died peacefully."

Corin was embarrassed. He should have asked, or at least mentioned some words of condolence, in light of the female's obvious grief. He did not like being put in the wrong, so his voice was gruff when he said, "I'm surprised. I thought the old bat—ah, the old lady—would have gone kicking and screaming, giving the Grim Reaper a part of her mind."

A smile played about Angelina's mouth. "And she would have, if she wasn't ready. But she was content, knowing her pets would be cared for and her foundation would be established. Her only regret was not seeing the primroses one last time, though."

The flowers that gave Primrose Cottage its name were magnificent, row upon row of red and yellow blooms bordering every path. They'd be out soon, but not in time. Angelina wiped another tear from her eye. "I am sorry for your loss, my lord."

Corin didn't know why, but he patted the female's bony shoulder, then found his handkerchief and pressed it into her hand. "And I for yours, ma'am." Either she was the world's finest actress or her sorrow at his aunt's passing was genuine. No matter which, he still intended to see Miss Armstead and the mutts out of his house.

The viscount didn't actually need the cottage. Lud knew, he had enough space at the Knoll to house Hannibal's army, elephants and all. It was a castle, by Jupiter. Then there were his three other homes, plus the hunting box in Scotland and the seaside cottage outside Brighton, without counting the plantation in Jamaica.

Corin did not need Aunt Sophie's small fortune, either, not when he was already one of the wealthiest men in England. He wouldn't have turned the money down, naturally, but he wasn't greedy. He wouldn't have minded if his aunt had left all her blunt to charity or to her faithful old retainers—anything but her dogs. Why, he'd be a laughingstock in Town when the terms of Aunt Sophie's will were made public. Corin, Lord Knowle, did not like being laughed at. It did not suit his sense of dignity, any more than having a dog hotel at his doorstep. Besides, he had plans for Primrose Cottage, plans that did not involve spinsters, setters, or superannuated servants.

To that end Corin detained the white-wigged butler after the old man handed over his hat and gloves. He'd known Penn his entire life, so felt entitled to ask, "Shall you be staying on here, Penn, do you think? Lady Sophie's bequest to you was a generous one, I believe. Enough for you to retire in comfort, I should think, especially if you invest it wisely. I'd be happy to give you some advice on the funds or the shipping trades."

"Thank you, my lord, I'm sure any advice would be welcome. But I could not repay my lady's generosity by abandoning her dear ones at their hour of need."

Corin bit the inside of his lip. "I see. And what of Miss Armstead, Penn? Do you think she'll take the cash and head for greener pastures, now that she is a woman of substance?"

"I could not presume to guess, my lord, but Miss Armstead has never expressed a desire to be anywhere else."

"Her family?" he asked hopefully, but Penn merely shook his head.

"None, my lord."

"Surely she has friends somewhere, school chums or old neighbors she'd like to settle near?"

Penn shook his head again. "Nothing, my lord. Nobody. In the years she's been here, there has not been one letter of a private nature delivered for her. Or received by her. I do not believe she has ever taken so much as a weekend holiday away from my lady. Perhaps that is why she seems most despondent. Why, if it weren't for the dogs, I believe Miss Armstead would go into a decline, so devoted was she to my lady—not that the rest of us weren't, of course."

Blast! Corin thought. The female would be even harder to dislodge than he had believed, but get her out he would—her and her ribbon-decorated dust mops. He had plans for the cottage, the vacant cottage. Corin snapped his beaver hat on his head and started to draw on his gloves. His fingers all poked through the ends of his right-hand glove. The wrist of the left one gaped open, except for one long shred of expensive, dyed-to-order, specially fitted leather. Corin just stared at the remains in his hand. His gloves, the personal effects of the seventh Viscount Knowle, a hero of the Peninsular Campaign, a rising star in politics, and a nonpareil in tonnish circles, had been put through a meat grinder.

The butler followed his astounded gaze, then hurriedly opened the door. "Sadie likes leather, my lord. She's not usually loose in the house, but Miss Armstead thought she was pining for the mistress. What with everything at sixes and sevens with the reading of the will, she must have been upset again."

So the bitch butchered an innocent pair of gloves? Two weeks, that's what Corin would give them. Two weeks and they'd all be chasing balls in Bath or Belfast or Boston. He didn't care which, as long as they were gone. Miss Armstead included.

Miss Armstead was upstairs, lying down. She had a cold compress on her eyes and an Irish setter on her legs. Thank goodness that was over, she thought. And thank goodness she'd never have to see Lady Sophie's toplofty nephew again.

Chapter Three

$\mathcal{V}$iscount Knowle traveled to London the next morning, armed with copies of the will and the deed, a fresh pair of gloves, and a deep determination to resolve this awkward situation before another day went by. Or another misanthropic mongrel took up residence at Primrose Cottage. There was more at stake here than Corin's pride and dignity, more even than his near feudal bond of ownership with his titled estate. National security was at risk.

"Sorry, my boy," the Duke of Fellstone told him, "you'll have to do better than that. We're counting on you."

As soon as Corin had delivered his documents to his own solicitor, with instructions to find a way to overturn that blasted will by nightfall, he'd headed for His Grace's office. It was in a private chamber in a secluded wing of a nondescript government-owned building near Whitehall. Few even in the War Office knew of the department's existence; fewer were admitted through its doors. A stepchild to the espionage division, the Duke of Fellstone's operation controlled sabotage, propaganda, and the dissemination of information Bonaparte wouldn't want his people to know—such as how many Frenchmen were dying in Spain, how many francs the emperor's ambition was costing France while the peasants went hungry. Unfortunately most of the peasants couldn't read, nor could the majority of Boney's troops, or Fellstone would have dropped enough broadsheets and leaflets on their heads to wallpaper every room in Paris. He had four hot-air balloons just waiting on his orders.

Lord Knowle had been drafted by His Grace after a musket ball ended Corin's army career. Viscounts weren't supposed to risk their lives, Fellstone informed Corin. They were supposed to be decorative dilettantes, hey-go-mad hedonists—and loyal patriots. With his noble contacts, the viscount could travel to courts all over Europe, amusing himself and amassing information, meanwhile passing messages among the department's network of provocateurs, sympathizers, and outright paid mercenary rabble-rousers. If some of their pay came from Corin's own purse, well, noblesse oblige and all that.

Now he had a new and unusual duty: to provide secret housing for the fleeing French author of the anti-Bonapartist newspaper *Le Commentaire*.

"No," Lord Fellstone was saying through the pall of cigar smoke surrounding him, "we owe L'Écrivain safe harbor for all the work he's done for us in the past, gathering news, spreading erroneous information about our troop movements, encouraging the Royalists. Besides, although no one knows L'Écrivain's identity, he knows some of our codes and contacts. Can't let him fall into the wrong hands, what?"

"Of course not, Your Grace. I know that the Scribe has been invaluable to the war effort, but surely there's a place other than the Knoll—"

"No, no, too late, my boy. The hidden print shop was discovered in a raid and the pressman arrested. It's only a matter of time before that poor bastard gives up the Scribe, unless he's lucky enough to die first. L'Écrivain's been warned, so he's most likely already making his way to the coast. As soon as your aunt died and you offered that vacant cottage, word was sent. Communication got to France before you got to Kent for the funeral, I'd wager."

Corin muttered an oath under his breath while His Grace sat back and admired his latest smoke ring and the efficiency of his department. "Good men, what? No recalling the message now. Don't even know where the fellow is, much less how long it will take him to make his way across the Channel. Our smuggling chaps have been told to be on the lookout. That's all we can do to help him until he gets here. Too risky to send anyone over there."

"Surely we can get word to him somehow."

"Too dangerous. Wouldn't do to draw attention to him, or to one of ours if the Scribe is taken. Besides, we don't even know the Scribe's real name, my boy, he's that cunning. He'll get out."

Not if he had Corin's luck, he wouldn't. "Let us hope so, Your Grace. Then, when he arrives, we can redirect him to another area. I have a comfortable, secluded property near Brighton."

"Where Prinny and his set congregate? Lud, the place may as well be a fishbowl, what? Besides, the Scribe's not going to arrive here in Town and announce his presence at the Horse Guards, is he? Not if he wants to see the next day's sunrise. No, he'll go straight to Kent, to the location we passed on. Also, it's closer to the coast."

Corin groaned.

"Don't worry, lad, it won't be for long, just till we can get the man back into France with another identity. He's too valuable to lose, and you know every bastard Frog bloodhound will be after his skin if they find where he's gone to ground. Violent bunch, those *Securité* blokes."

"It's not a matter of the length of time at the cottage—"

"Besides, we can't forget the man's a gold mine of information. We need him where everyone appropriate can have access, the foreign secretary, the War Office, the army. Your property is, what, less than a day from Town?

Perfect, my boy, perfect. And with the cover of that house party you're planning for right after the Season, no one will notice one or two government bigwigs among the company. Looking forward to it myself, what?"

Hell and damnation, Corin thought. His future career in politics just stuck its spoon in the wall.

The duke was smiling, thinking of the brief vacation he was going to permit himself. He might even get in some fishing. "No one will think anything amiss with a gentleman disappearing from the company for an hour or two. Shooting, riding, what? Normal country pursuits, like going for walks around the property. Couldn't be better, my boy. Excellent suggestion you had. I'll be sure to tell the Secretary."

Be sure to tell him not to wear leather gloves, Corin thought, but dared not say.

"And inviting Midas Micah Wyte was brilliant, lad, just brilliant. The man travels with an entourage befitting a Turkish pasha. The nabob's got so many servants and secretaries that my men won't even make a ripple in the countryside."

The duke puffed on his cigar. The smoke in the room was so thick now that Corin was feeling queasy, or perhaps it was the thought of Micah, Lord Wyte, coming to Kent, too, with his daughter. Lud, a defector, a deep-pockets nobleman, and a debutante, all tripping over his dead aunt's dogs.

"Don't look so downpin, Knowle, the end of the Season's not far away. Then you'll be able to get Miss Melissa Wyte all to yourself there in Kent, away from those young pups sitting at her feet here in London, what?"

If His Grace only knew . . .

"A few walks in the moonlit gardens, perhaps, or getting lost in the maze? I'm sure I don't have to give a downy cove like you advice, my boy, but if you stop this dillydallying, you can announce the betrothal while all

20

the company is still assembled. No need to toss another do, what?"

"My betrothal?" Corin choked. It was the smoke, he was certain. "There's nothing definite yet, Your Grace. How did you hear about that?"

"We *are* an intelligence organization, my boy, or did you forget? Excellent match, Wyte's daughter. Your blood's blue enough for both of you, but the chit'll bring another fortune to the family coffers, what? Not that you need it, of course. Lovely gel, I hear. A real beauty."

Melissa was a Diamond of the First Water, but Corin wasn't ready to commit himself. At eight and twenty, he needed a wife to fill his nurseries and ensure the succession, a chatelaine for his houses, and a hostess for his political aspirations. What he didn't need was a spoiled and demanding rich man's daughter.

"The visit is by way of an experiment, Your Grace, to see if Miss Wyte likes the countryside and the castle, to see if we'll suit. As you say, it will be easier to spend time alone out of the city, to get to know each other before we make the irrevocable decision. Miss Wyte might find some other, more eligible, *parti* before the end of the Season, someone with whom she prefers to spend the rest of her life."

"She'll have you, my boy. There's no higher title up for grabs this year, no greater fortune, either. Wyte's holding out for both, I hear. He may have bought his own title with the India trade money, but he aims to make sure his grandchildren come by theirs the old-fashioned way, in the blood. The chit won't mind pleasing her papa, either, not if you turn her up sweet the way you handled that French *comtesse* for us. The gel's Wyte's only chick, eh? Excellent. Excellent. I wish you luck, my boy."

His Grace stubbed his cigar out in the silver ashtray on his littered desk. The interview was over. "Oh, and my condolences on your aunt. Send Higby in on your way out, will you?"

* * *

"You've got to find a way, Abercrombie, you just have to! I absolutely have to get that female and the furballs out of Primrose Cottage—instantly!"

All the way to his solicitor's office, Corin had been thinking of alternative solutions to his French spy dilemma. He couldn't pass him off as another guest at the house party, not with that high stickler Micah Wyte inspecting him as a prospective son-in-law. Lud, Corin didn't even know if the Scribe knew which fork to use at dinner.

Whether he did or not, the viscount couldn't offend the War Office's ally by disguising him as a servant, not after he'd served Britain so well and at such great personal risk. Besides, the other footmen and the visiting servants were bound to notice, and bound to gossip about the new man. Corin thought about stashing him in the wine cellars or the attics, but that wouldn't do since so many people, all of them influential, were coming to consult with the heroic bastard.

Some remote gamekeeper's cottage or shepherd's hut? No, the local folk couldn't help noticing such odd comings and goings, to say nothing of a Frenchman in their midst. Did he speak English? Corin didn't know. Lud, how could he keep him a secret? And if Corin couldn't keep him secret, how the deuce was he supposed to keep the man alive?

Hell and confound it, the war was going to be over eventually, and when it was, Corin wanted to be a respected member of the ruling class, not just taking his seat in Parliament, but having a say in the welfare of the country. Who would respect the man who got L'Écrivain murdered? Thunderation!

Abercrombie was his only lifeline, and Abercrombie was letting him drown.

"I'm sorry, my lord," the solicitor reported, nervously realigning the documents on his desk. "But the will seems to be in order. I doubt you'd be able to prove mental incapacity, collusion, or coercion, not with the bishop's signature."

"That's it, then? There's nothing I can do?"

Abercrombie straightened the papers one more time. "I did find one clause of note, my lord, which perhaps escaped your notice."

"Yes?" The viscount was almost off his seat, his sudden movement disturbing Abercrombie's neatly stacked piles. "What did you find?"

"Ahem. In discussing the tenure of Miss Angelina Armstead, your aunt wrote, 'Until the last of my beloved pets joins me in Heaven, or finds a good home.' It would appear that all you have to do is find decent homes for the curs—ones this Miss Armstead cannot fault—then she'd have to leave and the cottage would become your property. Easy as pie."

Finding a home for a dog that hated men, or for one that loved leather? For three of the yippingest little terriers in creation? And what about Windy? Good grief, who'd ever take Windy? No matter, Corin vowed, he'd do it. He'd find homes for the ones he could, even if he had to bribe his friends and neighbors to take the plaguey pooches, even if he had to pay annuities for their upkeep. Even if he had to put an advertisement in the newspaper, he decided. And he'd just have to adopt the rest, that's what, take them all back to Knowle Castle with him. Easy as pie.

Chapter Four

The way Corin figured, he had a week, perhaps two, before the Frenchman arrived, not enough time to get all of the mutts adopted and out. No, he'd do better to clear the cottage of the hairy horde at one fell swoop, then work on getting rid of them one by one. That way he could see the last of Miss Angelina Armstead.

On his return to Kent, the viscount stopped first at Primrose Cottage, at the edge of the mile-long drive up to the castle. Deuce take it, the place was practically on his doorstep. So absorbed was he in his cogitations that he didn't bother to notice that the primroses were starting to show their vibrant colors or that a vase of daffodils stood on the mantel in Aunt Sophie's front parlor.

He should have worn mourning, he admitted, reminded by the scowls and somber black gown of Miss Angelina Armstead. But, dash it, spring had finally come, and he'd tossed off his greatcoat with its black armband. She might be sending disapproving looks toward his striped waistcoat, but, hell, he didn't think much of her appearance, either. The companion resembled a scarecrow in that shapeless black bombazine, something put out to frighten the birds and small children. And her nondescript hair was falling out of its bun again as she bent to pour their tea. Granted, she looked better than she had at the reading of the will, for her complexion wasn't all ruddy and splotchy. In fact, now that he could see her face, Corin decided Miss Armstead wasn't nearly as old as he'd imagined. Her eyes, no longer red and swollen, were actually quite fine, a soft shade of green, somewhere between a hidden forest glen and a moss-lined trout stream.

The popinjay might as well be comparing her to pond scum, Angelina fumed, the way he was rudely inspecting her, a sneer marring his handsome countenance. Handsome is as handsome does, she reminded herself, and Lady Sophie's nephew was a cad. She pursed her lips, set down her teacup, and said, "My lord, your plan to adopt the dogs yourself will not be acceptable."

Yes, she could be a passable-looking woman, Corin decided, with those eyes flashing fire that way. Then her words penetrated his connoisseur's automatic evaluation. "Why the devil not? I saw a handsome foxhound in the fenced yard as I drove up that would be a fine addition to my kennels. There was a capable-looking sheepdog out there, too; I'm sure one of my tenants could use a good shepherd."

"And the rest, my lord? What about the others?"

"Are you suggesting I wouldn't give them a decent home? I have an army of staff and miles of grounds. How could you possibly object?"

"Because you're never there, my lord. You'll be back in London by the end of the week, at some house party or hunting trip or off on one of your pleasure jaunts. The dogs will be left in kennel cages like your own hounds, or alone with your servants in that big empty castle."

"And what's wrong with that?" Corin wanted to know. "It's good enough for half the children in England." Hell, it was how he himself was raised, and all his friends and acquaintances. "We're talking about dogs, anyway, not infants."

Angelina didn't think much of the British aristocracy's system of child rearing, a prime example of which was sitting across from her, cold, heartless, and despotic. That wasn't the point. "Leaving children to governesses and nannies and tutors may or may not be the proper way to care for them, but it's not good enough for Lady Sophie's pets, my lord."

"Deuce take it, Miss Armstead, they're animals!"

"Exactly, and they need companionship, attention, and affection. They were Lady Sophie's friends, not just a collection of living knickknacks. With her infirmities your aunt could not get around as much or be as active as she wished. The dogs were with her constantly, her joy and her comfort in her isolated life. Can't you understand that she loved them and they loved her? They need to be around people, yes, but not some hired servants who come and go. I can let them go only to homes where I'm sure they will find that same kind of love, my lord. It would be dishonoring Lady Sophie's memory to do otherwise."

Corin was furious that this insignificant drudge had found him wanting. He brushed a crumb of poppy-seed cake off his knee and watched the three little ankle biters charge after it. They had gray bows in their hair today. Bah! The sour-faced spinster had grasped the mutts to her meager, unfulfilled bosom as the children she'd never had. Next thing he knew the woman would have them in little bibs and nappies. She'd never part with them, blast her to perdition. "What do they have now, Miss Armstead?" he demanded angrily. "What are you but a paid servant?"

That was unforgivably rude, and Corin felt like an outright dastard to be speaking to any female in such a manner, no matter how buffleheaded she was. Deuce take the woman, now he'd have to beg her pardon.

But Angelina wasn't giving him the chance to apologize. She rose to her feet, forcing him to stand also lest he appear even more of an unmannered brute. "Yes, my lord, I am a paid servant, one of those who are forced to make their own way in this world without being handed every advantage. I refuse to be ashamed of my status despite your arrogant attitude. Your aunt was my employer, yes, but I loved her as I would my own aunt, and I love her pets. Her other employees are equally as fond of the animals or they wouldn't all be staying on to see to their well-being. Even Lady Sophie's abigail is remaining to help with the grooming. So that is what the dogs have now, love that you would never give them with all of your fine houses and hirelings."

Angelina's hands were shaking. How could she have spoken so to Lady Sophie's nephew? She sank back down, as always making sure the chair behind her was empty. Drat the man for making her so angry she forgot herself. It was all his fault. Since she'd already blotted her copybook with his high-and-mighty lordship, Angelina decided she might as well be hung for a sheep as for a lamb and air another of her grievances. After all, she might work for her wages, but *he* wasn't the one who wrote the checks. "Lest you think the animals are neglected, my lord, by myself and the other 'paid servants,' the local children come in the mornings to help exercise the dogs. They come in exchange for lessons, because their patron, their landlord and resident potentate, hasn't bothered to hire a new schoolteacher since the last one ran off with Jeb Allen's daughter."

Damnation, another black mark against him! He'd forgotten all about telling his London secretary to see about filling the position. Corin didn't take his seat—the wretched female hadn't invited him to, and for now it was her house—but crossed to the window, which was open. This time he knew better than to close it, although he didn't see the old bulldog, only the three little beggars at Miss Armstead's feet, under the tea tray. The day was warm enough anyway, though growing overcast, and his

27

war-injured thigh was telling him foul weather was approaching. About as foul as his mood, to be so in the wrong so often with this cursed ape leader, in whose debt he now found himself. Knowing the answer beforehand, he still had to ask, "Who is it, then, who gives the children their lessons?"

Angelina merely nodded.

"Damn. I mean it was devilish good of you to take on the chore, Miss Armstead. I'll find someone for the position as soon as possible."

Angelina was busy crumbling bits of scone for the Yorkshire terriers. She nodded again, hoping his lordship would leave.

Corin couldn't go, not without getting the dogs and their *duenna* out of this house. Blast the woman for being a moralizing idealist anyway, with all her talk of loving the little beasties and honoring his aunt's last wishes. Hah! Most likely she was simply afraid of losing her lucrative sinecure. Miss Armstead could stay here, collecting her ridiculously exorbitant salary, for what? Ten or twelve years or however long one of these creatures lived. She'd be a moderately wealthy woman if she didn't spend her blunt before then, but she'd also be ten years older, ten years less likely to snabble a husband, whereas if she had even half the cash now, and a more fashionable appearance . . . His lordship sat down abruptly, invited or not. "Miss Armstead, I have a proposition for you."

The rest of the scone fell out of Angelina's fingers, but Corin was too rapt in his new scheme to notice. Money was the answer, by George. "I propose to pay you what you would have earned here in five years if you'll give me the dogs. They'll be well cared for, and you can set yourself up in a cozy house someplace else, someplace like Bath or even London, where you might meet eligible gentlemen while you still have your, ah, first blush of youth."

Angelina was blushing, all right, but at her own assumptions, not the viscount's heavy-handed attempt to buy her out of Primrose Cottage. Lord Knowle's reputation, though, and the way he'd stared at her, had her expecting a slip on the shoulder. She should have known better. His lordship was known to patronize only the highest-flying birds-of-paradise, not drab ladies' companions. Then again, he should have known better than to offer her money. "My lord, your aunt was kinder to me than anyone else in my life. I could not repay her so shabbily."

Shabbily? "Seven years' salary and a new wardrobe."

"You forget yourself, Lord Knowle. Money might mean everything in your world. It does not in mine."

"Very well, ten years', and my mother will introduce you to some of her cronies' sons and nephews."

Angelina's cheeks were scarlet by now. How dare the insufferable man be discussing her future as if she were a brood mare and he were paying the stud fees? Besides, she knew all about the viscount's mama from her sister-in-law. If Lady Knowle was so accommodating, Lady Sophie would have remained at Knowle Castle all these years. The viscount would be the owner of Primrose Cottage instead of sitting in its parlor, importuning its mean-time mistress. "I told you, my lord, that I do not want your money. And, although this is a highly improper conversation, I shall tell you that I hadn't thought to look for a husband."

"Nonsense, all women want to get married." Corin thought Lena might even be pretty, with the added color in her cheeks. Take away the wretched cap, add a few pounds or a bust improver, and his mother could easily find her a second son or a half-pay officer to wed.

"I assure you, I hadn't given the matter much consideration." How could she? No one married penniless females with no connections and less countenance. Angelina had never thought to have an establishment of her own, either, yet now she did. She'd been running Lady Sophie's household for years, of course, but always as her mistress's

29

deputy. Now she was mistress. Tradesmen deferred to her, neighbors called on her, the staff catered to her wishes. Even Lady Sophie's superior abigail had offered to help with Angelina's clothing and hair. Who would have believed it? Not scrawny little Lena Armstead, slaving for every crust of bread. But a husband? She never thought a home and family was to be her lot in life. Perhaps in a few years, when the shelter for homeless pets was built and she'd repaid some of her debt to Lady Sophie, Angelina would think about it. For now, she was content with the cottage, the dogs, and a project of her own.

Corin was getting desperate, for he couldn't recall ever having met a woman who wouldn't be swayed by the offer of money or, if not the cash itself, then the possibility of a match with a full purse. He absentmindedly rubbed his aching thigh. What else did women want? "Children. What about children, Miss Armstead? Haven't you thought about that?"

"Yes, I have, every morning when the noisy, uncooperative little rascals go home."

He smiled. "I understand from my married friends that one's own offspring are the most intelligent, adorable, and well-behaved creatures on the earth, each and every one of them. Surely you'd like infants of your own, ma'am, instead of the tenants' brats, instead of my aunt's animals?"

"Perhaps, but I am content for now." Angelina patted Lucky's head. The viscount was speaking so fondly of babies that she decided the rumors were correct, then, that his lordship was shortly to bring a prospective bride to the Knoll. Lady Sophie had thought it was well past time for her profligate nephew to settle down and start his nursery. He must think so, too. Then, why, she wondered, was he so concerned with Primrose Cottage? He'd been speaking with such familiarity, on such personal matters as husbands and children, that Angelina felt entitled to ask.

"Because I have made plans for the cottage, that's all you need to know."

Angelina could just imagine what his lordship's plans might be: a gentleman's usual use for a separate, secluded residence near his family seat. The dastard would set up his mistress in Lady Sophie's cottage whilst he entertained his betrothed at the castle! Not while Angelina Armstead had breath in her body, he wouldn't. "I am sorry for your plans, my lord, but I also have intentions concerning the cottage, and that is all *you* need to know. Accept it, my lord, Primrose Cottage does not belong to you." Angelina was clutching Lucky so hard that he yelped and jumped out of her lap.

The viscount hurriedly stood when it appeared the little dog might jump into *his* lap. His valet was already threatening to give notice over the shredded gloves. Dog hairs would send Doddsworth packing. Corin frowned down at Miss Armstead, who was all sparks and sizzle in her indignation. "By Zeus," he shouted at her, "it was my grandfather's and then my father's!"

"And now it is your aunt's!"

"No, Miss Armstead, it's not. I couldn't have cared less if Aunt Sophie had lived here for another sixty-five years. In fact, she'd have had my blessings, the tough old bird. But she's gone, and I don't own the cottage. You don't own the cottage. Her blasted dogs own the blasted cottage!"

So one of the owners bit him.

Chapter Five

"What do you mean, I shouldn't have shouted?" the viscount shouted. "Now it's *my* fault that your vicious little beast bit me?"

"You were towering over him, raising your voice, and gesturing with your hands. Of course Lucky felt threatened. Besides, my lord, it's only a small gouge in your boot. It's not as though a six-pound dog were going for your jugular vein."

Only a small gouge? There was a six-inch scrape on one of his his new Hessians. Now Corin needed a new valet in addition to a new schoolteacher. And a new career. He rubbed at the spot with the black cloth she handed him, until he realized Miss Armstead hadn't done any such thing. When she had bent down to inspect the damages, her hideous mobcap had tumbled off her head and into his hand.

His lordship might apologize for mistaking Lena's headpiece for a rag, but that was one faux pas he wouldn't regret. Now he could see why her hair was always coming loose: it was a mass of ungovernable ringlets. Who would have thought that the starched-up companion would have such wanton curls, like she'd just gotten out of bed, and a warm, well-tumbled bed at that? "My apologies, ma'am. I'll replace your cap, of course."

"No, no," Angelina quickly contradicted, her hands vainly trying to bring some order to her hair. "The cap is nothing, an old one of Lady Sophie's. No. It is the damage to your boots that concerns me."

Corin regarded her thoughtfully, wondering how her soft brown curls would look threaded through with ribbons and rosebuds, or spread upon his pillow.

Embarrassed by his scrutiny, knowing she looked the veriest frump with her hair every which way and unconfined, Angelina tried to bring the conversation back to its original topic, before Lucky's unfortunate interruption. "I still do not see why you are so wrought about Primrose Cottage that you are acting like the dog in the manger."

"I am not wrought, Miss Armstead," Corin stated, catching himself from wringing the black cloth between his hands, in lieu of the companion's neck. "And I am not acting like any dog in any manger."

"Begging your pardon, my lord, but you certainly are. With all your holdings, you do not need this one small property, yet you're like the dog trying to keep the oxen from the hay he himself cannot use. They are Lady Sophie's pets, Lord Knowle. Why do you dislike them so?"

"I do not dislike them in the least." Well, he wasn't fond of the runt with fangs or the glove gnawer, for that matter, but that wasn't the point. The vacant cottage was. How the deuce was he to convince this old maid to take her menagerie and leave? Corin wanted to get up and pace, which always helped him think better, but she'd only accuse him of being agitated. Besides, he could feel his sore leg stiffening into the limp that presaged a storm. Devil a bit if he would show Miss Armstead yet another weakness, moral or physical. Morals, that was it! He'd appeal to Miss Armstead's better nature, if she had one. Jupiter knew he'd tried appealing to everything else.

"You are an intelligent woman, Miss Armstead, caring

and responsible. I appreciate your devotion to my aunt's ideals, but how can you justify all this"—he waved a manicured hand at the room, the two fires going, the elegant appointments, the platters of cakes and tea—"to serve someone's pets, when there are children starving in orphanages?"

Angelina blinked. The man had a diamond in his neck cloth, and he was speaking of starving children? "I know all about orphanages, my lord. I was threatened with one half my life. Were you? And how can you justify the existence you lead, which is so much more lavish, yet which benefits no one but yourself?"

Deuce take it, how could she put him in the wrong again? "What, are you an anarchist besides?"

Besides what, she wanted to know, but didn't ask. "I don't believe any child should go hungry, ever, no more than I believe honest men should have to beg in the streets because they cannot find work. Veterans should be given fair pensions, farmers should not be thrown off their lands to make way for sheep or factories. There are a myriad injustices in this world, my lord, more than I with my entire inheritance could ever hope to affect in the least, much less resolve. Climbing boys, child prostitutes, impressed sailors—there isn't one blessed thing I can do about them. I cannot even vote for social reform." She stood in front of him, shaking her finger in his face to emphasize her passionate discourse. "You could do something about them, however, with your power, your voice in Parliament, and, yes, your fortune. What are you doing with all of your influence and wealth, other than denying some poor dogs a peaceful retirement?"

"I didn't de—"

"Furthermore, we are all God's creatures, all deserving of charity and mercy. Your aunt believed that, and I believe that. You can make a difference in a great many lives simply by giving the poor what you spend on wagering. I can make a difference, can relieve a tiny pocket of suffering, by helping to found Lady Sophie's shelter for homeless animals. I feel it is our God-given duty to help where we—"

So he kissed her. To shut her up, to taste those fire-breathing lips, to satisfy his own base urges, Corin didn't know which. Surely he wasn't attracted to the rag-mannered female.

It wasn't much of a kiss. He didn't even have time to touch those tempting curls. It was one hell of a slap Miss Armstead dealt him, however. Corin could taste the blood on the inside of his cheek, which was no more than he deserved, of course. "My apologies, ma'am."

"Why did you do that?" Angelina gasped. 'Twas a foolish question, she realized, for Lord Knowle was a rake, and taking liberties was what a rake did. But not with females past their last prayers. Angelina wasn't precisely past her last prayers, for she'd never had any prayers—certainly not of being mauled about by a well-born womanizer, no matter how handsome his countenance or how broad his shoulders.

"I did it because . . . because I wanted to show you how inappropriate your remaining here at Primrose Cottage is. Yes, that's it. You cannot remain here without a chaperon. No lady with a care to her reputation would stay alone."

"My lord, I am not a lady, I am a companion, so I have no need for one."

"Your reputation still matters. This used to be my grandfather's love nest, you know. A single woman, on the edge of my property . . . everyone will assume the worst."

"Everyone will assume I am doing what I've been doing for the last five years: caring for Lady Sophie's dogs, not her nephew! How dare you, my lord! First you accused me of cheating you out of your rightful inheritance by wheedling a legacy out of your aunt. You even declared her insane for writing her will as she did. Then you

35

thought my loyalty to her and her pets could be bought. Now you are suggesting that I am a loose woman!"

"Nothing of the sort. I was merely trying to suggest what others might think."

"You treated me like a trollop!"

"Good grief, woman, it was only a kiss, and I already apologized. Besides, living alone here, you leave yourself open to such familiarity. I was simply showing you how vulnerable you are to unwanted attentions while you stay by yourself in this cottage with its checkered past. You'd do much better to let me care for the dogs while you take up residence at some respectable boardinghouse, or with some distant relation or whatever."

Angelina counted to ten, lest she strike him again. Then she counted to twenty because her palm still itched. Through clenched jaws, she told him, "I have no distant relations, sirrah, and I am not in the least vulnerable to the importunities of any licentious lord."

So he kissed her again. What was one more sin? This time Angelina was so shocked she didn't push him away before Corin could deepen the kiss, could press her against the hard length of his firm body, could run his hands through those soft ringlets. When he did release her, Angelina's eyes were glazed, her lips were tingling, and her knees were threatening to abandon her altogether. She was pale and paralyzed.

"Breathe, Lena," Corin advised, admiring his handiwork with a self-satisfied smile but stepping back a pace from her punishing right arm.

"That's . . . that's Miss Armstead to you, sirrah," she managed to say.

He made a mocking half bow. "Do you see, Miss Armstead? Vulnerable."

Angelina had her wits gathered by then. She stepped closer to the open window, pursed her lips, and whistled. Then she crossed her arms and stood back, wearing a fairly smug smile of her own.

A huge black dog bounded through the window and took up position in front of Angelina, fixing the viscount in its small amber eyes. Keeping her hand on the massive head, Angelina quietly informed Corin, "I suggest you rethink your opinions, rather than repeat your actions. Ajax *usually* obeys my command to release his prey."

Ajax stood higher than Corin's waist and was as wide around as a sturdy oak. His teeth looked as big as the monoliths at Stonehenge, and the low rumble in his throat made the teaspoons rattle. The little dogs stayed under the chair. The viscount stayed unmoving. When it appeared that he wasn't to be swallowed whole, Corin exclaimed, "My word, that's not a dog, it's an elephant! Why, no one will adopt the beast, for only someone as rich as Golden Ball can afford to feed it!"

"Ajax is not up for adoption, my lord. He belongs to me, not Lady Sophie. She said I might keep him for my own after we rescued him from that gristmill. The miller's donkey had died of abuse, so he was using Ajax to turn his grindstone. Ajax was emaciated, covered in whiplashes, and near blind from never seeing the light of day. Lady Sophie cried, before she ran the miller over with her wheeled chair. A very nice family runs the mill now. They took one of the spaniels."

"And you ended up with a creature the size of the whale that ate Jonah?"

Angelina shrugged. "He needed nursing, so I kept him in my room. After that he wouldn't leave my side for nearly a year. Now he's never out of sight or calling. And he is very protective."

"Point taken, Miss Armstead." Corin's leg was getting even stiffer from standing rigid so long, so he asked, "Is there, ah, any way you can convince your bodyguard that I am harmless?"

"Are you?" was all Angelina replied, her hand still wrapped around the great dog's collar.

"Have I a choice? If my alternatives are good behavior

or getting eaten, I swear to conduct myself as a gentleman, on my honor."

Lord Knowle's idea of gentlemanly conduct mightn't quite coincide with Angelina's, but she didn't doubt his given word. She mistrusted his morals, his motives, and his methods of getting what he wanted—but not his honor. She bent slightly to Ajax's eye level, pointed at the viscount, and said, "Friend."

At which Ajax wagged his tail, clearing the table of teacups, cake trays, and two china figurines. He gave a happy woof that shook the floorboards and closed the distance to his new colleague in one mighty bound, landing with his platter-size paws on Corin's shoulders.

The viscount staggered under the weight while Ajax gave a slobbery lick to his chin, cheek, and ear. The monstrous dog also left huge, muddy footprints up and down Corin's shirtfront, neck cloth, and meticulously tailored coat. His leg had been right about the rain. Now it was right about collapsing. From his position on the floor, Ajax straddling his chest and the Yorkshire terriers yapping in his ear, Corin looked over at Angelina. "Couldn't you have told him I was a mere acquaintance?"

An hour later the habitually fastidious viscount was repaired to some kind of order—his clothing, at least, if not his dignity. Corin would not have visited a coal mine in his present state of dress, but it was adequate enough to go home in and accept his valet's resignation. Before he left Primrose Cottage, however, he was determined to make at least some headway toward getting the animals out of there.

"You don't object if I take one of the dogs with me, do you, Miss Armstead? You wouldn't stand in the way of finding decent homes for them, I pray." It was a challenge, and Corin knew it. He wasn't certain he was ready for another confrontation with the confounded female; he wasn't certain he'd won any of their skirmishes yet, except that kiss. Yes, the kiss was definitely a victory, making the defeats almost bearable.

Lena surprised him by being agreeable, likely out of remorse for his ruined clothing. "Of course I wouldn't object to seeing an animal find a good, loving home. Lady Sophie found new families for her dogs whenever possible. That's the principle of the shelter she was so eager to build: that people might come and adopt homeless strays. Of course, her own adopted pets were not to be included there, but, yes, I think she'd be happy knowing her next of kin was caring for one of her favorites."

"My sentiments exactly." Actually, Corin thought the old besom would likely have a good laugh to think of her nevvy saddled with one of her canine misfits.

Angelina's brows were furrowed. "Not Sadie, I don't think, since I suppose a gentleman to have a great deal of leather, gloves and boots and such. And not Puddles or Windy."

"Definitely not Windy. I had in mind that foxhound bitch I saw in the yard."

"Oh, I don't think Bunny is a good choice, my lord. She isn't—"

"Miss Armstead, please. I do know something about dogs. My father's pack of hounds was the finest in the county. I can take the dog—Bunny, is it?—out with me tomorrow, have a good ride, see if we can't hunt down old Reynard."

"But—"

Corin held up his hand, devoid of yet another pair of gloves, due, he was beginning to suspect, both to Sadie and the fact that he'd been too angry to tip the butler and footmen the last time he was here. "You said you wouldn't object, and I'm holding you to the spirit of my aunt's wishes. I am an active man, so none of the ancient articles will suit. Nor"—he shuddered—"will a creature with ribbons in its hair. Bunny is the dog I want, the dog I will cherish and tell my sons about, when I have sons, of course. I really must insist that I know best."

When Angelina ordered Bunny into the viscount's curricle, Corin was amazed she didn't make a show of tears and sad farewells. Perhaps Miss Armstead wasn't as fond of the mutts as she wanted him to believe. Perhaps her noble devotion was a calculated act after all, he speculated, to keep her at Primrose Cottage.

For Angelina's part, she saw no reason to say goodbye to the foxhound. Bunny would be back in the morning.

Chapter Six

*A*ngelina was waiting in the morning room, which overlooked the drive. She didn't think his lordship would keep country hours, rising with the dawn. He'd likely stay abed till nine, then take an hour to dress, another hour to break his fast. Angelina estimated that Lord Knowle would last approximately thirty minutes with Bunny. No, she amended her mental calculations, the viscount was the most pigheaded, stubborn person she knew. He hadn't given up on getting the cottage yet, by fair means or foul, and he wouldn't give up on Bunny for at least an hour before conceding. She was quite certain she wouldn't see Lord Knowle before noon.

Since his lordship was also the most practiced flirt she'd ever encountered, Angelina considered the extra time a bonus, especially given that kiss.

She didn't count the first, hasty touch of lips, only that second, heart-stopping embrace. It was her first real kiss, and the first time she'd been held since she was four. Unhappily for her peace of mind, Angelina had liked it very well indeed. Feelings she didn't know she possessed threatened to overwhelm her good sense. Why, she hadn't even slapped the viscount the second time. She hadn't set Ajax on him, hadn't screamed for the servants. Worse, she was desperately afraid she wouldn't protest the next time, either—if there should ever be a next time.

His lordship was merely amusing himself, Angelina knew. Dogs chased rabbits, as he must be discovering this very instant, and rakes tried to seduce every available woman. Therefore, she simply had to make sure that she was not available. Hence all the tables were cleared of bric-a-brac, and Ajax reclined next to her desk, next to the sofa, and next to the fireplace. The viscount would *not* find Miss Armstead an easy conquest.

Unlike the idle gentleman, Angelina had risen at seven, broken her fast, helped feed and exercise the dogs, and given the schoolchildren their lessons and assignments. She nibbled on a sweet bun while she contemplated the letters in front of her . . . and her future. Perhaps she should consider finding herself a husband, now that she had a dowry to bring to the marriage, and now that she'd briefly tasted the benefits of marital relations. Of course no man she met was like to equal the viscount's expertise in such matters, which was a good thing for unmarried women everywhere, and an unfortunate thing for married ones.

No, she decided, a husband was for the future. Today was for the dogs and for her own past. One letter was to the architect, asking him to call about beginning work on the proposed dog hospital. The other letter was to a London gentleman of Lady Sophie's acquaintance who dabbled in unsolved mysteries, criminal proceedings, and private inquiries. Mr. Truesdale had agreed to conduct an investigation on Angelina's behalf. She wanted him to expend whatever funds were necessary, hire as many assistants, offer as much reward money as would bring results. One day she might have a husband; once she'd had a sister.

* * *

Her estimation was off by an hour. Lord Knowle must have been even less willing to admit defeat than she'd supposed. In either case, Angelina was glad she'd dismissed the children early. Their vocabularies did not need such enrichment.

"The blasted bitch chases rabbits. Every rabbit, every which way. There's no holding her back, no calling her to heel."

"That's why she's called Bunny, my lord."

He was too angry to listen. "Rabbits are the only thing she chases, by Jupiter! A fox ran right across her path, and what did the featherheaded hound do? She kept on, after another rabbit. I had to drag her out of every spinney and hedgerow for miles."

And he looked it, too. His hat was missing, his boots were scuffed and covered in mud, his hair was littered with twigs and leaves. He'd have given up sooner if he hadn't had to confess his failure to this prune-faced prig in another shapeless black gown and floppy black mobcap. Corin noticed that she kept her elephantine protector between them at all times, reminding him of yet another lapse in his good judgment. "A pox upon the miserable beast. No one will ever make a decent hunter out of the bitch, and she'd ruin any pack she was run with."

"That's why Bunny is here, my lord. I thought you understood about Lady Sophie's pets. She took a lot of them in because no one wanted them. Squire would have destroyed poor Bunny, only because she isn't a very good foxhound, but she'd be an excellent companion for a young boy. And she does keep our gardens free of rabbits. Perhaps she could patrol your grounds?" she asked helpfully.

Corin snapped his riding crop, which he had refused to relinquish to the butler and the leather-eating Sadie, against his booted leg. Ajax stood. Corin decided to lay the whip atop the mantel. Now he had nowhere to vent his simmering spleen. Except at the interfering, in-the-way

Miss Armstead, of course. "Thank you for another brilliant suggestion, ma'am. You have been most helpful. But no, since I already have a competent grounds staff numbering hundreds, I do not believe I want a harebrained hound chasing through my gardens, digging up every bush she suspects might harbor a rabbit. What, are your attics to let?"

Ajax took exception to Corin's raised voice. He stood, the hairs at his neck ruffled.

"Are yours, you gudgeon?" Angelina answered, soothing the big dog. "I suggest you take a seat and stop shouting. It displeases Ajax. And me."

He sat, keeping a wary eye on the big dog. "My apologies again, ma'am. The morning has been somewhat trying." Especially for someone momentarily expecting the arrival of a French spy. Deuce take it, Corin couldn't have the Scribe knocking on Miss Armstead's door. In two shakes any Gallic gallant would also be knocking on the door of her bedchamber. Now that the companion wasn't looking so pulled, he decided, she was almost attractive. Lena would never be a beauty, but those wayward curls and wood-sprite eyes had their own appeal. Seeing her pointed chin and prim little mouth, no self-respecting Frenchman would be able to resist the challenge of melting Miss Armstead's icy unapproachability. Corin could barely resist himself. If not for his given word and the gigantic dog, he'd be sorely tempted.

No, he had to get rid of Miss Prunes-and-Prisms. Therefore, he had to get rid of the dogs. Making an effort at keeping his voice and his emotions—which had been composed and collected before he met the maggoty old maid—under control, Corin sat back and wondered how impossible his task was going to be. "Are all of Aunt Sophie's pets as hopelessly unadoptable as the foxhound?" he asked.

"Bunny's not in the least hopeless, except as a hunting

dog. And no, the others aren't necessarily here because they failed to meet someone's standards. There's Pug, for instance, whose mistress died. Her heirs sold the house and were ready to toss out poor Pug, who'd been fed kidneys and cakes his whole life, to fend for himself."

Corin hated pugs, with their protuberant eyes like nearsighted dowagers. Still, ladies seemed fond of them, so he'd have no trouble reducing the canine population at the cottage by at least one. He could send Pug to his mother in Bath. Which left . . . "Precisely how many dogs are there, anyway, ma'am?"

Angelina whistled, two short birdlike notes. Suddenly the room was swarming with animals, big, small, recognizable breeds and mixtures unrecognizable for ten generations back. Most were barking or jumping about for attention until Angelina managed to greet each one and pet each head. "These are the public rooms dogs," she informed the viscount, who'd managed to shut his mouth before it got filled with flying dog hair. "Then there are the upstairs dogs, the kitchen dogs, the servants' dogs, and the outdoor dogs. In all, I would guess—"

Corin held up a hand. "No, don't tell me. Let me have one more night's decent sleep. But I would appreciate a list of the animals, their breeds and so on, so I can ask around if anyone is interested in acquiring a new pet."

"Not without my approval, my lord," she reminded him.

"What, do you think I am going to send Pug off to the coal mines to detect poison gases?"

"I think that Lady Sophie entrusted me with her dogs' welfare. I shall not shirk that responsibility."

"Unlike some others you could mention if you weren't such a lady? I wrote to my man in London yesterday, about hiring a schoolteacher."

"And a doctor, my lord?" Angelina was shooing most of the dogs out of the room or onto cushions placed in

45

various corners. She stopped to rub an ear here, scratch a chin there.

Corin was watching her, appreciating her graceful movements, when her words sank in. "What, never tell me we don't have a doctor, either?"

"*We* have a physician, my lord, but he won't come out from Ashford to tend the farm laborers or the poor. Knowlton Heights should have a medical practitioner of its own." Angelina thought it would be nice to have a doctor who was familiar with veterinary medicine, too, but she believed she'd gone far enough in prodding the prickly peer.

Corin nodded curtly, thinking she'd stuck her busy-body's nose far enough into his business. "About the dogs, Miss Armstead. What's to keep you from rescuing another reject? Another runt? Another mistreated mongrel?" He brushed at the dog hairs on his sleeve. "You could make sure your position lasts indefinitely, and your salary, of course."

Angelina crossed her arms over her chest and glared at the viscount. How could she have thought him attractive? His eyes were a common gray and his hair an undistinguished blond. Why, his broad shoulders might be stuffed with sawdust or buckram wadding for all Angelina knew. And how could she have feared being affected by his practiced charm? The man had none. He was a boor and a cad and a popinjay more concerned with his clothes than with the plight of Lady Sophie's pets. She would *not* allow her feelings to be hurt that he still thought her a grasping, greedy female.

"My honor, Lord Knowle, will keep me from abusing your aunt's generosity, just as your honor will keep you from abusing my hospitality," she stated, reminding the viscount of his gaucherie and her possession of the cottage in one breath. "I will not, could not, sit back and let an animal suffer, but any new arrivals will go to the charity home in the village as soon as it is finished. At that time you may check the dogs remaining here against the list that shall be in your hands at the castle by tomorrow morning."

He noted that the list was to be delivered, not held for his next visit. Being cordially hinted away by the finicky female did not sit well with him for some reason. "I did not mean to disparage your honor, Miss Armstead. I have seen your gentle heart and tender sensibilities." Always directed toward the dogs, he recalled with a tad of jealousy. "I do not want you to be overwhelmed, is all."

Her icy glare of disbelief could have cooled the Sahara. Corin scrambled for a change of topic. "And what about babies? I mean puppies, of course. You'll be overrun soon if you keep all of these animals together like this." Corin prayed she wasn't such an uninformed virgin that he'd have to explain why one shouldn't keep the dogs and the bitches in the same room. He needn't have worried.

"Lady Sophie was very careful about not adding to the numbers of unwanted pets, my lord. Females in season are kept secluded, of course. As for the males, the butcher comes."

He sat up straighter. "The butcher? You slaughter them for being males?"

"Don't be absurd. The butcher comes and . . . and . . ." She made a snipping motion with her first two fingers.

"You have them gelded?" Corin crossed his legs, then tried not to look under Ajax, the poor wretch. No wonder that other dog hated men.

"Stallions and steers are, ah, gelded, all the time. Why not dogs if it keeps them from quarreling or straying or propagating litter upon litter?"

"That's very progressive of you, I'm sure. I am relieved." He was also relieved he wasn't a dog. That bit of jealousy over Miss Armstead's affection toward her pets died aborning, along with any attraction he might have harbored for the frowsy female. "My word, look at the time. I have outstayed my fifteen minutes."

Angelina smiled, satisfied with her day's work.

Chapter Seven

 $\mathcal{A}$ Knowlton never backed down from a challenge. Usually they were wise enough to avoid lost causes and rarely bet on long odds, hence the family's political and financial success throughout England's varied history. Corin wasn't ready to concede, but he was deuced glad he didn't have money riding on his chances of dislodging Miss Armstead and her army. No, he only had his career at stake, that and his future engagement. Let Papa Wyte hear a word of Miss Armstead's living unchaperoned on the viscount's property, Corin knew, and he could kiss the heiress good-bye. No, he wouldn't be allowed near enough to Lord Wyte's daughter to shake her hand, much less ask for it. No matter that the companion dressed like a crow and had a tongue like an adder, Lord Wyte would not tolerate the least hint of impropriety to sully his chick's innocence.

Midas Micah's wealth came from trade, was why. There was no higher stickler than a man trying to prove himself and his offspring worthy of social acceptance. Wyte's birth was respectable enough, if one respected genteel poverty. A third son of a cadet branch of an impoverished duchy, Wyte had married a mine owner's daughter. Instead of living on his father-in-law's largesse, however, Wyte took himself, his bride, and her settlements to India, to speculate and invest. He'd come home a widower with a purchased title, a fortune, and a stunningly beautiful daughter—and a set of morals that were as strong as his desire to see her accepted in Polite Society. Wyte wouldn't entertain an offer from a fortune hunter, a wastrel, or a libertine. At least Corin would still have his wealth when his reputation was gone.

Gone. Corin was going to see some of those outcasts out of his cottage or die trying. While his aunt's old groom, Jéd, now turned dog walker, went to fetch his horse, the viscount surveyed the dogs in the yard. Some were behind fences, some tied to trees and stakes. Why the devil couldn't his aunt have collected pressed flowers?

"I'm taking another of the dogs back with me, Jed," he told the grizzled servant, and added at the other's doubtful look, "Miss Armstead approves. Why don't you untie that spotted chap's lead for me? I'll take him back to the castle at a walk, so you can tell Miss Armstead the dog won't get tired."

Jed spit tobacco juice through the gap in his front teeth as he handed the viscount his reins and watched him effortlessly mount the chestnut gelding. "Domino could run for miles without slowin' to catch his breath, cap'n, but you hadn't ought be takin' him."

"Nonsense, he's the perfect coach dog. It's all the fashion nowadays for aspiring young whips to set a spotted dog on the seat next to them. Just hand me his rope like a good fellow."

Jed hooked his thumbs in his belt. "Nay, I won't be doing that, cap'n."

Corin supposed such insolence came when the servants had no proper hand at the reins. "What, are you afraid for your pension, too, old man?" He waved his hand at the crowded yard. "There are enough animals here to keep you in ale for the rest of your days. Botheration, I've never seen a group of people so goosish over a bunch of dogs." With that the viscount dismounted and tossed the reins over the gelding's head, knowing his well-trained hunter would stand. He stomped over to the black-and-white dog and untied the dog's tether from its stake. Domino wagged his tail and licked Corin's hand. "At least you show some sense," Corin said, patting the dog as they walked back to the patient horse and the grinning groom, "and respect."

Gathering the reins and remounting in one fluid movement, Corin nudged the gelding with his heel. As they set out, he held Domino's long rope to the side. Nothing happened until the dog felt the slack tighten on his rope, then the pull on his collar. Go with a horse? Never! Domino turned into a frantic, flying dervish, snapping at the gelding's legs, growling and lunging for its vulnerable underside. The hunter was used to noisy hounds milling beneath its feet, not ferocious creatures biting at its belly. The gelding was up on two legs, then the other two legs. Then it was on its way back to the safety of the Knoll's stables.

His lordship was on the ground, in the dust and the dirt and the mud. Domino was licking his face. Corin didn't have the energy to push the dunderheaded dog away. He merely lay on his back, staring at the clouds overhead and swearing. Of all the ignominious scenes, this one was beyond imagining. Not only had Corin, who prided himself on his horsemanship, come unseated, but things had happened so fast, before he'd gotten settled atop the gelding, that he'd also dropped the reins like the veriest green 'un. Lord Knowle still held the dog's rope, though. He tossed it away in disgust. Worst of all for the viscount's *amour-propre*, his horse had parted his company in the road, in front of Jed with his gap-toothed grin, and yes, in full view of Miss Angelina Armstead's morning room window. Even now, from his place on the ground, he could hear the door slam, hear her asking if they should send for a doctor, who was, of course, located in the town of Ashford, not in nearby Knowlton Heights village.

Corin sat up, reassuring Lena that he still lived—much she'd care, he thought—to discover a ring of servants and dogs. More than a few of them, he estimated, wore smiling faces. He also discovered that Sadie had also joined the debacle and was even now gnawing on his boot top. All his day needed was Caesar, the one who didn't like men.

His coat was ripped, his breeches were stained, and his boots were ready for the dustbin. His pride was in tatters—and his mood was as black as the dirt that clung to his hair despite the efforts of Aunt Sophie's old butler, Penn. Miss Armstead wouldn't hear of his walking home, not after such a grievous toss, so she was lending him the donkey cart. The donkey cart! He'd be tossed out of the Four-in-Hand Club next!

Before clambering aboard his humble conveyance, Corin threw open the gate of an ebony-colored spaniel's fence. He picked up the silky-coated animal and dumped it in the back of the wagon. Ignoring Miss Armstead's twitching lips, the viscount bowed, then stepped into the cart and flicked the whip an inch over the donkey's left ear. The donkey was so impressed, he turned around to look at the viscount.

It was, of course, Angelina, who, biting her lip to keep from laughing aloud at the viscount's sour expression, had to tell him, "I believe if you just say 'Hup, Dumpling,' you'll get home the faster. Oh, and do enjoy Spooky's company."

Spooky?

Angelina shook her head at male foibles, then went inside to spend the afternoon at feminine ones. She had decided, with the urging of Mrs. Penn, the housekeeper, and Mavis, Lady Sophie's abigail, to improve her appearance. Now that their Miss Lena was a woman of means, they had tried to convince her, she should look the part. She was the mistress of Primrose Cottage, gently born, with education and manners to prove it. She was a lady, not a scullery maid. Mavis insisted the scullery maid was better dressed and had a handsome beau to boot.

Angelina finally agreed. The constant intrusion of a certain London buck of the first stare had nothing whatsoever to do with her decision. The architect would be coming soon, and Angelina wanted to be sure he saw her as the administrator of the animal shelter, not a mere employee. He needn't run back to Mr. Spenser for every decision; Miss Armstead was to be considered a figure of authority.

In sprigged muslin? Angelina thought she should dress in somber colors and sturdy, practical fabrics, but Mavis swore otherwise. The architect, the builders, and the tradesmen would sooner respect a woman of fashion and taste than one who looked like a governess. Besides, wasn't there already a dress length or two gathering dust in the sewing room? And here was Mavis, with thirty years of experience dressing elegant ladies going to waste, and nothing to do but groom Lucky, Lucy, Lacy, and the other longhaired dogs to within an inch of their little lives.

As for mourning Lady Sophie, Mavis clucked her tongue. "Milady never cared for the trappings of mourning, don't you know. It had nothing to do with what's in the heart, she always used to say. And she made sure you'd have a new start at a better life, didn't she? Why, 'twould be disrespectful of her memory to go around looking like old potatoes in a sack."

So Angelina permitted herself to be convinced into modality. The weather was turning lovely and her heavy black bombazines weren't suitable for romping with the dogs anyway. Light, simple gowns were much more the thing. If the high waists and narrow skirts flattered her graceful, slender figure, that was merely a bonus.

"But what about my hair?" Angelina complained when Mavis was done poking and pinning. "I'll never look like a fashion plate with this unruly mop. Can you do anything with it?"

"Gladly," the maid replied, and set to it with a will and a scissors.

Angelina hadn't meant Mavis should cut all her hair off, but she had to admit that the short cap of little curls made her feel younger, more carefree. Now that she wasn't worrying over her mistress, staying by her bedside night and day and later grieving, Angelina was sleeping better and eating better. She was outside more, too, and the sun added a touch of color to her cheeks, a honeyed glow to her brown curls.

Yes, she was starting a new life, this elegant creature in the mirror, even if it was the one Angelina had been born to but had never known. Now she almost felt equal to meeting the granddaughter of a duke, her own sister.

Mavis was pleased with her afternoon's handiwork, too. "Don't you look a treat, Miss Lena. A real lady and no mistaking. Now that hard times is past, blood will show."

Angelina's blood was as blue as any in Debrett's. Half of it, anyway. The other half of her ancestry came from the minor gentry, respectable until Reverend Armstead heard the call from his Maker, and answered by making everyone else miserable. He didn't care about titles, fortunes, or worldly goods. Souls were all that mattered. His son Peter's soul was lost when he ran off with the Duke of Kirkbridge's daughter, Rosellen.

Both of their names were struck from their respective family Bibles, but Peter and Rosellen Armstead didn't care. With his earnings as a tutor and her small inheritance from her mother's estate, they lived comfortably enough for two people in love. After five wonderful years they died together in an influenza outbreak, leaving two orphaned tokens of their affection. Neither set of grandparents was willing to claim the little girls, Angelina and Philomena, yet the Armsteads were too full of Christian morality to throw them on the dole, and the Kirkbridges were too full of pride. So they each took one. That was the last Lena had seen of her sister.

Philomena would look like this, she thought now, staring at her reflection and half listening to Mavis's lecture about wearing a hat and not ruining her hands by bathing the dogs herself anymore. Mena would be a real lady. Lord Knowle would never mistake her for a servant.

Viscount Knowle was soaking his sore muscles in a bath. He'd left the dog in the stable, not knowing if Spooky was housebroken or not. The spaniel had been tied outside at the cottage, and Knowle Castle was filled with priceless antique rugs. Corin did make sure one of the stable boys would look after the dog, keeping Spooky with him at all times, especially at night. With a name like Spooky and a place in Miss Armstead's array of outcasts, the dog was most likely afraid of ghosts. He'd be better off in the stables, sharing a cot with the lad. Not that the castle was haunted, of course, despite local whisperings that Corin did not discourage, since they kept his formidable mama in Bath. No, he thought, scrubbing his hair again to get the road dirt out, the dog was undoubtedly named Spooky because of his black color.

He was a nice dog, too, friendly and intelligent without any demonstrative shows of drooling devotion. Corin decided he wouldn't mind having the spaniel around.

The castle was a big, empty mausoleum of a place. Why, Primrose Cottage could fit in the viscount's private wing. Here Corin was, rattling around by himself except for the scores of servants. It would be much nicer, he decided, to come home to a loyal companion, to uncritical and uncomplicated affection.

Yes, he'd offer for Miss Melissa Wyte, by George. The girl was a beauty and an heiress, and she'd make him an excellent hostess. With her background she wouldn't be too high in the instep to entertain members of the Commons, as well as of the Lords. Furthermore, she seemed like a pleasant, polite chit. She wouldn't make scenes or make a man uncomfortable. Miss Wyte would never contradict her husband, much less shout at him. She was certainly too well bred to laugh at him when he was down.

Chapter Eight

*E*arly the next morning, wearing an apron over the new gown that Mavis, Mrs. Penn, and two maids had stayed up sewing, Angelina proceeded to make the promised list of resident dogs. Some belonged to various members of the household, as their own pets, and would leave with Cook or the Penns or the gardener when those worthies retired. Angelina listed them in parentheses, to make sure his lordship did not accuse her of hiding any creatures. She also wrote down Ajax's name and the three little terriers she could never part with.

Upstairs, downstairs, Angelina double-checked with the maids and the footmen to make sure she hadn't missed a single animal before going outside. She made notes as the schoolchildren brought each dog back from its walk, and led the students on a counting session in the stable and barn. She did hope the vexatious viscount wouldn't take it into his head to verify her count in person, for she doubted a noted sportsman like his lordship would appreciate finding Foxy in the tally. But poor old Foxy had no teeth. He wouldn't last a week out in the woods without Cook's lamb stew and chicken pies and porridge.

Finished with the list, Angelina took it inside to make a neat copy of all six pages while the children were at their lessons. Since most of her pupils were needed at home to help get fields ready for planting or to move the sheep closer to the shearing pens, Angelina dismissed them early again. She handed the list to Tom, the youngest footman, for delivery to the castle.

Tom returned with the donkey cart and a grin. "His lordship wasn't in," the servant reported. "So I left the note with his niffynaffy butler like you said, Miss Lena. Uh, Miss Armstead. That's what Mr. Penn says we should call you now."

Angelina brushed his confusion aside. "Lena is fine, Tom. But what of Lord Knowle? Did the butler say where he was, or where Spooky was?"

"He said they was out together. Hunting."

"Oh, dear. With a bow and arrow?" she asked hopefully.

Tom's grin grew broader. "With a rifle."

"Oh, dear." Angelina opened the gate to Spooky's pen. Then she took off her apron.

Corin was enjoying his tromp through the home woods despite the slight drizzle starting to come down. He admired the new green leaves, the busy chirpings overhead, the fresh scent of growing things. The dog at his side was perfect company, not disturbing the serenity of the day with idle chatter the way a human companion would. Spooky was happy to nose through piles of leaves, investigate fallen tree trunks, and startle the occasional small bird. He'd stand still then, quivering in anticipation, waiting for directions.

"No, old chap, we're not interested in pigeons today."

Spooky would return to Corin's side for a job-well-done pat. Country life was delightful, the viscount thought. Perhaps, when the Corsican was finally defeated, he'd spend more time away from London. He'd go to Town for Parliament's sessions, of course, but maybe he wouldn't devote so much of his effort to the political machinations beyond taking his seat. He had responsibilities here in Kent, too, after all. A property the size of the Knoll didn't run itself.

Corin didn't think he'd miss London. He didn't pine for the late nights, the boring receptions, the interminable dinners, or the constant gossip and gambling. He didn't regret not seeing another production of *Romeo and Juliet* or another assembly at Almack's. Even his favored pastimes of sparring at Gentleman Jackson's or shooting at Manton's gallery could easily be foregone. Corin had exercise and camaraderie right here, in his own home woods.

All he'd need to be content, he thought, was a pretty little wife waiting patiently at home, puttering in the rose garden and providing him with the required heirs. The only thing he did regret missing, being in the country, was the chance to fix Miss Melissa Wyte's interest. Every gentleman in Town, it seemed, was throwing himself and his empty purse at her dainty little feet. Corin shrugged. There'd be other heiresses. There wouldn't be many days as perfect as this one, even if the viscount's corduroy jacket was growing heavy with moisture and his game leg was beginning to ache.

Then Spooky flushed a covey of quail. "Now that's more like it, sir!" Corin congratulated the dog, taking aim. Boom! went the rifle, "A-woo" went the dog. Thud went the falling bird, and thud went Lord Knowle as Spooky knocked him off balance by running right between his legs. A ghost couldn't have disappeared into thin air any faster than the spaniel fled the woods and the loud noise.

He'd strangle her this time, Corin decided as he brushed leaf mold off his shirtfront. No matter that she hadn't even been in the yard when he'd taken Spooky, it was all Miss Armstead's fault. Hell, his being in this benighted backwoods was her fault! If she'd just behave like a rational person, taking his money and her dogs elsewhere, he could leave Primrose Cottage to the spy, leave the Knoll to his stewards, and leave his card at Miss Wyte's house tomorrow afternoon.

Instead, he'd spend the cursed morning marching through miles of wet woods in sodden garments, looking for the world's most useless gundog. Poachers could be lurking in the woods, or itinerant bands of starving ex-soldiers. Lud knew what would become of Spooky if he fell into their hands. And Lud knew what would become of Corin if Miss Armstead found out!

Damn and blast, he had to find the muttonheaded mutt. So the viscount shouted himself hoarse and walked himself lame. He missed lunch and he missed tea, and most of all he missed his clubs and his comfortable town house. With every miserable mile, Corin got madder. Seeing Spooky happily gnawing on a meaty bone back in his enclosure at Primrose Cottage made the viscount see red.

"You could have told me the bloody dog was gun-shy, damn you!" he shouted, even more furious with himself for not realizing the dog could find his way back home more easily than Corin could.

"You didn't ask, did you?" Angelina replied from the front doorway where she stood, Corin noted, out of the weather.

He also noted six smirking servants and one immense, alert dog. Lowering his voice, he ground out, "I shouldn't have to ask, by all that's holy! No one keeps a dog that runs away at the sound of a rifle. He's useless!"

"Lady Sophie didn't think so. Spooky sat by her chair all the time." Angelina knew she was wasting her breath. "Oh, do come inside, my lord, before you take your death from the rain. I'm sure you'll blame that on me, too."

"Who else?" he muttered, but stepped through the doorway and wiped his muddy boots on the mat Penn had put there for the dogs. Then he saw Miss Armstead. That is, then he actually looked at Miss Armstead.

One look at her and Lord Wyte would pack his little heiress back to London, if not India. The sanctimonious old sod would be sure Corin couldn't resist making Lena his mistress. Hell, no man could resist. Seeing that artless elegance, the delicate blush, the perfect roundness, Corin wouldn't be surprised if Lord Wyte wanted her for himself, what with his wife gone these past years. No man was monkish enough to look at Miss Armstead and not see Aphrodite.

Miss Armstead wasn't beautiful, the viscount told himself; it was the change in her appearance that so stupefied him. He had to stop staring like a schoolboy who'd never seen a pretty girl before. He had to stop his heart from pounding loudly enough to send the little terriers into barking fits. First he had to run home to cancel his instructions about the new schoolteacher and doctor.

Only last night Corin had written to his man in London that he wanted energetic young fellows to fill the demanding positions. Now he wanted to hire foggy-eyed octogenarians. Married ones.

No, Corin realized. Getting the chit married off was the best solution to his problem, even if it wasn't his favorite solution. Deuce take her, Miss Armstead would likely marry his hireling and move the blackguard into Primrose Cottage with her, just to spite Corin. He'd have to check with his solicitor to see if she could do so.

Then again, thinking of her as another man's mistress didn't sit much better. Some lucky chap would be able to take her upstairs, or take her right here in the morning room. There must be a rug without dog hair on it somewhere in Primrose Cottage.

Confound it, the jade was all prettified to entertain a gentleman at Corin's cottage! That was the outside of enough, when she was looking at him like something that crawled out from under a rock. Most likely he smelled that way, too, after searching for Spooky half the day.

Corin had to get a hold of himself. The woman was no

enchantress; she was a nuisance sent to plague him for all his sins. So what if she had cherubic curls and tempting curves, milky white skin and swanlike grace? She had no business being here, and he had no business lusting after her.

Now that he had his head convinced that his aunt's bothersome companion wasn't worthy of his regard, his lordship could work on convincing his body. It was easier to turn away, to stare out the window.

What he saw outside could dampen any man's ardor. Dogs. And more dogs. "By all that's holy, isn't there one of the mangy beasts that I can take home?"

Angelina joined him at the window. "None of the animals you're looking at. They are working dogs, not used to being indoors, for the most part. And they don't have mange. What about Pug?"

Corin hated pugs. He loved lilacs, which was what she smelled of, drat the distraction. "What about that good-looking collie? I've always admired their intelligence."

"That's Gemma, Ti Wingate's dog. Ti is one of your tenant farmers."

"I do know the names of my tenants, Miss Armstead. I am not an absentee landlord."

Angelina raised one eyebrow, but did not comment. "Gemma is retired now, of course."

"What do you mean, retired? Not even Aunt Sophie would give dogs pensions."

"No, but she'd give them a loving home when they got too old to work. Gemma developed a limp," she said, as if that explained the dog's presence.

"If the dog is injured, why the deuce wasn't it destroyed?" Bad enough they were harboring singularly inept animals, but breakdowns, too? It would be like a breeder keeping every racehorse past its prime.

Angelina's chin rose a notch. "I notice you limp, my lord," she pointed out. "Has anyone suggested putting you out of your misery?" The sparks in her eyes seemed to indicate that the idea had merit.

"Devil a bit, are you comparing me to a dog?" He held up a hand. "I take that back, Miss Armstead. I don't want to know. I'd lose."

She ignored him in her eagerness to explain, to convince him, to break through his wall of cynicism and uncaring. "Gemma's not suffering. Look at her trying to herd the other dogs into one area. She's just slow, too slow to work Ti's sheep. But she worked them all her life: winter, summer, cold, and rain. Don't you think she deserves a peaceful old age?"

"Well, yes, but Ti—"

"Ti came to beg Lady Sophie to take her, and he is a proud man. It broke his heart to part with Gemma, and he still visits her when he can, but the old dog had to go when he bought a younger one. Ti simply couldn't afford to feed another mouth."

Corin hit his fist against the windowsill. "I suppose you hold me to blame for that, too, ma'am."

She shrugged. "Times have been hard." And he'd been in London, Paris, Vienna. "Your people needed you."

"My people are well looked after, Miss Armstead." And his land steward would be sacked tomorrow. "You are meddling in affairs and traditions you do not understand. The fact is that farmers and sheepherders do not keep pets."

"Precisely. That is why we need the shelter, my lord. I am meeting the architect out at the old Remington place this very afternoon to get started. Isn't that marvelous?"

"Splendid." Miss Armstead not only looked like a newly emerged butterfly, she was acting like one, too. The peagoose was flitting off to meet a total stranger at an isolated property somewhere. "Absolutely perfect. I'll drive."

Chapter Nine

"*Y*ou must have been one of those children who brought home every orphaned lamb and broken-winged sparrow," Lord Knowle commented later that afternoon when they were driving in his curricle to the abandoned estate. A hot bath and a change of clothes had restored his temper—that and the thought of Miss Armstead's being convinced to move her entire establishment to the new property. The sooner the better for his peace of mind.

She had on another new frock, he noted, with a matching spencer and a silly little bonnet all trimmed in silk flowers. The companion rivaled the sweetness of May, and it was only April. Spring wasn't the only thing rising. Corin shifted on the curricle's seat and dragged his attention back to his cattle. "I can imagine you with a lapful of kittens." He could imagine her many ways, but this was safest.

Angelina lowered her eyes. "I was not permitted to have a pet when I was a child."

"What, not even a canary?"

"My grandparents did not allow animals in the house."

"What about your parents?" he asked, blatantly fishing for information.

"They died when I was very young. My grandparents had the task of rearing me. They were religious," she added, as if that explained everything.

Corin didn't think much of a religion that denied a child a playmate, if only a fish in a bowl. He remembered all the frogs and snakes and mice he'd dragged home to terrorize his sisters, all the foxhounds his father kept indoors and out, despite his mother's protests. There was a tame crow, the kitchen cats, and even a ferret Corin had bought from the rat catcher. He wondered if his old nursery room still held that distinctive odor.

His had been a privileged childhood, his lordship knew, but even the poorest household in the parish kept a mouser or two. Miss Armstead was obviously educated and refined, which spoke of enough blunt to support a turtle, say, or a pair of finches.

"It wasn't the money," she said, almost reading his thoughts. "Reverend Armstead and his wife believed that anything that distracted from the worship of God was evil."

"I'm sure God rewarded such devotion." Corin spoke sarcastically, wondering how a child would fare under such fanaticism.

"They were eaten by cannibals."

So much for that topic of conversation. Corin felt he had perhaps a shade more information than he wanted. Cannibals, by Jupiter. "I pity St. Peter if your relations meet up with Aunt Sophie at the pearly gates. She was certain that all her little darlings would be joining her there. I imagine Reverend Armstead would protest vehemently."

"He'd be certain to treat St. Peter to a sermon on sanctity and the sin of worshiping false gods. Mrs. Reverend Armstead would be on her knees, scrubbing away all traces of the filthy beasts. Cleanliness is next to godliness, you know."

With more sympathy than he had believed he could feel for the usurper at his cottage, Corin asked, "What happened to you then, after your grandparents got eat—ah, went on to their final reward?"

"I stayed on at the school my grandparents chose for me, Children of the Divine Academy. Needless to say, there were no animals there, either, although I did manage to keep a cricket in my Sunday shoes for a week. I would have been forced to stay on there, as instructor or servant, if not for Lady Sophie."

What an abominable life. No wonder Lena had a sharp tongue and a prim outlook. And no wonder she was so loyal to his dotty aunt. "Well, you are making up for the lack of pets now," Corin noted, brushing at his shoulder where Ajax was slobbering onto Weston's finest Bath superfine coat.

The big dog was on the groom's bench behind them, with his head between Corin and Angelina. In addition, a small, furry white dog, Diamond, sat in her lap. A Maltese, Lena called him. A barracuda, Corin would have guessed from the puncture wounds on his hand. All he'd done was try to pet the little maggot.

"Diamond can't see very well," Angelina explained. "He must have thought your fingers were some kind of threat. Or perhaps a treat."

Fine, Corin thought, he was wasting his efforts transporting a female and two canines, one blind and one Brobdingnagian. Miss Armstead would have been safe with her two watchdogs, and he could have better spent his time going to London, groveling.

"It's so kind of you to drive us, for Diamond does like an airing now and again. Lady Sophie often took him in the carriage when we went calling in the neighborhood. I couldn't have brought him along in the donkey cart, my lord, so I am doubly grateful."

Then again, Corin decided, winning one of his first smiles from Miss Armstead meant his day wasn't wasted after all.

He was even more gratified that he'd escorted Lena

when they reached the Remington place and met the architect. Averill Browne was slightly younger than the viscount's own eight and twenty, and good-looking, if one admired the poetic mein, the long titian hair curling around his shoulders, dreamy eyes, and a soft, wet-lipped mouth. The nodcock was wearing a loosely knotted kerchief at his throat and yellow cossack trousers.

Browne obviously admired Miss Armstead. As soon as Corin handed Lena down from the curricle—incidentally earning the viscount another needle-toothed nip from Diamond—the architect dropped his portfolio and, it seemed, his heart at her dainty feet.

Clumsy clunch. Corin hated him on sight, and more so when the dirty dish started play wrestling with Ajax. The dastard even fed Diamond a bit of cheese without losing any blood. Then he proceeded to enthuse about the project ad nauseam, saying what pleasure he'd get from helping to build a shelter for their needy four-legged friends. Pleasure? Corin thought. Hah! Browne would be getting a big chunk of Aunt Sophie's blunt! And the jackanapes would be needing a new nose if he didn't stop pawing at Lena under the guise of showing her how the old house could be extended, how the barn could be converted to a hospital. The architect's enthusiasm was all for Lena's benefit, Corin swore. And damn if he didn't feel he had to invite the dastard to stay at the castle, rather than at the inn in town, so he could keep an eye on the loose screw. Not even her devoted dogs could protect Miss Armstead from falling for the architect's Spanish coin.

Well, that went fine, Angelina thought after the viscount left. Her very first curricle ride had rendered her so nervous she'd held Diamond tightly enough that the little dog got skittish. But it was so fast, so high, so exhilarating once she was used to it, that the drive home was much too short.

And the architect seemed a pleasant, competent, caring

man. She could tell he liked dogs, too. Mr. Browne might appear young, but his ideas were sound and he listened to her as to an equal. Mavis must be right, that he saw a lady, so he treated her with the respect due a lady. And Angelina's good impression of the architect was not simply due to his flattering attentions; even the viscount approved of him, going so far as to invite Mr. Browne to put up at the castle.

Work on the shelter was going to begin as soon as the solicitor released funds for lumber and carpenters, now that Miss Armstead had approved the final plans. Lady Sophie's dream of a place for strays was really going to come true. Angelina thought that dear lady must be smiling up in heaven, for the sun was shining brightly again.

Lady Sophie would be pleased to know that her nephew had behaved just as he ought also, asking Mr. Browne to hire local men when possible, offering his steward's assistance in selecting the best workers. He was a decent man and charming company, Angelina had to concede, when he wasn't ripping up at her or taking liberties. Why, he even took her advice about a dog to take home, a first for the prideful peer.

Lady Sophie had believed it was important to match personalities when picking a new owner for one of her darlings. In that case, his lordship should have a strong-willed, volatile, and unpredictable dog with a pedigree a mile long, which he'd hate. Angelina knew firsthand that the viscount resented anyone more stubborn than himself. He wouldn't want a fussy little dog or a placid rug warmer or a demanding player, either. No barkers, biters, or chewers; his lordship had no patience. Rough-and-tumble half-grown pups were out, as were any dogs without exemplary house manners. Angelina had been awed at her tour of Knowle Castle; she wasn't about to jeopardize the Ming vases and Aubusson carpets and polished hardwood floors, or give the viscount an excuse to banish the dog to the kennels. Squirrel was endlessly energetic, Cookie had a digestive complaint, Simon was unfortunately simple, and Puddles would be intimidated into an indiscretion if the viscount raised his voice. Which he did fairly frequently, in Angelina's experience. And his lordship did not like pugs.

Unfortunately, most of the dogs at Primrose Cottage were there because they weren't perfect. That is, Angelina thought each animal was perfect in its own way, just not perfect for the fastidious, formidable nonesuch.

If his lordship were a plain country squire or a farmer or the owner of an ordinary house, Angelina would have no problem. If he didn't half believe the world revolved around his wants and desires, she'd have a handful of dogs to offer. If she thought for one moment that he wanted a dog to love and to cherish, good traits and bad, the same way the dog would accept him, then she'd let him choose.

In the end she sent him home with Molly, a sweet, middle-aged bitch of indeterminate breed that they'd found starving at the side of the road. "Just feed her," Angelina advised, "and she'll be a good friend to you."

How could Corin refuse those big, soulful eyes? The dog had nice eyes, too, intelligent and warm, so Lord Knowle took Molly up with him in the curricle, where she sat like a lady. Walking her back from the castle's stables, Corin stopped at the kitchens, thinking of Lena's suggestion to keep the dog fed—or was it a warning? Something was grievously amiss with each of those other tail-wagging waifs, so what was Molly's particular vice? If the dog got hungry would she eat the furniture, the wallpaper, or the upstairs maid?

Corin never got to find out because his highly paid Belgian chef was delighted to have an appreciative audience for his culinary expertise. Henri fed the dog tidbit after tidbit from platters that looked suspiciously like the viscount's supper. When it was time to leave the kitchens, time for Corin to dress for his own sadly depleted dinner, Molly forgot her name and her manners. The dog had discovered Utopia. She wasn't leaving.

Confound it, his own dog didn't like him! Corin calculated the disloyal bitch had taken less than two hours to find someone she liked better. Lena must have known what would happen, of course. She'd most likely be laughing even now, but he'd have the last laugh. He'd finally gotten one dog out of Primrose Cottage. Corin might be bailing a big boat with a small bucket, but it was a start. Besides, now he wouldn't feel guilty about leaving Molly behind when he went to London in the morning.

Before Corin left, however, he had to stop by the cottage to warn Miss Armstead. "I know you think your reputation is solid as stone, but things have changed. Without Aunt Sophie, you're not an employee under her protection; you're a doggie do-gooder, subject to gossip and speculation. If you wish to remain in Knowlton Heights, remember that this is a small town whose residents have little to discuss except strangers."

"And you, their lord and master. You have always been the townspeople's favorite topic. I swear, the Glenmore sisters know the name of your latest London *cherie* before your first waltz with her is ended. So if you're preaching discretion, my lord, I suggest you look into your own behavior."

"Zeus, Lena, I'm a man. No one cares how many women I bed."

"Your aunt cared." And she cared, Angelina feared. The devil take the man, here he was, leaving her alone at last, and Angelina was greatly afraid that she was going to miss him. "That's Miss Armstead to you, sir."

"Very well, Miss Armstead, then try to remember you are a lady now."

She drew herself up. "I have always been a lady." Except for when he kissed her.

Except for when she kissed him back, Corin was thinking, which act he was tempted to repeat, except for the presence of Ajax. "Thunderation, woman, I am not accusing you of impropriety. I'm merely trying to warn you against spending your days alone with that architect fellow. It won't look right to the people you want to impress. At least take that maid of my aunt's, the one who's got nothing to do now anyway."

Angelina scratched the big dog's ears and allowed as how she would consider his suggestion, when it was convenient for Mavis.

Corin nodded. He'd done his best to spike the architect's guns. "Oh, and one other thing before I leave: Do you speak French?"

"Only what they teach schoolgirls. Enough to get by with your aunt's mantua maker in Tunbridge Wells. Why?"

"Nothing important. A certain Frenchman might stop by looking for a place to stay, that's all. If he does arrive before I return, send him on up to the castle. I'll tell Penn, too, and the men in the stables."

"Very well, what's your friend's name?"

Corin brushed a dog hair off his sleeve. He did not meet her direct green gaze. "I don't know."

"A foreign gentleman is going to stop at my home, and you don't know his name?"

"Dash it, it's a favor to a friend, and the Frenchman's name makes no never mind. I've already got a Byronic house builder up at the castle, what's one Frenchman more or less? Simply send him along like a good girl." Corin bowed and rode off, thinking that he'd brushed through that coil nicely.

Angelina was thinking that she finally understood why the viscount was so determined to get her out of Primrose Cottage. He didn't want it for his mistress, no, he had even more havey-cavey motives. The villain wanted to use Lady Sophie's home for a smuggling operation. A favor to a friend, hah! That's why Lord Knowle was never around, she reasoned. He was too busy directing an illegal-import band. Everyone knew the free traders operated on the coast, but they must need an inland loading station, too. The cottage would be perfect once the vile viscount had the place vacant, standing isolated as it was. His poor aunt must be having kitten fits in heaven.

One Frenchman more or less? How many spies was the viscount expecting to come ashore with the booty? Smuggling was bad enough but treason was even worse, and him a retired officer. The only questions in Angelina's mind were whether she should notify the magistrate or the Preventive Officers, and how soon after his traitorous lordship left could she go reclaim Molly.

Chapter Ten

"What's that, my boy, you want to go to France?" the Duke of Fellstone asked. His Grace blew a puff of cigar smoke Corin's way. "No need, lad, no need at all. And too dangerous now, what?"

Corin cleared his throat. "Yes, but I thought that since L'Écrivain hasn't made an appearance, I'd go help the fellow get out of France. As you say, as long as the Scribe is in danger of falling into Fouché's hands, none of our other agents are safe. If taken, the Scribe could cry rope on any number of our people, give up whatever codes he was using to pass on information to his contacts."

"No codes, and only one contact, Knowle; that's all the scribbler would deal with. Safer all around, what? Even if it meant we didn't know the bloke's identity. That chap, the contact, is already in London, safe as houses. We aren't complete codsheads, what?"

Some of them would be kippered herring before this was over, unless Corin managed to intercept the spy. His eyes watering from the smoke, he asked, "What does the man say? Our agent, that is, does he say where the Scribe is now? How soon we can expect him, which bit of coastline to watch? Anything?"

His Grace nodded his approval. "Good of you to be so concerned over L'Écrivain. One of the best anti-Bonapartists we've had, of course, deserves our solicitude. Brilliant essayist, what? But you don't have to worry, lad, our man says the Scribe is safe for now in some hidey-hole. Didn't know where or when—L'Écrivain was too downy a bird to tell in case our lad got himself arrested before leaving France—just that she'd be on her way soon."

"But how soon, dash it, and—She?"

"Clever, what? Never would have guessed it myself, a female propagandist. And that's not the best part."

"It's not?" Corin was suddenly yearning to light up a cigar, too.

"No, the best part is that our man knows her real name. He can tell us at this point because the game is over. If Mademoiselle Lavalier does get back to France, she cannot resume her identity. Too well known, what?"

"Mademoiselle Lavalier?" the viscount asked with a sinking feeling. "Not . . . ?"

His Grace chuckled, which turned into a coughing fit. Corin jumped up and poured him a glass of wine from the decanter on the desk. He poured himself one, too, not waiting for an invitation.

"Not Mercedes Lavalier, the dancer? Not the most popular courtesan in Paris?" If ever there was a time for God to answer prayers, Corin thought, this was it.

He obviously hadn't prayed loudly enough, for the duke slapped his thigh. "The very one. I couldn't believe it myself, but I had someone over there check. La Lavalier hasn't performed at the French court in a fortnight, and hasn't been seen on any officer's arm lately, either. Besides, her house was ransacked by the security police. That ought to tell you something."

Yes, that he was a dead man. "But . . . but . . ."

His Grace picked up another cigar and puffed and puffed until he had it lighted properly. "I know, I found it hard to reconcile myself, that dasher composing those essays. But it's no wonder she was able to get us such valuable information and so much of it. They say Mercedes Lavalier has been with every officer in Napoleon's army and every adviser in his cabinet. Brave and brazen, fine combination, what?"

"But I cannot bring the most notorious cyprian in France into my home!"

His Grace set the cigar aside. "Of course not, lad. Not fitting at all. Never expected it of you. That little cottage will do just fine."

Oh, hell.

"Couldn't be better, or safer for our ally. If anyone notices her, they'll think she's your *chère amie*. What could be less suspicious? A well-set-up chap like yourself is bound to have an elegant bit of fluff stashed away on the corner of his property."

Viscount Knowle already did. Several elegant bits of fluff, in fact. He still bore the tooth marks from one of them. "But it's impossible. All the company, the house . . ."

"The woman is an entertainer, my boy. What's more natural than for your gentlemen guests to go be entertained? Looking forward to seeing her dance myself. That is, looking forward to seeing what new details she's able to give us about the Corsican's operations. Big service to your country, what?"

What if he just threw himself on a French cannon?

Before leaving London, Lord Knowle interviewed applicants for the position of schoolteacher, rejecting every one of them. All of those who replied to his secretary's inquiries were studious, sincere, single young men. But Corin had heard the children laugh during Miss Armstead's lessons. He wanted someone like that, who would make learning a pleasure, not a self-righteous scholar like his own tutors and dons. In addition, none of the applicants admitted to liking dogs. They couldn't even understand what the viscount's question had to do with informing young minds. Corin wasn't sure, either, but he was certain it was important.

He visited his clubs to hear the latest *on dits*, thankful that his name wasn't one of them yet. He stopped by Tattersall's to look over the newest batch of auction horses. The Knoll's stables didn't boast of many ladies' mounts, discounting his sisters' ancient ponies. If he was having guests this summer—Gads, would he have to mount Mademoiselle Lavalier also? On a horse, that is. No, she wouldn't be in Kent long enough. Corin fully intended to ship her off to another of his properties before those blasted primroses bloomed. National security be damned.

Next the viscount paid a courtesy call at Wyte House, one of the largest, most ostentatious residences in Belgrave Square. No chance of his gloves getting chewed here, not with four footmen and the underbutler standing guard over them while the butler escorted Lord Knowle down a corridor filled floor to ceiling with statues and still lifes, artifacts and urns of flowers.

Miss Wyte was not in, but her father received Corin in his study, which, instead of works of the great masters like the hallway, was decorated with the work of a great white hunter, and mediocre taxidermists. The spacious room was filled with stuffed hunting trophies, their dull glass eyes reflecting Corin's dismal future.

Lord Wyte was pleased to see Corin, for now. Of course he was; he didn't yet suspect that Viscount Knowle was strewing Kent with kept women. He'd find out quickly enough, Corin knew, for Mercedes Lavalier was not one to remain tucked safely away, and, once seen, she was not easily forgotten.

He'd been meaning to write, the nabob told Corin while they waited for three servants to pour two glasses of cognac, intending to ask the viscount if he and his poppet Melissa might move their visit ahead by a month or two. Or three, since the viscount was fixed in Kent for a while, paying respect to his aunt's memory. His little girl was getting sadly pulled by the hectic pace in Town, her doting papa reported. Not that Missy was delicate in the least, Wyte reassured Corin, waving his beringed fingers in the air. She was simply more used to the quieter country ways. Of course she'd be a fine hostess, for Melissa knew her way around Polite Society already, did his precious. But she was yearning for fresh air, flowers, and proper horseback rides, not the tame park excursions available in Town.

Corin was happy he'd bought that sweet little bay mare until Lord Wyte announced that his Missy had her own Arabian filly they'd bring along with them to Kent. Looked a real treat, she did, her proud papa informed the viscount, a fine rider. Wyte had seen to that. He waved the rubies and diamonds toward the stuffed heads on the walls. Melissa had even been on one or two of these hunts with the nabob, it seemed. Corin politely mentioned that he kept a pack of foxhounds, and they might have some good runs, but Wyte just laughed, a loud braying kind of laugh, worse than Dumpling the donkey's.

"Precious might find it tame sport after tigers, heh heh, but she won't embarrass a noted Corinthian like yourself on the field. A lot in common, you two, heh heh."

All of which Corin took to mean that he was no longer the hunter, he was the prey. He glanced again at the bearskin rug, the elephant's-foot cane stand, and the zebra cushions. He didn't think he cared to be on this end of the safari.

Either no better suitor had come up to scratch or Miss Wyte was forming an unsuitable attachment her father wanted to discourage—or she liked Corin. She could ride in Richmond, she could rest in Bath, she could admire flowers at the Covent Garden markets. She did not, therefore, need to arrive in Kent early. Especially not now. But what could he tell her father? No, you and your paragon of a daughter cannot come early because the roof of Knowle Castle is undergoing repair, or Cook has a toothache. He couldn't say he was expecting a French whore on his doorstep, a doorstep which was, incidentally, littered with dogs' calling cards. No, Corin didn't think he could tell Midas Micah Wyte any of those things.

"It will be my pleasure whenever you and Miss Wyte choose to grace my humble home, my lord. Except . . ."

Lord Wyte leaned forward, fixing Corin in his intense glare. "Except?"

Corin thought he understood how the rabbit felt in the hunter's sights. "Except that I have no hostess at the castle right now. Not that you aren't a proper chaperon for your own daughter, my lord, but I would be remiss to permit Miss Wyte to visit a bachelor's establishment without a respectable older woman in residence. I am only thinking of milady's reputation, you know."

Hell, Lord Knowle was thinking of saving his own skin. Papa Wyte would have Corin's head on this very wall if little Miss Melissa should be contaminated by the likes of La Lavalier. Then, too, there was that avaricious gleam in the nabob's eye that Corin distrusted. He wanted a proper dragon so no one could cry compromise. The viscount wasn't going to be coerced into any forced marriage, nor would he permit the girl's ambitious father to push her into an unwelcome alliance.

Melissa Wyte wasn't an unfledged deb, Corin knew. She was closer to twenty, but her father had kept her so wrapped in cotton wool that she retained a sweet innocence that appealed to the viscount. Now he feared that Melissa was too weak-willed to stand up to her father if she did indeed prefer to wed another man. Then again, if she really went tiger hunting with the old jackass, it was Corin who was in danger.

His mother was scheduled to arrive at the castle in June. Lud, Corin didn't want her there any sooner, not harping on his duty to marry and beget more little Knowltons lest Cousin Arlo inherit. She'd have Corin engaged to the heiress so fast his head would spin. And heaven knew what Mama would think about Miss Armstead.

Now there was a woman who wouldn't let any man tell her what to do. It didn't make her any less feminine, Corin surprised himself to admit, just more difficult and more interesting.

The viscount was brought back from his musings by Lord Wyte's clearing his throat. "As for a chaperon, Knowle, I've already thought of that. Met your sister at Almack's t'other night, and she thought spring in the country would suit her and her children to a cow's thumb."

Corin groaned. Florrie was always ready to attend house parties; they were less expensive than paying her own upkeep. She was especially fond of visiting the Knoll, where she could try to wheedle a better position in the government for her ne'er-do-well husband out of Corin's influential friends. And she always thought her brood should know their Knowlton heritage. Corin thought they'd be better off knowing some discipline, from what he'd seen of the little monsters. Still, the castle was large enough to lose the two brats. And maybe they'd like a dog!

He nodded, agreeing to consult with Florrie about the earlier date for his house party, a party that would see the destruction of his reputation and his career and his prospective betrothal—and his sibling's fond regard. There was a silver lining after all.

But maybe it wouldn't be all that bad. Mercedes could dance, Lena could get her dogs to do tricks, and Miss Wyte could ride bareback on her Arabian filly. He'd call it a circus and charge admission.

It seemed to the viscount that his life was suddenly sliding out of his control. Usually matters proceeded in an orderly fashion, like a well-plotted military campaign. No sloppy execution of orders, no surprises. Corin was the general of his own fate—before now. Now, since encountering Miss Angelina Armstead, he couldn't tell friend from foe, whether to stand or retreat. Hell's bells, he didn't even know where to point his own pistol. His life had been ambushed.

Chapter Eleven

*H*e was going to have to beg. That was all there was to it. Corin had made no headway dislodging the buffle-headed female, and he'd only managed to get one dog away from Primrose Cottage for one night. Molly had been reclaimed, his cook lamented, because Miss Armstead said they were feeding her too much rich food. The usurpers were firmly entrenched.

Pleading was beneath his dignity and beyond his principles, but Corin could see that prostrating himself at Miss Armstead's feet was the only chance he had of getting her to take in Mercedes Lavalier. He could not appeal to her patriotic loyalty, for L'Écrivain's identity was too dangerous a secret to entrust to a civilian, nor to Lena's better nature, for her charity seemed to end at the canine kingdom. He could try to bribe her, of course, since keeping all those dogs was an expensive proposition and the proposed hospital could use a higher endowment. He'd try bribery first, *then* he'd beg her to let the Frenchwoman stay at Primrose Cottage.

Since she couldn't be told her guest was a spy, Lena didn't even have to know La Lavalier's real name. That would be safer for both of them if any vengeful Frenchman tracked the Scribe to Kent. The starched-up companion certainly didn't need to know that the visitor from abroad was a whore. Although knowing the ballerina, which the viscount had last year for two exciting, expensive weeks, her second profession would be obvious at a glance to anyone with the least bit of social expertise. Miss Armstead wasn't worldly, thank goodness. He'd figure out later how to explain all the officers and diplomats who planned on calling on the escaped spy. He was sure there'd be more gentlemen, once they learned mademoiselle's real name.

If all else failed, his lordship was prepared to invoke the power of the military, which he did not possess, but the Duke of Fellstone did. 'Twould be a novel experience, having Miss Armstead do his bidding for once. The deuced female was too independent for his taste. She was prickly and opinionated and disrespectful of his position.

And she was crying.

Angelina had been busy while his lordship was away, so busy that she didn't have time to think about him, not more than thrice an hour. Fashioning a fashionable wardrobe took a lot of her time, and all of Mavis's efforts. And it was the month for spring cleaning, which at Primrose Cottage meant giving all the dogs baths and haircuts.

In addition, Mr. Averill Browne made frequent calls to consult with Angelina about details of the construction, stopping at the cottage on his way to the Remington place in the mornings, and back to the castle at the end of the day. Angelina invited him to share her breakfast and afternoon tea so the young man did not have to take all of his meals in solitude. Conscious of Lord Knowle's warnings, she made sure to leave the doors open, or to have Mavis nearby.

She needn't have bothered. The architect seemed to

like the dogs better than he liked her. They reminded him of his boyhood, he said. Mr. Browne often took one or two dogs to the construction site with him in his gig, claiming they gave him a different perspective on the building, a new inspiration. Bunny got to chase rabbits to her heart's content, and Digger was permitted to help with the excavation instead of being yelled at for uprooting the roses. Averill's favorite animal, though, was Calliope, a beautiful Irish setter he was hoping to take with him when he went to his next commission. That wouldn't be soon, Angelina couldn't help thinking, if Mr. Browne kept romping with the dogs all day. Calliope had long, flowing hair almost the color of Mr. Browne's own artfully disarranged auburn tresses. The setter was also as deaf as a doorknob, but the architect didn't care. Lady Sophie had chosen well.

Angelina was also busy interviewing sisters. Her advertisement had been very specific about Mena's name, date of birth, and coloring. It was amazing how many young women there were like that, liking the chance for the reward. Mr. Truesdale wrote that he was having as little luck, what with the Kirkbridges both dead, their solicitor having passed on, and all of their old servants pensioned off elsewhere. No one he could find knew what had become of the little girl. Most weren't aware there had ever been an orphaned child at Kirkbridge House.

Why did they have to be so cruel as to keep Lena and Mena apart? It wasn't the sisters' fault that their parents had disobliged everyone by wedding. Neither set of grandparents wanted the reminder, but what harm could a letter now and again do? Lena had tried once, as soon as she knew how to write well enough, but her letter had been returned unopened, and she'd been assigned an extra hour of prayers and two more hours of chores. She had tried again from her school after the Armsteads left for Africa, selling her Sunday desserts to frank the letter.

That one never even came back. When she wrote from Lady Sophie's house, she did get a reply, but it was from a solicitor. Their Graces were deceased, he wrote, with no acknowledged grandchildren. She was, therefore, not entitled to any part of the estate. Angelina didn't want any of their wretched money, which hadn't brought anyone much happiness that she could see. She wanted to find her sister.

Instead she was finding a great many needy young women. Some she gave their coach fare, some a few coins. Some were grateful for a hot meal. But this last girl claiming to be Philomena Armstead was the worst, bringing tears to Angelina's eyes. She'd always pictured her sister content, the laughing golden cherub she remembered. Why shouldn't Mena be happy, taken in by the next thing to royalty? The image had sustained Lena through her own years of abject misery. But the Duke of Kirkbridge hadn't kept his beautiful little granddaughter; he'd sent her away to a foster home somewhere within the week. Why, Lady Sophie spent more time than that finding a good home for one of her strays. Then the dastard duke had the nerve to die without leaving a scrap of information behind. Mena might be dead, too, or worse.

Corin forgot all of his intentions. His firm resolve dissolved with one salty tear. "What's wrong, Lena? Did someone hurt you? Harm one of your dogs?" She might be a thorn in his side, but Lena Armstead was *his* thorn, and Corin wasn't about to let anyone else torment her.

Without inquiring too deeply whence this protective streak, the viscount simply told himself that since she was on his property, Miss Armstead was his to defend. And comfort.

He opened his arms, the most natural thing in the world, and she fit perfectly, dampening his shirt collar.

Some women could look attractive when they cried, dewy-eyed and interestingly pale. Not Miss Armstead.

She went all splotchy and swollen, and her nose dripped. Corin thought her adorable. He handed her his handkerchief. "Was it the woman I passed on the way in? Did she insult you?"

Angelina blew her nose and shook her head, too overcome to look up at the viscount. "She wasn't my sister."

"Lud, I should hope not! That female was a . . . That is, she . . ."

"Was no better than she ought to be," Angelina supplied, still sniffling.

"She blew me a kiss on her way out." For a moment he'd feared she was Mercedes Lavalier, arrived beforetimes, in a blond wig. But the woman today was taller and broader and, no matter the danger, Mercedes would not masquerade as a common whore. She might be a prostitute, but she was anything but common. "What the deuce was a female like that doing here anyway?"

So Angelina twisted his handkerchief into a wad and told him about looking for the sister who'd been lost without a record. "Who knows what happened to her? She could be dead, too, or forced into a life of shame like that unfortunate female."

"Plaguey things, sisters," he said, trying to console her. "Always nagging at a fellow. Moody, conniving—and you can't wallop one like you could a brother. Trust me, you're better off without."

"That's easy for you to say with all your aunts and uncles, nieces and nephews. But I have no one. No one in the whole world to call my family." And she started weeping again. So Corin started patting her. He got to touch those little curls clinging to her nape; they were as silky as they looked.

Angelina stepped away before Corin could disgrace himself by taking advantage of her unhappiness and vulnerability. "I have to find her," she said, sniffling. "I just have to, to know that she's safe. Now that I have funds, I could help her if she needs me."

"But you said they must have changed her name when your grandparents gave her up for adoption, so how will you know it's your sister? Surely you don't expect to recognize her after, what? Fifteen years? Children change too much. Their hair gets lighter or darker, even the color of their eyes can alter with time."

"I'll recognize her by our shared memories, the pet names my parents had for us, a million things no stranger would know. Surely Mena would remember something."

"But what if she doesn't? You said she was younger. I understand little children often forget memories that are too painful to recall."

"She'll remember the happy times with our parents. I do, and I am only a year older. If by chance she does not remember being adopted at all, if the new people never informed her and never told Mena her own name, then I suppose it won't matter. She wouldn't answer my advertisement."

"Advertisement? You put a notice in the paper?" Corin put more distance between them so he'd not be tempted if Lena started to weep again. Sympathy was quickly being replaced by outrage, a much more typical emotion for him when confronted with Miss Armstead's freakish starts. He almost forgot how nicely she felt in his arms, how her softness against his chest made up for any number of ruined neck cloths. The woman was a blight, was all. "You invited every orphaned female in England to pop in at Primrose Cottage?"

"How else am I supposed to find my sister? The heir to the Kirkbridge dukedom was a distant cousin who doesn't know anything and cares less. I think he's afraid both Mena and I will end up being his dependents, for he ordered his new man of affairs not to let me look through the old papers." She started pulling at the handkerchief, just thinking of the man's intransigence. "And Mr. Truesdale hasn't had any luck tracking down any of the old duke's retired retainers, either."

"Truesdale? Nigel Truesdale? What the devil has that basket scrambler got to do with anything?"

"He is a connection of Lady Sophie's in London who is helping me search."

"Nigel Truesdale is no such thing. He's my cousin on my mother's side, no relation to Aunt Sophie at all. Their only connection was that she used to hand him a coin now and again, which he managed to gamble away in minutes."

"Yes, when Lady Sophie suggested I hire him, she did mention that he used to be a knight of the baize table. Mr. Truesdale has turned over a new leaf, embarked on a new career of handling just such investigations. He knows everyone in the ton."

"And everyone knows him and his spendthrift ways. That's why he hasn't managed to snabble himself an heiress: no rich papa is going to entrust Nigel Truesdale with his fortune, much less his daughter. The only reason he's still accepted is because of his family connections."

"Which are considerable. Who better, therefore, to find out what happened so long ago? Some dowager is going to recall some tidbit of gossip, a cardplayer at White's might have taken a hand with His Grace of Kirkbridge."

Corin had to admit that Nigel did have the entree everywhere, and he must be making a success out of this new venture for he hadn't come to his cousin to pull him out of River Tick in ages. Nigel wasn't a bad sort, Corin supposed, or he wouldn't be when he stopped being a useless ornament of Society. "You should have waited, then, if Nigel is making inquiries, to see what he turns up. Servants pensioned off so long ago could be anywhere. Publishing an advertisement was an addlepated thing to do. You'll have every hungry female knocking on your door, every adventuress and out-of-work actress."

"Any one of whom might be Philomena. That's why I cannot leave Primrose Cottage. Not because of the dogs—I could and would take them with me wherever I went—and not to be disobliging. But my sister might read the notice. She could be coming here any day."

And pigs might fly, but Corin didn't say it because Penn was wheeling in the tea cart. One look at Miss Lena's ravaged face and his lordship's disordered neck cloth and the butler assumed the worst. He slammed the tray down on the table, took up a place near the door, and stood glaring at the viscount. "That will be all, Penn," Corin said, but the butler purposely looked to Lena for directions. She nodded, so Lady Sophie's loyal retainer was forced to leave. He didn't have to leave his new mistress alone with a confirmed rake, however. Until Mavis could be rousted out of the sewing room, the dogs would have to chaperon. Penn sent in three to join Ajax near the plate of raspberry tarts.

While Angelina poured the tea with hands that still trembled, the viscount bent to ruffle the ears of a Pekingese that came sniffing at his boots. The small dog didn't seem interested in chewing the tassels off his new Hessians, so Lord Knowle kept stroking its shiny coat.

Angelina was handing over Corin's cup. "Oh, don't pet him on his—"

The dog fell over, legs thrashing, eyes rolling. Angelina jumped up, spilling the hot tea onto Corin's lap. She stuffed the viscount's already damp handkerchief into the dog's mouth and crooned calming words. They didn't work for his lordship, but in a few minutes the dog stood up and spit out the handkerchief. The Pekingese tottered over to the hearthside, looking confused but none the worse for wear, unlike the viscount and the handkerchief Angelina handed him back.

"Tippy is a good dog," Lena told him, "as long as you make sure you don't—"

"Pat him on the back. Yes, I gathered as much." Corin had also gathered his wits. "Do you know, Lena—Miss

Armstead, I have been thinking of your investigation, and it's the damnedest coincidence. You're not going to believe this, but I may have found your sister. She's been living in France. . . ."

Chapter Twelve

Corin just couldn't do it. He couldn't watch Lena's eyes light up as if someone had put to flame a hundred candles in the room. He couldn't raise her hopes this way. The peahen really believed she'd find her missing sister, changed name, hidden records, and all, just as she really believed she was making the world a better place by nurturing a dog that fell over if someone pet it.

No, he simply could not lie to Miss Armstead. She'd never believe him, anyway. Mercedes had dark hair and eyes and was older than the lost girl. As for a family resemblance in their temperament and attitude, Corin could sooner have believed Miss Armstead was related to the Pekingese rather than the Frenchwoman.

Angelina's eyes were already dimmed and narrowed. How could he have found Philomena when he hadn't known she existed two minutes ago? "It would seem that you know a great many foreigners." She was sorry she hadn't consulted Squire Hardwick, the magistrate, about her suspicions concerning Viscount Knowle. She wasn't sorry she'd spilled tea on him.

His lordship was still dabbing at his inexpressibles with the serviette. "I have traveled extensively."

"I bet you have," Angelina said, thinking of his smuggling operation. "Oh, and your French visitor never arrived here. Did he go directly to the castle, then?"

Gingerly accepting the tray of thinly sliced bread and butter Miss Armstead passed him, the viscount faltered: "Not yet. That is, he isn't coming. Well, he is, but he isn't a he."

Angelina raised her eyebrows.

Corin cleared his throat. "The French gentleman who was due to arrive is actually a female. That's what I meant about your sister. Mademoiselle La—La—" He looked around. La Pain? The Bread? "Lapine. That's it, I forgot for a moment. Does that ever happen to you, when a name is on the tip of your—never mind. Miss Lapine is coming to this country and needs a place to stay. I thought, that is, I wondered, if she might bide here with you a bit. She could be like a sister to you, until you find your own, of course."

Angelina choked on the piece of bread she was swallowing. "What? You want me to take in your mistress?"

"Deuce take it, the female is not my mistress! Wherever did you get that ridiculous notion?"

"From your stuttering, for one, and from the fact that you aren't inviting your guest to your own house. Well, if you won't foul your own nest, you certainly shall not foul mine."

"She's not now and never has—She's not my mistress!"

"Aha!"

"There is no 'aha!' about it. Mademoiselle Lapine cannot stay at my house because it is a bachelor residence. I have no chaperon for her there. It wouldn't be proper." Corin believed he'd had this same conversation quite recently. It had ended the same then, too.

"Invite one of your sisters. Mrs. Talbot is always happy to visit the Knoll."

"Florrie is coming for the house party, but not yet. And

I thought mademoiselle would be happier here, in your friendly company." Friendly? One of Lord Wyte's stuffed tigers was friendlier than the stiff-backed Miss Armstead.

"She's a spy, isn't she?"

Now Corin swallowed wrong. "Florrie? A spy? Don't be ridiculous."

"And don't be condescending, my lord. Mademoiselle, whoever she is, is a French spy. That's why you don't want her at the castle, where all the servants can see her."

He put his cup and plate down where they'd be safe, so he'd have his hands free to throttle the infuriating female across from him. Then he remembered the dogs. He held out a slice of bread and butter. "Good dog, Ajax."

Angelina tapped her foot. "My lord?"

He was thinking. "A spy? You are letting your imagination run away with you, Miss Armstead. Perhaps you should stop reading those gothic novels my aunt always had around the house."

"It does not take much imagination, sirrah, to detect something decidedly skimble-skamble about the whole affair. The lady is a spy, isn't she?"

"Deuce take it, how did you come to that conclusion?"

"Other than that we are at war, living near the coast, and you are up to your eyebrows in hugger-mugger? Even your aunt used to comment on your comings and goings, my lord, how you were never here when the London journals reported you ruralizing in Kent. You, sir, are a smuggler."

He jumped up, making sure no decrepit dog was under his feet. "What, give good English gold to the French so they can buy weapons to kill Englishmen? The devil, you say."

"The devil indeed! You want Primrose Cottage to store your booty, and now you want it to store your spies. Bringing French spies into the country is even more reprehensible than bartering gold for wines and lace. It is treason, pure and simple. You could hang!"

"My word, Miss Armstead, is that what you think of me?" He stepped over the paroxysm-prone Pekingese, careful not to touch it with his foot.

Angelina was having trouble believing the worst, while his lordship looked dreadfully hurt and confounded by her accusations. And he had served with the army in the Peninsula before being wounded. Still . . . "You made no secret of wanting us gone from Primrose Cottage."

"I want my family's property properly united. That doesn't make me a spy. Deuce take it, I work for the government!" Corin's disclosure at this point made no difference anyway, because his work in France was done. Safeguarding Mercedes Lavalier was to be his last covert assignment. He wasn't sure why he'd told Lena now, except that he couldn't bear her thinking so ill of him. He wanted her to see him in a better light. It worked, for the little dancing yellow flashes came back on in her eyes. A better light, indeed.

"Oh, I wish you had told your aunt. She would have been so proud! Why, she wouldn't have called you a fr— Oh, dear. More tea?"

Corin shook his head. Aunt Sophie would have called him a fribble if he'd single-handedly defeated the French legions. She had no use for anyone who laughed at her menagerie of misbegotten mongrels. "Anyway, I am helping the War Office, and they wish to interview Mademoiselle Lapine in a private, secure location."

"She is a spy, I knew it!"

"Blister it, will you forget about spies? The female is a friend to England. That's all you have to know. She fled her homeland and needs a safe haven for a brief time. May she stay with you?"

Angelina was nibbling on a macaroon. "Why not at the

castle? You could make the lady a grand welcome, in appreciation for her service to the country, rather than asking her to stay in a small cottage with few servants and many dogs."

"The castle is too public, especially with a houseful of guests coming soon. Mer—Maria wouldn't be safe."

"But she'd be lost in the crowd. I think that's a much better solution, my lord."

Corin brushed at his damp thigh one more time. "Miss, ah, Lapine would not precisely get lost in the crowd. More likely she'd stick out like a sore thumb."

"Ah, the lady is from the lower orders. I see. But still, your sister can make her welcome, I'm sure. Mrs. Talbot was always more than kind to me when she visited Lady Sophie."

"Deuce take it, you're not a servant, and neither is Mer—Maria. And my sister would definitely not make Maria welcome at the castle." More likely Florrie'd screech down the centuries-old walls. Miss Wyte's papa would have fits worse than the Pekingese's, and as for Mama—It was better not to think about Viscountess Knowle sitting down to dine with Mercedes Lavalier.

Angelina was pleased at how adamant the viscount was in denying her lowly position. Perhaps he did see her as more of a lady now that she was wearing another of Mavis's creations. Then his words sank in. "Your lady friend is not a lady, is she?"

Corin felt his cheeks grow warm. Hellfire, he was blushing like a youth! "Not precisely."

"One either is a lady or one isn't, my lord! Either this Maria Lapine is suitable to introduce to your sister and your houseguests or she is not."

He sighed. "She is not."

"But she is good enough for the likes of me. Is that it, you black-hearted bounder? You won't bring her to your own house, but you'd bring some light-skirt here to mine? How dare you!"

He ducked, but nothing was coming. "You're the one so casual about your reputation," he replied when he deemed it safe to come out from behind the big dog. "Your jumped-up carpenter told me how gracious you were, inviting him to take his meals here. Breakfast, by George! What do you think the neighborhood will make of that?"

"Exactly what it was, a polite visit between two acquaintances who have a mission in common. Can you say the same for your dealings with Maria Lapine?"

Not without perjuring his soul, he couldn't, so he ignored the question. "Besides, I never implied that you weren't as much a lady as my sister. I thought that, with you looking for your sister, and women like the one I passed outside coming by, you could tell anyone curious enough to ask that Maria was another of the claimants."

"Who happened to stay on for a month? Foolish beyond permission, my lord, to think no one would notice a thing like that or that the servants wouldn't gossip."

"Your people are the most loyal, closed-mouth group I've ever encountered, whereas the castle will be filled with the guests' maids and valets and extra servants hired just for the house party. Maria would not be safe."

"Safe? You mean it's dangerous besides? Someone is trying to harm your French harlot, and you think nothing of endangering me or your aunt's employees? Or did you expect old Penn and the rest to defend her?"

"Lud knows you've got enough watchdogs to guard Buckingham Palace. But there is no danger," Corin told her, not precisely lying, for he had every intention of stationing half the militia in the garden to guard the cottage. "I would not put you, the old servants, or the dogs in jeopardy, Lena."

"That is Miss Armstead, my lord. No one gave you permission to be so familiar."

"Your pardon, it's merely habit from hearing my aunt say what a treasure Lena was, what a joy Lena was. The nickname doesn't suit you, either, Miss Angelina Armstead. You should be called Angel, of course."

Angelina looked down at her hands so he couldn't see her blushes. She'd never had such a compliment in her life. Too bad his lordship wanted something from her in return. "There is no reason to pour the butter boat over me, my lord. No amount of flattery is going to convince me to let a bird-of-paradise nest at Primrose Cottage."

She was wavering, he could tell. "Maria's not any common bachelor fare, you know. She's one of the premier demimondaines in Paris."

"And *that* is supposed to convince me? That she is better paid than the rest of the frail sisterhood?"

"No, that she is an intelligent, elegant woman with exquisite manners and incredible artistic talent. I daresay she could pass for a lady in any court in the world."

Flattery to herself was one thing, Angelina thought. High praise for a high flier was another. She scowled at Ajax, who went instead to lean against the viscount's legs.

Trying to stay upright under the dog's weight, Corin said, "I know I am asking a great deal, Angel—Miss Armstead, and undoubtedly it will put you in an uncomfortable position. But you would be helping your country. And I will make a contribution to the new shelter, so you can feel you are helping the dogs, too. Not bribery," he added quickly before she could take umbrage, "but repayment for a debt of gratitude."

"It means that much to you?"

"It means the world, my dear. Why, I'd even take home that dog who hates men if I thought that would convince you to help Maria and help your country."

"And she is not your mistress?"

"I swear it on my honor."

"And never has been?"

"I—" He swallowed. Lena would know soon enough.

Mercedes was as liable to throw her arms around him as she was to land in his lap, and she'd never been reticent about her career, either. "We were friends, once."

"Get out."

Chapter Thirteen

"Very well, I'll pay the expenses of Aunt Sophie's shelter for two years, and I'll take this nice dog here off your hands." Corin was petting a medium-size, curly-coated terrier who'd rolled over to have his underside scratched. "He seems like a good fellow. What's his name?"

"Homer. He's an Airedale, and you cannot have him."

Corin was learning. "Homer, as in the blind poet? Long-winded?"

"Homer as in pigeon. You can't have him because he won't stay with you any more than he's stayed at the four other homes Lady Sophie found for him."

"Let me try. You've got nothing to lose except one hungry mouth to feed." Corin was determined to pry at least one dog loose from Lena's tender clutches. He had to prove to himself that he could do it, and he had to prove to her that he was worthy of one of her pets. "If he doesn't stay at the castle, I'll put another hundred pounds toward the construction."

Angelina nodded. "You may as well take him, then. He needs the exercise, and we need the money. Homer always returns here anyway, maybe because of all his friends. I'll have Penn find you a leash." She turned for the door, to summon the butler.

"Wait. Two years' support of the shelter, half the building cost, and I'll take Molly, too. Why not? I already have your poetic puppy at the castle. Your architect fellow is endlessly enthusiastic about the noble undertaking, the noble animals."

"Mr. Browne is devoted to the dogs. Did he ask your permission to keep his setter Calliope at the castle with him? He was awaiting your return to bring her there."

"What's another dog or six? Especially if it gives the cawker something to do after supper so I don't have to converse with him. Chasing sticks ought to be a good diversion for the whelp."

"Calliope is not a young dog."

"I didn't mean the dog."

"Mr. Browne is very dedicated," Angelina defended the architect, a trifle too vehemently for Corin's taste.

"He's a good businessman," he countered. "But about the other dog, Molly. My cook grew attached to her, and he promises to prepare better meals for her if you'll send a list of her requirements." Just like a demanding dowager, Corin muttered to himself. He didn't say whom he felt was being difficult, the mongrel bitch, the brown-haired chit, or the Belgian chef for threatening to resign unless Corin brought his dog back. The viscount's toast was burned and his eggs were cold this morning. Henri understood blackmail.

So did Lord Knowle. "Of course I cannot force you to let me have either dog, no more than I can force you to play hostess to Miss Lapine. If you absolutely refuse to give up the dogs, though, I shall find it necessary to go to the gentlemen overseeing my aunt's estate and inform them that in keeping the dogs from excellent homes you are not acting in the animals' best interests."

Angelina laughed. "Since one of those gentlemen was Homer's original owner, I don't think I have anything to worry about. The vicar couldn't keep the dog with him for more than a week at a stretch before Homer would disappear. Of course his name was Redemption then, which high standard, Lady Sophie used to say, caused the animal to bolt in the first place. Nearly every Sunday sermon ended with a prayer for Redemption. No, the vicar won't think the less of me for not sending Homer where he won't stay. Besides, my lady's will said nothing about *having* to find new owners for her dogs. She was content knowing they could live out their days at Primrose Cottage."

Unlike Corin. He sighed. "Three years, all the construction, new collars all around. That's my final offer."

"How long?"

"How long should the collars be? How the deuce should I know? I suppose it depends on the dog."

"No, my lord, how long shall your spying strumpet be foisted on me and the servants here?"

"Not long at all, I shouldn't think." Corin couldn't imagine Mercedes Lavalier rusticating in the country away from adoring gentlemen for any length of time. If she couldn't return to France, she'd be off to Italy or Austria to find herself a new Golden Ball. "Does that mean you agree to do it? You'll welcome Maria?"

"I'll never welcome her, my lord, but I am thinking I might accept her. Not for the money, you understand, although donations are always appreciated. What I want in return for permitting a fallen Frenchwoman to stay here is your promise."

Corin would promise his firstborn son at this point. "Anything."

"I want your promise that you will cease your badgering ways, that you will stop trying to weasel me out of Primrose Cottage."

"Badger? Weasel? Me?" Blast, his last birdbrained promise kept Corin honor bound from making sheep's eyes at this pigheaded female. Her new demand placed the viscount firmly under the cat's paw, robbing him of the greatest challenge he'd faced in dogs' years. But he had to swear it, to resolve this mare's nest. After his cowhanded handling of the last interview, Corin was too chickenhearted to face the Duke of Fellstone again with Miss Armstead's mulish refusal. Rats.

Dinner at the castle was excellent. Henri was once more in fine form, although Lord Knowle had to wonder if the mutt in the kitchen was getting a better cut of meat than the master in the dining room. Conversation wasn't exactly scintillating, as Averill Browne chatted about his work on the shelter and his admiration for Miss Armstead, her generosity, her noble purpose. Corin knew all about her noble purpose: to drive him insane.

Listening to the sprig sing Miss Armstead's praises throughout the meal was better than listening to him sing to his deaf dog after. The setter sat by the gudgeon's feet all evening, her head on his knees, her gaze worshipful. Molly couldn't be coaxed out of the kitchen, not when Henri was preparing tomorrow's menus. And Homer, Corin's chosen companion, had chosen to return home ages ago. The not-so-addlepated Airedale had waited until Corin walked him on a lead through the formal gardens, which would never be the same with three dogs in residence, and fed him with his own hands. Then he'd gone out the French doors when Corin stepped out to blow a cloud.

At least he didn't have to chase the dratted dog through the home woods, Corin reflected, watching Homer bound across the lawns in the direction of Primrose Cottage, proving the blasted female right. Again.

It was the devil's own bargain he'd made, Corin thought as he stubbed out his cigarillo. Now the companion would be here on his doorstep in perpetuity, tempting and tantalizing—and there wasn't a deuced thing he could do about it, the proximity or the appeal. Lena was safe from him on all counts.

Of course after Mercedes Lavalier left, and once Lena got that goosish notion of finding her sister out of her head, perhaps he'd see if her principles were still so firm. He'd promised to behave like a gentleman, that was all, not a monk. If Miss Armstead turned willing—No, not even then. Her tale of the lost sister had more than one implication: Angelina Armstead had rogues for relatives, but she was a lady.

Corin didn't know the current Duke of Kirkbridge and didn't want to know any cad who disowned a female who should have his protection. If the dastard were here now, Corin would have to call him out. Then again, if the duke cared about his distant cousin, and knew the viscount's thoughts, he'd have to call Corin out. Either way, her honor would be defended.

She was the granddaughter of a duke, by all that was holy. If his oath hadn't stopped Corin from trying to get Lena out of Primrose Cottage and into that little jewel box of a house he maintained in Kensington, her birth did. He did not seduce gently bred virgins. Not even if they were willing, had no male protectors, and looked as entrancingly tousled as if they'd just stepped out of bed. Blast, Miss Armstead could send him to Bedlam without half trying.

Besides, he ruefully acknowledged, by the time Mercedes was gone and Lena was reconciled that she'd never find her sister, he'd be firmly affianced. Or married. Lud, married. Why had that seemed like such a good idea last month—and such a wretched one this month?

Angelina missed Homer. That must be why she was so blue-deviled, she told herself as she sat alone to dine. Mr. Penn no longer let her eat in the kitchens with the servants. It was not fitting to her position, the butler and the house-keeper insisted. Angelina had to smile at that. She was still a paid companion as far as she was concerned, only now she was better paid and her charges were all dogs instead of dowagers. She was still the same Angelina Armstead, wasn't she?

Perhaps not. Perhaps now that she had fancy feathers, she could fly a trifle higher. For a bit she had even wondered if the viscount would invite her to any of the parties sure to be held at the castle to entertain the houseguests. Mavis was counting on it, fashioning a rose silk ball gown.

Angelina had never been to a ball where she didn't stand behind Lady Sophie's chair all night. The viscount might even—No, Mr. Browne was sure to ask her for a dance. Angelina did not think she'd disgrace herself, having watched for so long.

Homer came home after dinner, and so did Angelina's wits. The viscount might be democratic enough to invite the vicar and the squire and others of the local gentry to his parties; he wouldn't be inviting a French *fille de joie*.

No, Angelina wouldn't be invited to the castle. She wasn't a paid companion anymore, she was hostess to a prime piece of Haymarket ware. That's what the viscount thought of her, the dastard.

The dastard showed up at breakfast the next morning. To fetch Homer, he said. Angelina had to invite him to partake of Cook's muffins, for Mr. Browne was already there, helping himself at the sideboard like one of the family.

No wonder she took his offer, Corin thought in disgust as he watched the architect eat his second breakfast of the day. The blasted builder was eating Lena out of house and home. But damn, those were excellent muffins.

The viscount glared at Averill until the younger man took the hint and allowed as how he had to get to work, so the unfortunate doggies in the neighborhood would have a place to stay all the sooner.

Tomorrow, if Corin had his way. "Deuce take it, what

is that puppy doing running tame here? I warned you that people are going to talk, Miss Armstead, if they haven't already."

Angelina kept spreading jam on her roll. "Not as much as they are going to talk when Miss Lapine arrives. I can't see how Mr. Browne, who is in my hire, can do my reputation worse harm than Miss Lapine. An actress, did you say?"

"A dancer," he mumbled so low she had to strain to hear.

She went on as if he hadn't spoken: "For that matter, your presence here is most suspect of all. We are related neither by birth, marriage, nor the bonds of employment. And frankly, my lord, your reputation can only reflect poorly on mine. I'll bid you good day, then."

With the barest of curtsies, she sailed out of the morning room to greet the arriving children. Children of his tenants, by George. The viscount stood and watched for a moment before taking himself and Homer off to the army base. Damn, he owed the female more than a check toward expenses. More than a slip on the shoulder, too.

Corin didn't much care for the man the post commander assigned to head the security detail. Something about Sergeant Fredricks rubbed him the wrong way, most likely the officer's leer when told he'd be guarding two attractive women.

He wasn't any better pleased at Fredricks's response to learning he'd be stationed at the Knoll's gatehouse. He was a soldier, he protested, not a bloody servant for the nobs who didn't want to get down to open the gate for themselves. And as for protecting a Frog informer, the sergeant declared the mort ought to be here at the army base under lock and key.

Corin looked toward the senior officer, who assured him that Fredricks was a crack marksman and a good soldier, precisely the man for such an important mission. Fredricks saluted, turned, and marched out, directly toward where Homer was tied. The dog had to scramble aside to avoid being stepped on, which bit of inconsideration rankled the viscount further.

"I say, Sergeant, there are going to be a great many dogs around the cottage. It's a breeder's kennel, of sorts. If you don't think you can deal with them, speak up now and I'll find another man."

Fredricks saluted again. "I knows my duty, cap'n."

Another man would have stepped around the dog, or would have stopped to pet Homer. Petting Homer's curly head himself, Corin thought that perhaps he should speak to the commander anyway. No, he decided, he was overreacting from being around Miss Armstead too long. You couldn't judge a man by how he treated a dog. Could you?

Chapter Fourteen

*H*omer came back to Primrose Cottage later that evening: later at night, and later than the evening before. Viscount Knowle must be making more of an effort, Angelina thought as she opened the door to Homer's barking. She wished he hadn't tried so hard, for she was exhausted but hadn't wanted to go to bed until Homer was accounted for. Now she was asleep almost as soon as she found room in her crowded bed, not bothering to recall whose turn it was to share her feather mattress.

Less than two hours later, Angelina was awakened by dog barking, all the dogs barking, inside and out, from the Yorkshires' high-pitched yips to Ajax's windowpane-rattling roars. The viscount was right about not needing to worry over intruders at Primrose Cottage.

This wasn't any sneak thief or cracksman, not even a wandering deer crossing the yard. It was a determined rapping on the front door. Mademoiselle Maria Lapine had arrived, at three of the clock in the morning.

Angelina struggled into her robe and slippers, then went downstairs to greet her guest, who was standing in the foyer surrounded by baggage, dogs, and half-dressed servants.

"*Bonsoir,* Mademoiselle Lapine," Angelina called into the chaos. "Welcome to Primrose Cottage."

The woman turned and threw back the hood of her ermine-trimmed pelisse. She was petite, dark-haired, and absolutely the most beautiful woman Angelina had ever seen. No wonder Lord Knowle was ready to sell his own mother to get her here. Not that Angelina would have taken his mother.

Miss Lapine's voice was lilting, her smile charming. Her clothes were elegant, and her figure was lithe rather than voluptuous. She might never see twenty again, but there wasn't a wrinkle, a sag, a gray hair, or the slightest hint of faded glory. This woman was the most gloriously vibrant creature imaginable. Angelina couldn't discover a single blemish, could not find the most minor of faults in her guest except, of course, that she was not Mademoiselle Maria Lapine.

"Mademoiselle Lapine? Who is this Lapine person, *cherie*? Didn't *mon ami* Knolly tell that I was coming? Me, I am Mercedes Lavalier, the premier *danseuse* in all of France. You have heard of me, no?"

Angelina blinked her sleepy eyes. "Knolly?"

"This is the Primrose Cottage, *oui*?"

"*Oui,* I mean, yes, this is, and yes, we were expecting you, mademoiselle. I am your hostess, Angelina Armstead."

"Angelina? Angelique, in my country, no? But you, you are *mon ange*." And the Frenchwoman grabbed Angelina with surprising strength for such a slight female, pulled her close, and kissed first one cheek, then the other. "You saved my life, *ma chérie*. Homeless, I was, and at the mercy of every *scélérat* in France, until you so kindly opened your door to me." Mercedes dabbed at a tear with a pristine white scrap of lace. Her eyes were not swollen, her cheeks were not red. Angelina was green with envy. "Now I am your friend, yours and my sweet Knolly's. But you must not fear I will—how do you say it?—hunt on your preserves."

"Oh, but his lordship and I—"

"*Mon cher* Knolly is an excellent *chevalier*, no? I wish you much joy with him."

Angelina was not quite sure what Mademoiselle Lavalier meant by *chevalier*, but she knew what she meant by joy. "No, no, mademoiselle, you mistake the matter. Lord Knowle and I are barely acquainted. I used to be his aunt's companion, which is how I ended up in this cottage. That is all."

Mercedes looked Angelina up and down, from the top of her disheveled curls to her encompassing flannel nightgown and tattered robe. Angelina had seen no reason to put Mavis to work on garments no one would see. Her old, faded bedclothes were good enough.

Obviously not for Miss Lavalier, who sniffed her disdain. "A little lip color, a bit of rouge, we fix that, no? *Mon cher* Knolly is no, *qu'est-ce que c'est*? a slowtop."

Angelina should have held out for four years' support for the shelter. "But, Mademoiselle Lavalier—"

"No, no," the Frenchwoman declared. "You shall call me Mercedes, no? And I shall call you Angelique, *mon ange*. We are friends forever, no?"

"Forever? Ah, that is, how long do you think you'll be staying?"

From the amount of baggage piling up in the hallway under the direction of Penn without his wig and an older, black-gowned Frenchwoman without a speck of English, Angelina feared forever, indeed. For a fugitive, mademoiselle outdid Marco Polo. Angelina expected her servants to unload a camel next.

What they did unload was even better, a tall white female poodle with a topiary haircut. The dog looked as if her last grooming had been performed by a demented gardener, or a blind one. The dog had pompoms and frills, bare patches next to little clumps of tight curls. She also had a diamond collar around her neck, ribbons in her hair, and gold paint on her toenails. The viscount was going to love her!

Angelina's dogs were sniffing 'round the newcomer. The poodle raised her nose like a *grande dame* lifting her lorgnette, but *"Mon Dieu!"* Mercedes exclaimed. "This will never do, my friend Angelique. My Juliette, how do I say it politely? The reason I gave her such a name, she is always in love."

The bitch wasn't in heat now, or Angelina would have a dog riot on her hands. It figured the French seductress would have an oversexed pet. It also figured that Knolly— Knolly, by Heaven!—wouldn't mention the dog when he was negotiating for Mercedes Lavalier's room and board. "Things seem calm right now. We shall keep a close eye on her, shall we? But the matter is not so grim, for most of the male dogs have been neutered. We can keep the others separated when Juliette comes into season, ah, falls in love."

"Neutered? *C'est merveilleux.* They should do the same for men, no? We would have no wars, no duels, no *imbécile* neck-or-nothing steeplechases."

Angelina knew the first gentleman she'd nominate for the honor, but Mercedes was going on: "Ah, but then we would not have the pretty jewels and the furs, no?"

No. Women like Mercedes would be out of work, along with warriors, weapon makers, and witless wagerers.

All of the baggage seemed to have been unloaded, so Angelina started to lead the way up the stairs. "I have given you the Blue Room, Miss, ah, Mercedes. It is just down this hall."

"A room, my friend?" Mercedes waved a graceful arm toward the mountains of boxes, baskets, and trunks filling the marble-tiled entryway.

"Perhaps the Oriental Room is larger." Angelina turned down the opposite hall. "It is right this way."

"And where shall my maid sleep? I need her nearby

me, in case I wake at night, *n'est-ce pas*? When inspiration calls, I must be up and practicing, composing new dances, writing down my thoughts. Then I need refreshment, or hot water for bathing. What an affront to your hospitality, *mon ange*, to awaken your household."

Angelina tried to hide her yawn, and her dismay at having her sleep disturbed every night when she had to get up and teach the dogs and exercise the children, or the other way around. "We'll be sure to set up a cot for your maid in the dressing room."

"Ah, but my Jeanne snores. She is the hairdresser par excellence, *mais oui*, but she snores. And I, I am a light sleeper."

Angelina made another about-face, almost tripping in her weariness. "Then we'll put you in the Rose Suite, ma'am. You can close the connecting doors between you and your maid and the sitting room, but Jeanne will still be within call. There is plenty of room for your baggage and for Juliette, too." Angelina had been keeping the best guest suite in readiness for her sister, but getting to bed and letting the servants get to theirs seemed more important. "It's right here, at the top of the stairs."

"At the top of the stairs? *Mon Dieu*, that will never do. The noise, the comings and goings, why, I could never sleep! Quiet, I need, *absolument*. In my house in Paris, no one was permitted to stir until noon, lest they disturb me, no, not even Juliette. Except when she was in love, *naturellement*."

"Noon?" Angelina's household had accomplished half its chores by noon.

Mercedes was wiping another tear from her eye. "But of course noon, after I danced half the night. Ah, but I no longer have a house of my own, do I, my angel? I will be strong, do not regard my tears."

"Lady Sophie's rooms are in the rear, overlooking the gardens. They have recently been refurbished." For Angelina's own use, but she hadn't been ready to move into the master suite, where her beloved mistress had died. She led her small caravan in that direction, a frown marking her brow.

"Do not scowl, *petite*. It leaves the lines. We have enough to fix already, no?"

"I was merely worrying that even the best bedroom will not be quiet enough for you. This many dogs can create quite a stir, you know, and then there are the children that I teach in the mornings."

"I thought you were the companion, no?"

"I was, but the viscount hasn't found a proper instructor for the local children, so I have been helping."

"An angel, *vraiment*."

"No, they help with the dogs, but, you see, Primrose Cottage is not an entirely restful place. The gardens are coming along nicely, and there are lovely walks into the village, but I am afraid the cottage is simply too small to grant you absolute quiet. It is not as spacious as you are used to."

"*Non*, my Angelique, do not distress yourself. Your little house is *très charmant*. I shall be happy in the country, you will see. This walking?" She shrugged. "I do not know about walking. The sun, the wind, *n'est-ce pas*? You would do well to avoid the outdoors, *chérie*. But me? I shall rest after my great escape and rejoice that no one is trying to kill me, no? I shall visit with my new friends and my dear Knolly, and I shall busy myself writing."

"Oh, I didn't know you wrote, too, besides dancing."

Mercedes smiled. "No one knows, *chérie*. I scribble now and again, but I mean to try writing my memoirs while I recover from my so terrible ordeal."

Mercedes was inspecting her new quarters while Jeanne directed the placement of the luggage. Angelina sent one of the maids to help Cook fix tea, and another to fetch hot water. Mercedes nodded. "You are the perfect

English lady, Mademoiselle Angelique. If the French *chiennes* had been half so gracious, my poor France would not be in such turmoil." Another tear, then another smile. "I shall return someday, *certainement*. Meanwhile we shall be as happy as English grigs, *oui*, and I shall sleep and write and practice. You have the ballroom, yes?"

Angelina could barely stand up without holding onto the back of a chair. The hall clock had just chimed four bells. She'd have to tell Penn to remove the gong in the morning, after he muzzled all the dogs and children. A ballroom? There was a lovely one at Knowle Castle.

"I am sorry, Mercedes, but no, Primrose Cottage does not have a ballroom. Lady Sophie did not entertain on a grand scale."

The Frenchwoman's big brown eyes filled with tears. "My house, my homeland—but my art? Am I supposed to give up my very life's blood?"

Not on Lady Sophie's Aubusson rug. "I suppose if we take up the carpet in the music room, you might have enough space to practice. That is, I've never seen you dance, but the music room is nicely proportioned."

"*Très bien, très bien.* I shall make do. And you shall play for me, no?"

"Me? No! That is, I am not proficient enough to play for a real performer."

"Bah, you are too modest. Every wellborn *jeune fille* can play the pianoforte adequately."

Not when their grandparents were religious fanatics. "I'm afraid I only had a few years of lessons at school." After the Armsteads had left England and before they died. Her tiny legacy did not cover additional instruction.

Mercedes was not fazed. Of course, any woman who could cross war-torn Europe without breaking a fingernail was not going to be upset by an unaccomplished accompanyist. "Then we will practice together, no? You will be the *demoiselle* most perfect when I leave. You see, Angelique, how many ways I can find to repay your kindness?"

"Oh, but I don't expect you to—"

"Don't frown. And it's no trouble, *mon ange*, no trouble at all."

Chapter Fifteen

*N*o trouble? It was no trouble for Mercedes to turn Primrose Cottage on its ear. Angelina could not blame her, could not even dislike the charming Frenchwoman. She could, however, dislike being wide awake at four in the morning, and she could blame her discomfort on its ultimate cause. She sent her youngest footman to the Knoll, therefore, with a lantern.

"You won't have to awaken *his* staff, Tom; there is sure to be a night watchman on duty. Make sure Lord Knowle receives the message himself, though. Tell him that his important package from France has arrived. Oh, and take Homer with you."

Satisfied, Angelina went back to sleep. The dogs had kept the bed warm for her.

"What the deuce?" It was black as night—hell, it was night—and Corin was awake. How could he not be, with his irate valet shaking his shoulder and holding a candle in his eyes?

This was not what Doddsworth was used to, the valet made sure Corin knew before giving over his message. Dogs, damaged clothing, disturbed rest, why, no gentleman's gentleman should have to deal with such irregularities.

"What, you woke me up to extort a higher salary? Not a good career move, Doddsworth, even if you can tie a cravat properly at the first try." Corin rolled over, to come against soft curls. For a moment he thought—But, no. Homer licked his face. "Thunderation, I suppose you want something, too?"

Doddsworth cleared his throat. "Ahem, milord, there is a footman with a communication from Primrose Cottage. He will not explain his errand to the night guard, who rightfully fetched me, nor to myself. As if I would not give milord his messages in proper form. The insolence, the inconvenience—"

"The purse is on my dresser," Corin said, jumping out of bed and belting his robe. A moment's reflection stopped the pounding of his heart: if there was trouble, the footman would have been shouting for help, not caring who heard. "Take what you think a night's sleep is worth and get out. No, lay out my riding clothes before you go. I'll most likely be going to the cottage."

"It is dark, milord."

"Don't worry, the dog knows the way."

So Mercedes Lavalier had arrived. Blast, it should have been one of the soldiers at the gatehouse who came to tell him, not one of Aunt Sophie's old servants. What if Mercedes had been followed from the coast? She'd be leading ruthless killers straight to Kent, straight to Primrose Cottage, with the guardsmen none the wiser. The devil take it, Corin knew he should have had that fellow Fredricks replaced. He called for his horse and his pistols.

Everything seemed quiet at the cottage when Corin got there. Either they were all asleep or all lying murdered in their beds. He didn't want to go too close, to chance setting off the dogs and thus waking even the dead, but Homer trotted right to the front door and barked. A few dogs barked back, halfheartedly, it seemed to Corin, before the door opened and Homer went inside. He couldn't hear the angry words, but he thought it was the same footman who had come to the castle. So nothing was wrong, except that his dog would rather be anywhere but at Corin's side.

Corin couldn't blame him. Homer was most likely asleep on some soft cushion right now, near a banked fire, surrounded by warm bodies. His lordship would not think of which warm bodies, or body, Homer cuddled with as he patrolled the circumference of the property in the cold and damp early spring air.

The viscount stayed near Primrose Cottage until after dawn, when smoke rose from the chimneys, dogs poured out of every door, servants went about their chores. Then he rode for the gatehouse to destroy the peace and tranquillity of the birdsong morning.

Fredricks wasn't even there. A lowly private was, fast asleep in the chair next to the window, but not for long. Corin was disgusted. The boy didn't look as if he could shave, much less shoot.

"My orders was to guard the Frenchie when she got there, not afore," the sergeant claimed after Corin rode to the army barracks to complain. Fredricks wiped egg off his mouth with the back of his hand. "We wasn't on duty yet."

"You are now, Sergeant, so I suggest you get yourself and the rest of your men to the Knoll before the lady has her morning chocolate. If Mercedes Lavalier puts her nose out of doors without one of your men there to wipe it for her, you'll all be at the front before Napoleon takes his next bath."

Which wasn't as often as should be, Corin had heard, but the threat had Fredricks and his men in a wagon headed toward the gatehouse. "And see you don't frighten the children or the dogs," the viscount yelled after them before riding home cross-country. There'd be the devil to pay if Miss Armstead got wind of the danger.

There'd also be the devil to pay if Lena got to Mercedes Lavalier before he could. Corin urged his gelding into a quicker pace.

What was he thinking to plunk the worldly courtesan into the midst of such innocence? He was thinking of himself, that's what. She'd be safer at the castle, especially with the dunderheads from the army guarding her, even if his own reputation would suffer. His sister wouldn't come to Kent if Mercedes was there, which was a mixed blessing. And an alliance with Melissa Wyte would be out of the question, of course. That was what he should have done, however, brought Mercedes to the Knoll, let the scandalmongers have a feast—and left Miss Angelina Armstead to her unsullied solitude.

But then he'd have no excuse to go visit Primrose Cottage except for Homer. Well, he decided, what was done was done, and now he had to make the best of it. He'd take Mercedes aside, explain about the name change, about all the government people coming from London to speak with her, and about her hostess's different set of moral standards. Then he'd pray she wouldn't mention their former liaison. He'd also pray that one of the men coming to the house party was wealthy, witty, and wicked enough to take Mercedes Lavalier away with him when he left.

So Lord Knowle didn't know Mademoiselle Lavalier so well after all, Angelina concluded when Penn informed her of his lordship's arrival at Primrose Cottage before eleven in the morning. Anyone truly familiar with the Frenchwoman would know to visit in the afternoon, when Mercedes would appear, most likely as fresh as a rosebud with dew still on it. Instead the viscount would have to make do with Angelina in her old black, dog-washing bombazine, with her eyes still puffy and shadowed from lack of sleep. So what if she looked like a hag? she asked herself. He hadn't come to see her anyway, Knolly hadn't.

She took her time about dismissing the children while he waited in the parlor. Then she decided she really could not face such a handsome, polished gentleman looking like something from the coal scuttle.

In her new pink dimity, Angelina was satisfied she was looking her best, even with little sleep. She was also satisfied that his lordship hardly knew Mercedes at all when he stated the reason for his call: "I thought I would walk you ladies down to the gatehouse to meet Sergeant Fredricks and his men. They should be able to recognize whom they're defending, while you should be able to identify the soldiers from the skulkers. If there should be skulkers, which I doubt."

"And I doubt you'll be able to entice Mercedes out into the sunshine."

If Corin was bothered by Angelina's use of the Frenchwoman's real name, he didn't mention it. "What, is she that fearful? I'll drive both of you myself and call out half my stable men to ride alongside. I doubt any highwayman is lurking in the gardens between here and the gatehouse."

"It's not the dangers of the road that Mercedes fears; it's the dangers of the air, the sun, and the wind. The out of doors is not good for one's complexion, *comprendez vous*?"

Corin understood. He grinned and said, "I prefer women with some life to them. A sprinkle of freckles is like a dash of salt on eggs; it adds a bit of flavor."

Angelina wasn't certain if she'd been complimented or likened to breakfast, but to a female unused to flattery, Lord Knowle's words were sweet indeed. Especially since that woman was sporting her usual springtime splash of sun spots across her cheeks. The viscount was forgiven a multitude of sins, even more when he let one of the Yorkshires jump into his lap.

"So what else did you and, ah, Maria talk about when she arrived? You two couldn't have had time for a lengthy conversation, could you?"

Angelina smiled. Sometimes this infuriating man was as deep and dark as a bottomless well. Other times he was as transparent as a pane of glass. "If you are worried that your name was mentioned, my lord, rest assured that *Mercedes* thinks very highly of you."

Corin mistrusted Lena's smile, as rare as it was. The plaguey chit only laughed at his expense, usually. Trust Mercedes to say the first thing to enter her mind, and trust that to be the last thing he wanted her to say.

It was actually a lovely smile, though, Corin thought, transforming a passable female into a beauty. Not a beauty like La Lavalier's seductive appeal, nor yet the porcelain perfection of Miss Wyte. Lena had a quieter kind of beauty, mixed of sunshine and sweetness. He couldn't, wouldn't let that innocent quality get lost.

"Surely you found other topics of more interest."

Angelina couldn't think of a single one, with him staring at her so. "We spoke of this and that. You know, war and traitors and assassins."

He stood so abruptly Lacy tumbled to the ground. The little dog turned to attack his boots, growling at the insult, but Corin picked her up and absently stroked the tiny terrier into forgiveness. The viscount did seem to have a way with females, Angelina noted. But he wasn't getting around her so easily. "It seems," she said, "that you neglected to mention precisely how much the French were irritated with Mercedes, among a few other things you forgot to tell me when we discussed her staying here. Things like how Miss Lavalier believes we lesser folks are placed in her path to smooth her way."

Waving her indignation aside, Corin said, "Yes, yes, Mercedes can be demanding, but what did she tell you? Does she know who is after her? Did anyone follow her here? Did she tell everyone she met along the way that she was L'Écrivain?"

"The writer? Who is that?"

"Oh, lud. Forget I ever mentioned it. Please, Lena, for your own safety."

"Then there really is that much danger?"

"I won't know till I speak to Mercedes. I have the soldiers on duty, and I'll have my own people keeping an eye out for strangers, too. Perhaps it is best if Mercedes doesn't go out of the house yet, her complexion bedamned."

"I don't think you have to worry. Mademoiselle has a busy schedule of resting, reading, practicing, and writing her autobiography."

"Damn, if word gets out that Mercedes Lavalier is writing her memoirs, naming her past liaisons, her life really will be in danger. Deuce take it, Lena—Miss Armstead, I am sorry I foisted Mercedes onto you without giving you all the particulars. I do know that Mercedes can be difficult. But I had no choice. You'd never have taken her in, else."

"I don't find her difficult at all. In fact, I think Mercedes is quite charming," Angelina said, and meant it. "She must be the bravest woman I have ever met, so it is a privilege to have her as my guest."

"I hope you feel that way when she starts having gentlemen callers. No, not that kind of caller. These are government types who need to hear her latest reports, but still another imposition. I sent a message to my sister, so she'll be arriving shortly with some of her cronies to start planning various entertainments. I'll arrange to have Mercedes invited up to the castle to dance. That way she can mingle with the guests with less suspicion. The sooner she speaks to every minister and cabinet member, the sooner she will leave." He put the dog down, gently. "Meanwhile I'll send Sergeant Fredricks to meet you both so you won't be frightened when you see him on the grounds."

"The dogs don't like strangers on the grounds, you know."

They didn't like Fredricks, either. The dogs never settled down after his arrival, never ceased barking or growling or walking stiff-legged, heads down, ears back, tails tucked. They were acting so threateningly, Angelina believed, because the soldier kept shouting at them to stop. Lady Sophie's dogs were not used to being shouted at. They didn't understand "Stubble it."

And Angelina couldn't understand how the man could be impervious to Mademoiselle Lavalier's charms. Even in all her new finery, Angelina knew she looked the drab companion next to Mercedes, so she hadn't expected the soldier to do more than acknowledge her presence. He hadn't, but neither had he smiled when the Frenchwoman thanked him so prettily for taking care of her.

Mercedes shrugged when Angelina asked about it, after Fredricks left. "The man is a swine, *enfin*. A man who does not like dogs is one thing." She gave a Gallic shrug. "And a man who does not like women is another. Unfortunate, but it happens. Ah, but a man who hates women and dogs, this man is no good, *mon ange*. No matter, we don't need the pig. We have all your precious doggies, no?"

Yes. They even had Homer, who decided that the white poodle bitch at Primrose Cottage was a lot more interesting than anything Lord Knowle had to offer at Knowle Castle. Less than forty minutes after the viscount dragged him off by his collar, Homer returned to the cottage, sans collar.

Mercedes was reassured, Angelina was amused, the viscount was aggravated, and Juliette was . . . in love.

Chapter Sixteen

$\mathcal{S}$ometimes Angelina felt that she could teach Ajax to fly sooner than she could teach the estate children their letters. This morning she had the youngest students, since the older boys and girls were helping their parents in the fields instead of helping Miss Armstead keep their younger siblings quiet and attentive. The children were too excited to learn anything today, having seen Juliette and Homer, one of the few unneutered male dogs, playing leapfrog. Since the creation of puppies was not on Angelina's agenda or in her curriculum, she was not well pleased. A bucket of water had dampened Homer's ardor, and a severe lecture to Mademoiselle Lavalier's maid—half of which the Frenchwoman could not have understood—saw Juliette firmly confined to the master suite.

With all the noise, it was a wonder Mercedes still slept, but she'd stayed up half the night, it seemed, drilling Angelina in pianoforte fingerings while she stretched and turned. When Angelina finally pleaded exhaustion, Mercedes declared she was now ready to begin her writing—after she slathered crushed strawberries on Angelina's cheeks.

Mercedes slept, and Angelina had the headache. She'd never be competent enough on the pianoforte to accompany a dancer of Mercedes's stature, and she'd never sleep if she had to worry about staining the sheets all night. Or about his lordship and his former paramour sharing theirs.

When the viscount and Mr. Browne had come by after dinner the previous evening, Angelina had been curious to see that Mr. Browne was still mostly interested in the dogs. How could he look at Mercedes Lavalier in her crimson gown of sheerest muslin with every nuance of her perfect figure perfectly delineated, and not fall *bouleversé* at her feet? Her painted-toenail feet, besides. The viscount couldn't. While the architect and Angelina discussed the day's progress at the work site over tea, Lord Knowle and Mercedes sat apart, with him hanging on her every word. While Averill Browne played with the dogs, Lord Knowle played with Mademoiselle Lavalier's fan. Angelina was tempted to fetch another bucket of water. Government business never looked so amorous before.

No wonder she had the megrims today.

About mid-morning, and long past her tolerance with the rambunctious children, Angelina was surprised to see a woman enter the makeshift schoolroom.

The stranger bobbed a curtsy. "I was waiting in the hallway, but I heard the children so I followed the noise here. My name is Elizabeth Gibb. May I?" She gestured toward an empty bench and Angelina nodded, studying her intently.

Could it be? Elizabeth was blond and blue-eyed, with a touch of green in her eyes that matched Angelina's own. She looked to be about Angelina's age, although it was hard to tell, she was so careworn and thin. Her clothes were poorly made of inferior goods, but Miss Gibb carried herself well and spoke like a lady. Could this one finally be Philomena?

Angelina tried not to get her hopes up; she'd been disappointed too often. So she just watched in amazement as Miss Elizabeth Gibb scooped up little Harry Elkins, a hellborn brat if there ever was one, onto her lap and proceeded to sing a rhyming song about letters and words. The children quickly joined in, making the right responses, laughing, listening, and actually learning something! Miss Gibb had received all the patience in the family if they were, indeed, related.

"My goodness, Miss Gibb, you surely have a knack for that," Angelina congratulated the other woman after the children were dismissed.

"I've had a great deal of practice," Elizabeth said, letting Ajax rest his head in her lap. "And I like children. And dogs," she added hurriedly, when three others entered the room.

So they had something in common. Not much else, it turned out. Miss Gibb had been adopted when she was three or four, as Angelina's advertisement had mentioned, but she recalled her own parents perishing in a fire. "My sister must have died then, too," she sadly acknowledged. "The names Armstead and Kirkbridge meant nothing to me, but I called my sister Angie."

"No one ever called me that, I'm afraid. Angel or Lena, but never Angie."

"I . . . I had to try."

"Yes, of course, I'm glad you did. Were you—That is, I know it is none of my affair, but were you adopted by a nice family?" Angelina had to know, as if she could somehow divine her own sister's past from this young woman's.

"The Gibbs were decent people, a wine merchant and his wife, with a houseful of boys. Mrs. Gibb took me in because she wanted a daughter to help keep house, I think. She did let me study with the boys' tutors, however, so I was able to find a position as a governess, after."

"After the Gibbs died?"

Elizabeth rubbed her worn gloves on the planked bench. "After one of my 'brothers' attacked me in my bedroom."

Angelina gasped. "Oh, no! How terrible! I hope the dastard went to prison!"

"He went off to sea, a naval hero," Elizabeth answered bitterly. "I was sent into service so no one had to be reminded of my shame."

"Your shame? That's ridiculous. What did you do wrong that anyone should be ashamed of you?"

"I was born a woman in this day and age, that's what. They said I must have tempted him, I must have led him to believe I was willing. I wasn't, I swear."

"Your own brother? Of course not!"

Elizabeth smiled slightly at her hostess's indignation. "Oh, how I wish you were my sister, Miss Armstead. There was a child, you see, a girl."

Angelina looked around, almost expecting a moppet to appear from behind Miss Gibb's worn skirts.

"No, she is not here. I was fifteen, Miss Armstead, and disgraced. I could not feed myself, much less an infant. Mr. Gibb took her away, to a home."

"An orphanage?" Angelina could have cried for the poor baby, for the poor girl. Her own life with the Armsteads and the harsh schoolmistresses was heaven compared to this horror.

Elizabeth nodded, her hand stroking Ajax's head. "They named her Robinet, for she was such a frail, birdlike little thing. They told me she was too weak to survive anyway, that they were sparing me the heartbreak."

"I am so sorry, Miss Gibb, and sorry you had to be reminded of your sorrow."

"Oh, but my Robinet didn't die. Before I took up my governess position, I searched through Mr. Gibb's papers and I found the name of the orphanage. He had a receipt! Can you imagine, as if my daughter was a consignment of wine he'd delivered. I saw her, my baby. She was too sickly for anyone to adopt, but she was strong-willed enough to live, to wait for me. No one will take on a governess with a child of her own, however. I send whatever salary I earn, so the matron has agreed to keep her until I can . . ." She shook her head. "You see why I was hoping for the reward you promised."

Angelina was already wondering how much money she could offer to Elizabeth without offending the young woman's pride. "I will repay your coach fare, naturally. I do it for everyone who takes the bother to come. And recompense for your lost day's wages, of course."

"Oh, no, this is my holiday—without pay. My charges are visiting with their cousins, where there are scores of nursemaids. I would have visited Robinet, but I decided to try my luck here instead."

"Forgive my prying, but do you like your current charges, Miss Gibb? Do your employers treat you well?"

Elizabeth laughed. "I am the governess; I never see my employers. As for the children, they are all dears, except that there are six of them."

"Six? Why, you might as well"—Angelina jumped to her feet, books and chalks and papers flying—"be teaching school!"

"She'd be perfect, my lord, I know she would!"

"Why, because the female spun you a sad tale? By Zeus, Lena, you and your tender heart would believe any taradiddle, wouldn't you?"

"That's Miss Armstead, and there is nothing wrong with my mind, even if my heart is soft," Angelina countered. "I do not believe Elizabeth is my sister, just as I don't believe Mercedes Lavalier is a mere casual acquaintance of yours."

"What the deuce has my relationship with Mercedes— my nonrelationship, by all that's holy—got to do with this stranger you want to take in like one of your strays?"

"Only to show that I am not as gullible and naive as you assume. I'll agree that I cannot swear to the truth of Elizabeth's story, but it should be easy enough to verify. She has references, but the best one of all is Harry Elkins. The little beast sat in her lap reciting his ABC's, whilst I've been trying for months to teach the brat to hold a pencil, unsuccessfully, I must add. Elizabeth is a natural teacher, one who adores children. Perhaps if you ever get around to hiring a schoolteacher, Miss Gibb could take on the younger children. Lud knows, there are enough of the little devils for two teachers. And she could stay here for now, so you wouldn't have the added expense of housing her. I'll even pay Elizabeth's salary. It will be worth it to me, not having to drum letters into Harry Elkins."

"Gammon, the schoolteacher is my expense, I'll pay the salary. In fact, if she stays here, I'll be paying you for her room and board also. I'm already paying three years' upkeep at the new kennels, I can stand the nonsense for one more female."

"Don't forget the new collars all around."

Corin smiled. "As if you'd let me. That bargain did not include new diamonds for Juliette, you know."

Smiling back, Angelina agreed. "Juliette wasn't part of the negotiations. But does your offer to pay her keep mean that Elizabeth can stay?"

"Well, I suppose we might take her on, as a trial."

"You'll be pleased, I know it. So will Mercedes. Elizabeth speaks excellent French." The two women were even now conversing in Mademoiselle Lavalier's tongue. Any minute Angelina expected the French-woman to start criticizing the governess's wardrobe, but for now they were conversing about the dogs.

"Very well," the viscount said. "You have convinced me, pending a check of her references."

Angelina thought that it was the French speaking that

had convinced him. Anything to keep Mercedes Lavalier content. "Of course."

"I'll have my man in London get on it tomorrow. If he approves, Miss Gibb can give notice and be back here in a week or two to start her new position."

"Notice won't be necessary, my lord, since her employers are away for the month. And they aren't even paying her."

"And you don't think that's too convenient a story?"

"I think it's lucky for you and the children."

He sighed. "Very well, she can start as soon as she gets her things together. I'll send a carriage back to London with her tomorrow."

"That's excellent, my lord, for I am sure your solicitor won't find anything amiss with her references. There is one tiny problem, however."

"How tiny?"

Angelina pursed her lips at the sneer in his voice. "About as tiny as mademoiselle's dog that you neglected to mention when we discussed her visit."

"Deuce take it, how was I supposed to know Mercedes Lavalier would escape Paris in the dead of night with a big white dog in a diamond collar? I'm amazed they made it past the first guard post."

"What, did you think that Mercedes would abandon her pet? She couldn't have left Juliette behind, no more than Miss Gibb can leave her daughter."

"Daughter? You did say *Miss* Gibb? Hell and damnation, woman, what are you using for brains now that you've cut your hair? Why, the woman is no better than she ought to be, and you think I ought to hire her to teach my tenants' children?"

Angelina lowered her voice. "She was fifteen, and she was assaulted. Her daughter is sickly and needs the good country air and the attention we can give her."

"That is unfortunate and Miss Gibb has my sympathy,

but Society sees her as ruined. Neither a sickly child nor a fallen woman belongs in a schoolhouse."

"*She* belongs in your aunt's bed?" Angelina asked with a nod toward the sofa where Mercedes Lavalier was holding court.

Corin had no answer. "But what about your rep—" No, he was on thin ice there, too. In fact, he was already drowning.

Angelina was far ahead of him. "We can say Elizabeth is a widow. *Mrs.* Gibb. Her stepparents would not dare come forward to dispute the title, and many young mothers are without husbands nowadays because of the war. No one will think anything less of her for supporting her child in so genteel a fashion. Teaching is one of the few decent positions open to women of her background."

"But you already introduced her as Miss Gibb." Corin knew he was clutching at particularly thin straws. "How can you suddenly make her a widow?"

"I made an error, that's all. A slight misunderstanding."

"She has no ring."

"She took it off for the journey because she was afraid of highwaymen. Or else she sold it for the war effort, to buy medicine for her husband."

"Perhaps you're the one who should be working for the War Office," Corin muttered, but Angelina wasn't paying attention.

"Besides," she concluded, "the only ones who would notice her change in status or the lack of a ring are my own servants, who would never gossip, and Mercedes Lavalier, who isn't one for casting the first stone."

"What regiment?"

"Excuse me?"

"I said what regiment did her husband serve with?"

Angelina grinned. "It's too upsetting for dear Elizabeth to talk about."

Chapter Seventeen

$\mathcal{N}$ow this was heaven, Angelina decided, waking up and not having to face the children. In fact, she decided not to get up at all. For the first time in her life others were feeding the dogs, others were doing the chores, and others were teaching the children. Elizabeth was going to wait for the afternoon to set out to Town, in order to hold morning classes for her. Angelina pulled the blankets over her head and rolled onto her back.

Mademoiselle Lavalier's habits must be catching, she thought, staring up at the canopy, determined to stay abed till luncheon. Except that she was wide awake and hungry. And Ajax didn't like the men at the gatehouse, and Diamond liked to be handed his food, and Windy couldn't eat liver. She got up.

Elizabeth was already in the morning room, sparklingly eager to start the day, anxious to prove herself to the viscount. If he accepted her, she could send for her daughter on the instant. She'd hardly been able to button her gown, with her fingers crossed from hoping so hard.

Averill Browne was also in the breakfast parlor, as usual, Calliope at his side. What was unusual was that neither Averill nor Elizabeth was talking, neither was eating. They just kept staring at each other, mesmerized.

Angelina was amazed. It seemed Juliette's habits were the ones that were contagious, not Miss Lavalier's.

Miss Armstead wasn't surprised when the architect mentioned going to London that day to gather some new plans and order special materials. He'd go along with Mrs. Gibb in the viscount's carriage, with her permission, thus saving expenses. Of course he wouldn't ride in the coach, which would cast unwelcome shadows on the lady's reputation; he'd ride on top with the driver. That way, Averill added, he'd be protecting Mrs. Gibb's good name and protecting her person from footpads, like the dastards who'd stolen her wedding ring.

She'd have another one soon, if Angelina didn't mistake the situation. It was early days yet, but the two seemed as if Cook had served up a slice of destiny along with the rashers and eggs. Angelina hoped so. Averill Browne was an intelligent, hardworking man, and Elizabeth was a kind, intelligent woman. If he was a shade too dramatic, her somberness balanced him nicely. They would make a good match, if the heavens and Viscount Knowle smiled on them.

Angelina decided she wouldn't mention anything about the moonstruck pair to him. His lordship was too liable to find a sinister motive behind such a sudden attraction. Angelina would be willing to wager her entire savings that Lord Knowle did not believe in love at first sight. Why, if rumors were true, he was bringing some heiress to the Knoll for the sole purpose of determining her suitability as his viscountess. Like testing a new pistol before he bought it, Angelina thought indignantly. She herself, of course, believed in marrying for love, which she hoped would develop from the instant infatuation she glimpsed over the gooseberry jam. Miss Gibb deserved some happiness in her life. Miss Armstead might not have found her sister, but she had found a friend.

As for the little girl, Robinet, Angelina was determined to make her feel as welcome as any child ever felt. There was no nursery at Primrose Cottage, since it had been built for a rich man's mistress, not his butter stamps. After that, Lady Sophie had taken up residence, so there were no old toys in the attic. Dog beds and baskets, furniture too delicate and valuable to put out in a houseful of hounds, but no toys. Angelina could only hope that Elizabeth's daughter liked dogs.

After breakfast and a walk with Ajax and some of the others, Angelina checked on the rooms the servants were preparing. She thought the child would be anxious among strangers, and she also thought that Elizabeth wouldn't want her daughter out of her sight, not after being apart so very long. Angelina and Mrs. Penn had selected the Yellow Room for Elizabeth, with its attached dressing room that now held a small bed and dresser, a cane rocker and a bowl of the first daffodils. The maids, Mrs. Penn and Mavis—none ever having had a child—agreed that the room was perfect, except for one thing. It needed a doll. The poor little mite needed something to cuddle in addition to a dog.

"Confound it." The viscount stepped into the book room unannounced except for the dogs' barking. "Never tell me you're taking in orphaned infants now, besides sisters and strays." He took out his quizzing glass to survey the little garment in Angelina's lap.

"Of course not, it's for a doll for Elizabeth's daughter. Mavis is constructing the doll; her stitches are tighter than mine."

Dolls came from shops. Expensive shops, Corin was well aware, from years of his niece's importunings. "Why don't you just buy one? I'm sure the everything shop in Knowlton Heights has dolls."

"Homemade is better. It will show how much we care. All the maids are sewing hats and knitting scarves. Mr. Penn and Jed Groom are building a cradle."

They were going to so much trouble for a stranger's ill-gotten girl child? Corin's own castle staff was cringing at the thought of his sister arriving with her brats, and Florrie had been born there. They'd sooner make them cages than doll cradles. "You are so sure she'll be staying, then?"

"Not for long," Angelina answered cryptically. "But yes, her references are impeccable."

"Good, for I've decided that it is a good thing she'll be here, as a widow, of course. There will be men coming back and forth to see Mercedes. A proper young widow will add a bit of respectability. Not much, since she's so young, but some, to counteract Mercedes's, ah, flamboyance. I wouldn't want any of the military types to consider you fair game, ah, less than respectable by association."

"Just what kind of men do you have coming, that I'd need Elizabeth at my side? She is going to be at the village schoolhouse most of the day."

Any kind of man, he thought, would make the obvious connection between Mercedes Lavalier and an attractive young female in her circle. For surely Mercedes could not be counted on to keep the intelligence officers in line. She was more likely to encourage them in outrageous behavior that could offend Miss Armstead. And if he, Corin, warned them off, they'd only assume he was marking his territory. The mousy Miss Gibb was Lena's only protection against forward males. Mrs. Gibb, that was. Damn and blast, why did he have to develop a conscience about Lena's reputation? Why did she have to be a duke's granddaughter?

"The military can be discouraged by the dogs, and you do not have to worry about the government officials coming to gather information from Mademoiselle Lavalier," he lied. "Trust me, they have more on their minds than seducing ladies' companions." There, now she'd have Mrs. Gibb, the dogs, and her own prickly personality to preserve her from indiscretion, he thought.

Angelina believed he was putting her in her place, that no gentleman was going to lower himself to her level. He only cared about her reputation lest anyone think she was *his* paramour. "I am sure I will manage. As I have said before, my reputation is no concern of yours. But if you are so worried over it, my lord, perhaps you should leave now, since we have been closeted here alone for long enough to set the scandal broth simmering. Mrs. Gibb is teaching, Mavis is upstairs sewing, and Mrs. Penn has a hundred better things to do than play propriety. Mademoiselle Lavalier, of course, is still sleeping. I suggest you return after two if you wish to converse with her."

Corin hadn't meant she should throw *him* out. After all, she had his oath not to go beyond the line. He thought she might enjoy a drive, since she was relieved of the schoolchildren, but, now that she mentioned it, people would be sure to talk if he was seen squiring a pretty young female around. With a young widow and an ever-young cyprian also in residence, the townsfolk were sure to think he was starting a harem. Lud, Lord Wyte and his daughter would be arriving any day. Corin stood up to leave. "Yes, well, you can tell Mrs. Gibb that she is hired. She may as well fetch her daughter today when she brings the rest of her belongings."

"Elizabeth will be thrilled."

"Do make her swear not to mention Mercedes Lavalier's presence to anyone."

"To whom? The footman at her place of employment or the matron at the orphanage? Unlike your French friend, who tells everyone she had to flee Paris because of her subversive activities, Elizabeth knows how to keep her own counsel. You won't be sorry."

Well, he was, but she was right, he had to leave any-way. "Oh, before I go, there is something else, the dog."

"What, have you given up on Homer already? Didn't we have a wager about that?"

"I do not renege on my wagers, Miss Armstead, and I do not give up. Homer can make the trek between the castle and the cottage for the next ten years, for all I care. I'm just afraid that the next time he goes through the nearest window to get out, it might be one on the second story."

"And I must admit that with Juliette here your chances of keeping Homer there are greatly reduced, which neither of us could have foreseen at the time. I shan't hold you to our bet, my lord."

What, did she think him less than honorable? "A bet is a bet, Miss Armstead. Oddsmakers don't forgive a debt simply because the horse comes up lame. That's why they call it gambling. Play and pay, that's the only decent thing."

What, did he think her so removed from Polite Society that she didn't understand the gentleman's code? "Very well, my lord, if it pleases you to toss your money away, I thank you and the dogs thank you, and I should think Homer thanks you for not making him run back and forth all day."

"I'd like another dog."

"Ouch!" Angelina pricked her finger again. Sucking on it so the blood wouldn't get on the little dress she was sewing, she asked him why. "You don't even appear to like any of the dogs. Why are you so determined to have one of them?"

Because he didn't give up and he didn't renege on wagers, even with himself. He'd sworn to reduce the population at Primrose Cottage and, by George, he was going to do it. "I like some of them very well," he protested, standing farther downwind of the old bulldog by the fireplace. "I liked Molly till she found the kitchens, and Browne's dog is wondrously well behaved.

I even liked Spooky and Bunny. Why do you persist in thinking me an animal hater?"

"Perhaps because Spooky and Bunny are in my yard right now, not yours. Or because you never stopped thinking that the lot of them are useless burdens kept alive by an eccentric old lady."

"I never said you were old."

"I meant your aunt!"

"Oh. Well, you are wrong. I no longer think of them as worthless. I have a perfectly good use for one of the dogs. My sister is coming with her brats—ah, her brood. A boy and a girl. Eight and ten, respectively. I thought they'd like a pet of their own." He thought a dog would keep them occupied and out of his hair. "Doting uncle and all that."

"Eight and ten are good ages. Children aren't so clumsy by then, and can be taught a sense of responsibility. They can also go for walks and rambles in the woods. Let me think. You wouldn't want a very big dog that couldn't come inside, nor a tiny one that couldn't play. I know: Pug would be perfect. He adores children. He even lets the village girls put bonnets on him. He doesn't bark or chew or snap. The children will love him."

They'd better, enough to take Pug along when they returned home. Corin hated pugs. He hated them more when this one had to be carried in his buttoned-up waistcoat so it wouldn't slide off the driver's bench and out of the curricle. Corin felt like a fool, with that pushed-in phiz and those pop eyes staring out of the top of his vest.

He didn't feel as much the fool when Angelina stood up to see him out. She'd sewn the doll's dress to her own skirt.

Corin was content with the morning's work. Elizabeth Gibb seemed a pleasant enough female, who would relieve his guilt about having his aunt's heiress teaching his dependents. Too bad she wasn't a doctor, but he was working on that. She'd also relieve some of his guilt at ruining Lena's reputation by association. He'd make sure everyone knew she was a respectable widow, and Mercedes Lavalier was an eminent *artiste*.

His content lasted about as long as the drive to the gatehouse, where he stopped to make sure Fredricks and his men had the list of government functionaries. Everyone else was to be escorted to the castle, not permitted to turn off for the path to Primrose Cottage. Fredricks allowed as how there'd been no strangers, except the dowdy doxy what walked down to the village that morning.

"She's the new schoolteacher, Sergeant, a respectable widow."

Fredricks only held a dirty finger alongside his nose. "If you says so, cap'n, but she didn't have no ring, and yesterday she was a miss, not a missus. Iffen she's a schoolmarm, next you'll be telling me the wispy one is a fairy princess and the French whore is a nun." He winked.

Oh, lud, Corin thought, the man had the mind of a slug and the mouth of a snake. He was most likely spewing his filth at the village tavern besides, if not at the army barracks. The world and its uncle would believe Corin was keeping three loose women at Primrose Cottage. No, they wouldn't think it was a harem; they'd believe it was a bordello, by Jupiter!

Well, at least he was still satisfied with his plan to bring Pug home to his niece and nephew. One less dog at Primrose Cottage, one less thing for the brats to whine about. If the dog kept them happy for an hour, it was worth the price of the waistcoat Doddsworth was burning. And if Corin's avuncular attentions proved acceptable to his sister, perhaps she'd be more amenable to helping him stop the gossip.

This time his sense of satisfaction lasted for two hours, until his sister started screaming the house down that he was trying to murder her babies.

Chapter Eighteen

*H*ow the deuce was he supposed to know the little brats were so allergic? Then again, he did remember Florrie going all swollen and splotchy when they were children, but they always had dogs and cats. And she was always broken out and blotched. He'd thought it was something she'd outgrow. Obviously not.

She hadn't outgrown ripping up at him, either. While Florrie ranted and raved, Corin reflected that, as plug-ugly as the pug in his arms was, Florrie's puling, pouting progeny were homelier. He supposed that did make him the unnatural, unloving uncle Florrie was screeching about.

"Dash it, Florrie, I was only trying to—"

She wouldn't listen, this tigress defending her cubs from deadly dog hair. He couldn't strike her or shake her or strangle her, so Corin resorted to his boyhood answer to his sibling's sermons. He called her Flat-chested Florrie, to which the mother of two reacted in her own ages-old inimitable fashion: "I'm going to tell Mama."

Lud, not Mama. "Blast it, I'm taking the dog away. I'll send for the physician if you think—" No, there was no local physician. Corin couldn't see dragging a doctor five towns away to look at a case of hives. "I'll buy the brats anything they want. Just don't write to—"

"And heaven only knows what she'll say about your scandalous behavior, carrying on with Aunt Sophie's companion that way!"

Corin was rethinking his tenets about not striking a woman. "I am not carrying on with Miss Armstead, by Jupiter, and she's no longer our aunt's companion; she is a lady in her own right."

"And I suppose all those other females are visiting royalty, you libertine, you profligate, you—"

"You are trying my patience, Florrie. There is nothing improper about my relationship with the women at Primrose Cottage. Any of the women."

"Well, I won't ask that French dancer to the castle and you cannot make me. Entertainment, indeed! We know what kind of entertainment she'd provide."

"What, are you worried Talbot might stray? It's a wonder he doesn't if you treat him to your temper tantrums. But you don't have to worry, the lady would not be interested in your husband." Mercedes never bothered with weak-chinned widgeons.

"The *lady* is not coming near Talbot. Mama would have seven kinds of spasms if I invited Mercedes Lavalier to the castle."

"Mama doesn't have to find out, you peagoose. And what do you know about Mercedes Lavalier anyway?"

"I know that she was notorious for her affairs in France and she came straight to you, her former lover, her *cher* Knolly. Everyone knows that. She told half the innkeepers along the way where she was headed, you dunderhead. I'd be surprised if Mama hasn't heard already."

Oh, hell. "Whether she has or has not is immaterial. This is still my house and my house party. I say Mademoiselle Lavalier will come to dance at least once, and will join the company for dinner before and tea after. She will be treated as an honored guest in my home. Is that understood?"

"I understand that you are trying to ruin us all. First you try to sicken the children, now you want to destroy my social standing in the ton. Next you'll be demanding I invite your new ladybird Lena, or that strumpet you've hired as schoolteacher. What happened to your good sense, Knolly?"

"If I had any good sense, I'd have drowned you years ago. For the last time, Lena is neither a maidservant nor my mistress. Mrs. Gibb is a proper governess and an excellent teacher."

Florrie snorted, not a very ladylike sound at all. "And what about those other females your insolent gatekeeper brought up to the castle? I suppose you're going to say they are ladies, too? Ladies of the night, or my name isn't Florencia Camille Annabelle Knowlton Talbot."

"What other ladies? I didn't invite any strangers."

Florrie sniffed again. "They said they were Miss Armstead's sisters. I sent them to the roundabout, you can be assured. Sisters, hah! Lena never had a sister all the years she was with Aunt Sophie. As plain as she is, she wouldn't have a sister like those women, either. I don't know what kind of rig you are running now, but I won't—"

"Lud, what if one of them was Angelina's sister?" She'd never forgive him.

"Those light-skirts? Humph! She'd be better off without."

Corin thought amen to that if they were like his own fishwife of a sibling. He had to go talk to that flat, Fredricks, about sending soiled doves up to the castle. He had to go talk to Lena, return the dog, find her sister, find a physician, buy the brats presents. Lud.

In the end Corin bought a toy for Mrs. Gibb's daughter, not his niece and nephew. He thought that child needed a gift more than those two, and the white stuffed dog with black button eyes reminded him of that half-blind dust mop Lena carried around. He was not hoping to find favor with Lena by selecting something to her taste for the little girl. That's what he told himself, anyway. It was just that the porcelain dolls looked too fragile for a real child to play with, and their glass eyes reminded him of Lord Wyte's stuffed trophies.

Which in turn reminded Corin that his chances of pleasing his prospective father-in-law were as dim as his current reputation. Thunderation, even Mrs. Culpepper at the emporium tittered when he purchased the dog. Old Rupert at the livery where he left his horse kept winking at him, and not only because his lordship asked the ostler to watch Pug for an hour. The viscount's own butler was giving him the cold shoulder for disgracing the family name, and his valet Doddsworth—well, Corin was going to miss how the fellow tied a cravat.

There would be no redeeming his good name, either, not while Mercedes Lavalier was in the neighborhood and unattached. Corin reviewed his guest list for possibilities, feeling only slightly like a procurer. Mercedes would find her own gallant. She always did. At least Corin would be exonerated of trifling with Miss Armstead, which in fact he had done, but not recently. Everyone would know her for a lady as soon as he could get her up to the castle and introduced properly.

As for Elizabeth Gibb, Corin didn't think he'd have to worry about her, not the way Averill Browne had gone on about her goodness since they'd come back from London, nor the way he was sitting on the floor now, playing with the child when he wasn't staring at the mother. Let the architect marry the schoolmistress, the viscount prayed. He'd set them up with a house in the village, host the wedding breakfast, anything to make matters more respectable.

The viscount hoped Lena wouldn't be too disappointed at losing her *parti* to the governess. The frippery fellow wasn't good enough for her, anyway. No, she didn't look downcast in the least, Corin noted, watching her as she watched the scene with a fond smile playing about her soft lips. And his sister thought Miss Armstead was plain? Gads, Florrie hadn't seen Lena recently. Why, the chit became more lovely day by day, and not just because he'd been without a woman for too long. Mercedes Lavalier was the most beautiful woman of his experience, and available, but he wasn't one whit attracted to her. Perhaps one whit, he amended, for he was a male, after all, and Mercedes was a goddess of femininity. Lena was a real woman. Deuce take it, that was the problem. She was laughing now, as she left Mercedes's side and came toward where he stood by the window in her parlor.

"Don't feel badly," she told the viscount, noticing his frown. "Robinet didn't like our gifts, either."

He saw the discarded doll in Lena's arms and his stuffed toy in a corner of the room. The little girl had one thumb in her mouth and the other wrapped in one of the outdoor dogs' fur. Corin raised an eyebrow.

"She got out of the carriage, took two steps across the yard, and saw Gemma, our lame collie. They haven't been apart since."

"But the dog is so large, and the child is such a little wisp of a thing. She looks more like three than five. Are you sure she won't get hurt?"

"Gemma's the most gentle dog I know. She wouldn't let anything happen to her little lamb. Look, she doesn't mind her fur being pulled or her tail getting stepped on. I don't think she'll go outside again, if it means leaving Robinet."

And Homer hadn't even greeted him with a tail wag, Corin thought, envious of a five-year-old.

"Do you believe in love at first sight?" Angelina was asking.

"The dog and the child, or the two mooncalves?" He nodded toward the architect, who was still on the floor, gazing up at Elizabeth, who was wiping tears of joy from her eyes—with Browne's handkerchief.

Angelina smiled. "Every one of them, I suppose. Robinet is certainly her mother's daughter, giving her heart on the instant. Isn't it wonderful to see them all so happy?"

"If it lasts. Browne is a mere stripling, subject to sudden enthusiasms. What if he is infatuated with another woman next week?"

"How cynical you are, my lord. But Averill isn't a womanizer. He wouldn't pay such particular attention to a woman without deeper feelings. Why, he doesn't even flirt with Mercedes."

"You mean there is a man immune to her fatal charm?" he asked, stung by her implied criticism. Mercedes Lavalier was a beautiful woman, blast it.

"Only Mr. Browne so far. Even Penn is trying to learn French. Oh, and Sergeant Fredricks doesn't seem to find her attractive, but he doesn't seem to like much of anything, so he doesn't count."

"And you don't mind?"

"Why should I mind if my gardener stares in the windows all day and my stable man finds a hundred errands in the house?" And Lord Knowle gaped at the Frenchwoman's gaping décolletage like a trout at a fly.

"It doesn't signify anything, you know," he told her now, and meant it. "That's just her way."

And the way of the world, Angelina thought, not her world, but his. Still, she couldn't resent the Frenchwoman for being beautiful, not when she was helping defeat the Corsican, not when she was making Angelina's freckles disappear, and not when she'd cried when Elizabeth walked in with her daughter. Her insistence on a practice session every night with Angelina struggling at the keyboard was another thing, but that was an artistic issue, not a moral one.

Lord Knowle brushed at a speck of lint on his sleeve.

"Ah, Mercedes has a big heart, but she can be a trifle indiscreet."

Angelina laughed. "Indeed she can be—if, that is, you're referring to how she told everyone in the village she is your dear friend."

"Then you've heard the gossip?"

"How could I not when every servant has a relative in town, and all the tradespeople have been making their deliveries in person? They all believe she is your mistress, precisely what we knew would happen, even without the lady's own testimony."

"And you're not upset?"

Angelina shrugged. "Why should I be? As long as they think Mercedes is your mistress, my own reputation stays moderately untarnished."

So she hadn't heard the chitchat that had him keeping a stable of fillies at Primrose Cottage. Corin didn't think he'd mention that particular rumor right now, when Lena was in a cheerful mood. He did have to warn her, though. "The tattlemongers will have a field day when the ministry fellows start to call. I thought, ah, that is I expect the first of them tomorrow, and it might appear better, for the servants, don't you know, if—"

"What is it you don't want to tell me, my lord?"

Corin took a deep breath. "That Primrose Cottage is going to resemble a brothel."

'Twas a good thing the doll they'd made did not have a porcelain head, as it fell out of Angelina's fingers to the floor.

"But I've thought of a solution," he hurriedly added. "We can say the men have come to look over the dogs, with the intention of adopting a new pet."

The doll's head was stuffed with sawdust; Angelina thought his lordship's must be also. "What, the under-secretary to the War Office is looking for a dog that wets the carpet? General Wellesley's aide asked you for a gun-shy spaniel? Or perhaps Old Hooky himself wants a horse-hating hound. That should go over well in battle."

"Yes, I can see where the plan needs some refinement."

"What it needs is for you to stay away. Without you and your rakish reputation, the doings at Primrose Cottage won't seem half as interesting to the local people. In fact, if you'd stayed away in the first place, there would have been no gossip."

And there would have been no kisses, no curricle ride, no verbal sparring, no awareness of him as a man. Angelina watched the viscount bow over Mercedes's hand, kissing every finger, and felt she was losing something she'd never held. Mercedes would always have her men and her muse; Elizabeth would have a whole family, with luck. Angelina had the dogs.

Chapter Nineteen

No, she would not indulge in a fit of the blue-devils, Angelina told herself the following morning. Her life was richer than she'd ever expected, more secure and comfortable than she could have imagined. She had friends and responsibilities and perhaps her sister.

Penn had sent Mavis to say that a lady had come about the advertisement and was waiting downstairs. The abigail sniffed her disapproval that the woman did not give her name, but she did allow as how Penn distinctly said a lady. Lady Sophie's butler could discern Quality better than an Almack's patroness, Angelina knew, so she took extra pains with her appearance. The short curls were a definite improvement, and the ribbon Mavis threaded through them gave her a girlish look. She wouldn't shame her sister.

The woman waiting in the parlor was well dressed and well groomed, with a strand of enormous pearls draped over her imposing chest. She was obviously a lady, and just as obviously old enough to be Angelina's mother, not her sister.

"I'm sorry, but there must be some mistake," Angelina said, her welcoming smile fading. Then she rushed forward before this distinguished visitor could pet the Pekingese in her lap with a diamond-ringed finger. "Tippy goes off if you pet his back wrong. We think it's a brain fever."

"Then I won't pet the darling's back, will I? You like your ears scratched better, don't you, Tidbit?" She looked up at Angelina and explained, "I used to have a Pekingese when I was a girl."

Almost a half century ago, Angelina estimated, wondering what such a *grande dame* was doing in her parlor. She wasn't one of Lady Sophie's friends, unless she was a correspondent who had never visited before. But Penn had said she was there about the notice in the papers, and yes, there was the column with Angelina's inquiry atop the woman's beaded reticule next to her on the loveseat.

"I'm sorry, Mrs.—ah, my lady, ma'am. I didn't get your name."

The woman didn't answer for a moment, staring at Angelina. "You're very like her, you know. Your mother, that is."

"You knew my mother? Oh, do I resemble her? I've often wondered, for it's been so long I cannot remember, and there was never a portrait or miniature for me to look at. If you knew my mother, ma'am, pray, do you perhaps know what happened to my sister? Is that why you've come?"

The lady shook her head no. "I'm sorry, my dear, I only knew your mother briefly when she had her come-out. I was already married by the time Rosellen Kirkbridge took the ton by storm, she was just such a beauty as you."

"Oh, but I'm not—"

"There was a dreadful scandal when she ran off with some vicar's son, but that was the last I ever heard of her until word came that Rosellen and her husband had perished. I never knew there was a daughter." She looked at the scrap of newspaper. "Daughters."

147

"Then why . . . ?"

"Why have I come? No, you are not being impertinent, child, and I must beg your pardon for not being more forthcoming. I suppose I wished to appraise your character before discussing my private affairs."

"Oh, but I would not betray a confidence, ma'am." She hadn't told anyone that Mercedes Lavalier was a spy or that Lord Knowle was working for the government or that Elizabeth was in love with the architect. She couldn't imagine what secrets this stately lady could have to tell.

Still petting the Pekingese, who had rolled over in ecstasy at having his belly scratched, the older woman nodded. "Yes, your mother had such strength of character also, besides her beauty. She needed it, to stand up to Kirkbridge and marry the man of her choice. I didn't."

"You knew my grandfather, ma'am?"

"No, but my own father was such a one. When he arranged a match for me, I was too weak to resist his dictates. The man he chose was unexceptionable: wellborn, well to pass, well favored. Hathaway was some fifteen years older than I was, but had all his hair and teeth."

"Hathaway?"

"The Earl of Hathaway." She nodded. "It would have been an excellent match, except that I did not love my husband."

"And he? Did he—Forgive me, my lady. I do not mean to pry."

"No, Miss Armstead, do not apologize. I came here to tell my story, so you would understand. No, Hathaway did not love me, he did not even care for me. He had his so-called outside interests. He wanted me to give him an heir, that was all, and I failed him in that. There were no children at all for many years, and then I bore him a daughter whom he ignored. A year later, I was blessed with another daughter. Hathaway was furious—more, I think, that he had to continue our farce of a marriage than anything. We hardly spoke, so you can imagine the

148

unpleasantness for both of us when—No, you cannot imagine, I hope, being a young miss."

Angelina smoothed the fabric of her skirt. "But I can understand, my lady. Do go on."

Lady Hathaway's gray eyes were fixed on the dog in her lap, but she was looking at the past. "There were no other children. I didn't mind, for I had my girls, Catherine and Belinda, my little angels. And then . . ." She reached for her handkerchief.

"Please, my lady, if it is too painful, please don't go on."

Lady Hathaway dabbed at her eyes. "I must. When they were four and five years of age, Hathaway insisted we leave the girls to visit some house party or other, where he could indulge his debauchery. They were kidnapped and held to ransom."

"Oh, no, how terrible! Those poor little girls. Did you—that is, were they recovered?"

A tear fell on Tippy's fur. "Hathaway refused to pay the ransom."

"Their own father? But couldn't you . . . ?"

"I had no funds of my own save some pin money. My jewels were all in Hathaway's vault, so I could not sell them for the cash. My father was dead by then, and my brother was traveling abroad. There was no one to help me, no one to listen to my pleas. Hathaway said that if we gave in to the blackguards' demands, no man of wealth would ever be safe. He did send for the magistrate, I'll grant him that."

"And did Bow Street find your little girls, ma'am?"

Lady Hathaway shook her head. "Not even a clue. We never heard another word."

While Angelina was expressing her sorrow and pouring another jot of brandy into Lady Hathaway's teacup, the older woman was gathering her composure. "That was sixteen years ago, Miss Armstead, about the time you and your sister were orphaned."

"Yes, but we weren't stolen by Gypsies or anything, ma'am, although that might have been better. How can there be any connection?"

"To you and your sister? Of course there is none." She tapped the newspaper article. "But who knows what young women might come seeking their pasts? What missing girls might turn up here, hoping to find their own lost identities? I thought, that is, with your permission, that I might stay nearby and speak with the young women, the ones who aren't your sister."

"But what of Lord Hathaway?"

"Burning in hell, I sincerely hope, for his sins. We lived apart after the misfortune. A younger brother inherited the title and estate, but I am a wealthy widow, now that it is too late to buy my happiness. Please, Miss Armstead, I have nowhere else to turn."

"Yes, you do, my lady. I am paying a gentleman in London to help me with my investigation. I am sure he would be happy to undertake another assignment. Mr. Truesdale is discreet and reliable. I know a great deal of time has passed, but he might unearth something for both of us."

"Nigel Truesdale? A connection of the Knowltons, isn't he? I'd heard he was setting himself up in some kind of business. Good for him, trying to make something of himself."

"Yes, that's what Lady Sophie thought. Shall I get you his address, then?"

Lady Hathaway nodded, then walked to the window while Angelina searched through her desk. Tippy was still in her arms, tongue curled and tail brushing along the dowager's substantial girth. "If you don't mind," she said, "I'd still like to stay in the vicinity in case your notice brings results. I'd forgotten how lovely the countryside is in spring. The village inn I stopped at for tea and directions seemed clean and pleasant."

"An inn? I wouldn't hear of it. Why, Lady Sophie

would never forgive me for not offering the hospitality of her house. And you ought to be here to see the young women for yourself, to ask the right questions, and to meet with Mr. Truesdale in person when he comes next week."

"Oh, but I couldn't impose."

"Please, ma'am, you must stay here, especially since I can see you like dogs so well. We have a few others, incidentally." Angelina rushed on rather than discuss how many dogs constituted a few. "The primroses are not quite blooming yet, and truly that is a sight not to be missed. Please, my lady, I would be honored." And she would be chaperoned.

"Thank you, my dear, I will accept your gracious invitation if you are sure you have room. And thank you for not laughing at an old lady's foolish, forlorn hopes. Your mother would have been proud of you."

"Oh, we have room." Angelina had room and dogs and primroses—and Mercedes Lavalier. Angelina had a problem. "Ah, before you accept my invitation, I fear I have to confess to another guest who might not be to your liking."

"Mercedes Lavalier?"

"But how . . . ?"

"You shouldn't be surprised. I took tea at the inn, recall. Your French visitor is the most exciting thing to happen to this little village since someone's cow kicked in the church door."

"That would have been Widow Maloney's Sugar. But Mademoiselle Lavalier's presence was supposed to be secret, for her own safety."

"Spying, was she? No, my dear, do not look so stricken. You have given nothing away that everyone hasn't surmised, with the most famous ballet dancer in France fleeing in the dead of night. If I hadn't heard all the conjectures, I'd still have wondered, seeing that contingent of soldiers at Viscount Knowle's gatehouse. No, I would not mind staying in the same house as Mademoiselle Lavalier.

In fact, I would consider it an honor to be given the opportunity to see her dance. The Corsican upstart has much to answer for, including depriving us in England of a magnificent *artiste*. Has she performed for you?"

"Only in practice. Do you play the pianoforte, my lady?"

"I have spent many lonely hours at my instrument. The music gives me solace."

"Then you might be honored every night when Mercedes practices, for I am nowhere near proficient enough for her."

"To play for a real ballerina?" Lady Hathaway set Tippy on the floor, making sure the little dog was firmly on his feet. "Oh, I couldn't."

"Well, I cannot, so you would be doing me a great favor. In fact, if you would see your way to staying here, you'd be doing me an incredible service. Mercedes Lavalier is a woman of magnificent passions: for her country, her muse, and her men. She is excused much because of her art, but I—"

"Need to satisfy the conventions if you are to live in the ordinary world, correct?"

"Precisely. But if you were here lending your countenance, then we may all be comfortable again. Oh, do say you'll stay, my lady. We also have a little girl who desperately needs affection, Mrs. Gibb's child just rescued from an orphanage. And Mr. Browne, the architect, is here all the time, more so now because of Mrs. Gibb, who is an excellent teacher. Oh, and there's to be a house party at the Knoll, but many of the gentlemen guests are expected to visit Mercedes at the cottage, except they are to say they are looking at the dogs."

"My, and I thought the countryside was a place for peaceful relaxation." Lady Hathaway laughed. "Are you trying to convince me or discourage me, my dear? Is there anything else I need to know? Perhaps a wicked stepmother, a troll in the garden?"

"Viscount Knowle was troublesome at first, but I don't know that I'd call him a troll."

"If you did, you'd be the first female in his experience to do so, I believe. So the young devil has been troublesome? That wouldn't be why you need a chaperon, would it? No, my dear Miss Armstead, I'll spare your blushes. I'll be pleased to stay to see your primroses and play for your prima donna and spoil your pets and your little poppet. I also consider it my duty to safeguard your reputation, as I would have done for my daughters, as your mother would have done for you."

Chapter Twenty

"What, have you taken in another stray? The guards said a woman called but didn't leave." Lord Knowle was in Angelina's parlor, pacing. Ajax kept his eyes on the viscount; the viscount kept his eyes on Miss Armstead, who was looking like dessert in a strawberry mull gown with a cream lace fichu. "Deuce take it, haven't we got enough in our dish without adding another tidbit to the scandalbroth, Angel?"

"That's Miss Armstead, Lord Knowle, and my new guest is not a stray." She was combing one of the little terriers. Mavis was so busy making dresses and pinafores for Robinet that the grooming chores were being delayed.

"Pardon, another sister. What is this one, a Covent Garden flower seller?"

"She's not quite a sister, more a fairy godmother, so you should be pleased. She is going to relieve you of at least two burdens. First, she's going to take Tippy."

"The furball that has fits? Excellent. You're right, I'd do better to welcome her. I'll even pay her coach fare back to London, with a bonus if she takes the blind dust mop, too."

"Coach fare will not be necessary, for she is going to

154

stay on as chaperon. Since you have been so concerned for my reputation, that should gratify you."

"If she stays, does that mean the dog stays, too? Blast." Corin grimaced at the other two rat-size dogs chasing after the swaying tassels on his Hessians. At least he wouldn't have to listen to Doddsworth complain when he arrived home with battle scars on his boots. Then again, his footman could not tie a cravat. Bother!

"Furthermore, I shudder to think what type of woman you'd find appropriate for a *duenna*. You picked an unmarried mother for schoolteacher, so what's this one?"

"A countess."

The viscount stopped so short the little dogs tumbled into his feet. He looked up to see golden lights twinkling in Lena's green eyes. "A genuine countess, I swear," she told him. "Lady Lillian Hathaway is her name. I believe you are acquainted."

"Lady Hathaway? Why, she's a veritable pillar of Society, one of the most respected gentlewomen of the ton. What the deuce is *she* doing here? No," he said when Angelina gurgled with laughter, "I didn't mean it that way. I mean why has she come and why is she staying?"

"She was a friend of my mother's," Angelina replied, "who saw my advertisement." That was the story she and Lady Hathaway had decided to tell, rather than broadcast that lady's sorrow. Not giving the viscount a chance to make further inquiries, Angelina continued: "I asked her to stay to lend her countenance. I think it shall serve, don't you?"

"In spades. There has never been a hint of scandal attached to the lady, not when she was married to that dirty dish Hathaway, not since she's been a widow. But where is your new watchdog? I should pay my respects."

"You should be gone altogether, rather. Didn't we decide you should not feed the rumor mill by calling here?"

He sat down, relaxed now that the question of the new female at Primrose Cottage was so happily resolved. He even let Lucky—or was it Lucy?—jump into his lap. "Yes, I was going to stay away, but I had to bring Major McKennon to interview Mercedes."

- "What, an officer in His Majesty's cavalry couldn't find his way through the home woods? He found his way to my morning room well enough," she said. She had not been pleased when the mutton-chopped officer curtly dismissed the servants and the hostess alike, firmly shutting the door behind him and the Frenchwoman. Everyone had heard the key turn in the lock. Everyone had deduced they weren't merely discussing government business. "And you surely didn't have to wait to see him back on the path. One cannot miss it, with the primroses nearly out."

"I wanted to see how the little girl was settling in."

"Well, thank you. She went off to the school with Elizabeth this morning, and with the collie, of course. Now she is resting, again with the collie. But you could have asked Penn, my lord, rather than sit in the drawing room, leaving your motives open to conjecture."

"My motives, dash it, were to get out of the house. My sister still thinks I was trying to murder her children by bringing a dog home. Anyway, there won't be any conjecture now that Lady Hathaway is here." He tweaked the ribbon out of Lucky's hair and stuffed it between the seat cushions while Angelina was distracted by the dog she was combing. "She *is* here, isn't she?"

"Lady Hathaway assured me that she is the perfect dragon, a regular fire-breather, until nap time."

"Capital, I always thought the ideal chaperon was one who let her good name and good sense play propriety. Let's take advantage of her largesse and go for a walk. The day is lovely, and I didn't get to see all the primroses."

The afternoon was perfect, and the primroses wouldn't last for long. Neither would his lordship's attentions, Angelina knew. He'd go back to London, back to his tonnish life that certainly did not include a former companion. Angelina decided to enjoy the day, and his company, while she could.

First she had to fetch a bonnet. Wearing the pesky thing was easier than listening to Mavis and Mercedes complain about her complexion.

Corin just said, "Of course," to cover his disappointment that Lena was going to cover those disordered ringlets he found so fascinating. He hadn't lied about his motives for coming—bringing the major, inquiring about the child, avoiding his relations—but he hadn't been totally honest, either. The fact was, he couldn't stay away. There was just something about this woman, this woman in the wrong place at the wrong time, with the wrong birth and the wrong beliefs, that drew him like a dog to a bone. She didn't fit into any of the comfortable categories: servant or master, light-skirt or lady, wife or mistress. Corin knew he couldn't trifle with her; he didn't know why he couldn't stop thinking about her.

"Charming," he said when she reappeared in a flower-strewn straw bonnet that made her look like a bouquet of violets. Not so charming, he thought when she invited half the dogs in Kent to join them in a stroll.

"We'll go toward the back garden, shall we," Angelina asked, "so we are in sight of Lady Hathaway's rooms? I find I care more for her good regard than for whatever the villagers might be saying."

The dogs frolicked around them, ecstatic to be out of doors and off the lead. Bunny treed a squirrel—no rabbits would dare invade her territory—and Digger set out to dig to China, via the rosebushes. Windy trundled to a spot in the sun, and the three little terriers chased bees hovering around the early blooms. Ajax stayed at Angelina's side, whichever side the viscount chose to take, so Corin started tossing sticks for the big dog. Ajax brought them back every time, to Angelina. His lordship gave up on getting rid of the monster and took a deep breath of the spring air.

Lilacs, he thought, although he didn't think they were in season yet. Lena, he decided, smiling.

"Something is amusing, my lord?"

"No, just pleasing. There's nothing like spring in the countryside, is there? One forgets, in the city."

"Because there are so many other diversions: theater, museums, parties. Some of us provincials take these days for granted, but others need to make nature our entertainment, don't you know. And, of course, there are the farmers, whose livelihoods depend on the sun and the rain."

"That reminds me, the farmers. I have been visiting with some of my tenants these past few days."

"I'm sure they appreciate it, knowing you care enough to come by in person to listen to their problems or commend their progress. A steward is merely a paid overseer, but you are part of the land to them."

He was dirt to some of them, he knew, for their leaking roofs and outmoded equipment, but he meant to see the cottages and holdings brought up to snuff. Corin was ashamed that he'd needed a chit's reminder that he'd let his responsibilities slide. "Yes, well, I don't mean to be so much the absentee landlord. The estate suffers. By the way, some of the tenants mentioned that you had been making calls in my stead."

"Not in your place, my lord, in Lady Sophie's. She always said it was your family's duty to look after the people who earned your wealth. Noblesse oblige, and all. I went along with her for many years, getting to know all of the families. With you not here, I felt I should continue after my lady's passing. Mrs. Rice needs her rheumatism medicine, and Sarah Cummings has delivered her sixth babe, so I took some new blankets to her."

"I wish you wouldn't."

"Take Sarah blankets? I assure you Primrose Cottage can stand the expense, or I could pay the cost myself."

"No, I wish you wouldn't be going about like that, visiting my tenants."

"Oh, I see." Angelina whistled the dogs back to her side, to return to the house. "I have overstepped my position. My apologies, my lord, if I inadvertently usurped your mother's duties or your wife's. I am sure your tenants will be relieved when you marry, so they might have a real lady to look after their interests."

Corin found himself alone on the path except for old Windy. He called out to Angelina, "Wait, dash it, that's not what I meant. And no, I shan't pick you up. Not you, Angel, this bloated bulldog of yours that's looking at me so piteously."

"He's old and tired and his joints ache, just like Mrs. Rice's, but I wouldn't expect you to help. After all, he is my responsibility, as the tenants are yours." She bent to pat the wrinkled old dog, telling him they'd wait till he was ready to go home.

"Hell and damnation, woman, I'll carry the malodorous mutt if he needs it. What is one more waistcoat? But I will not let you go off in a huff like that."

"Oh, no? And how do you intend to keep me from going where I want to?"

"I will—" He wouldn't. Ajax was between Corin and Angelina, showing his teeth and growling. "Blast, that dog hates me."

"He doesn't like shouting or threatening gestures. Neither does Caesar."

Caesar was the one who didn't like men at all. Corin looked down. "Bloody hell! The whole garden and he's got to use my Hessians? Of all your ill-trained, rag-mannered mongrels, Miss Armstead, this one is the worst. And I did not intend to insult you, by George."

"Didn't you?" she asked, telling Caesar what a naughty dog he was, while she scratched under his chin.

"No, blast it. I do appreciate what you've done for the estate, but I don't want you going visiting because it's not safe. There are too many strangers around, too much uncertainty about Mercedes and whoever might be looking for her. She's made no secret of her presence here, so our only hope of protecting the peagoose is keeping her inside or close to the house. That goes for you, too. And that is all I meant. When the world knows that Mercedes Lavalier has left Primrose Cottage, you may visit every one of the tenants, every day, with my blessings."

Had he really been worried for her safety? Angelina couldn't tell, except for the little warm glow in the vicinity of her heart. "There is no need for your concern, my lord. I told you, the dogs won't let anything happen to me."

"What, is Ajax protection from a bullet? Do you think an assassin will be discouraged by wet shoes? It's not safe, and I am tired of your arguing with wiser heads about situations you do not understand, and I am tired of you 'my lording' me all the time, Angelina Armstead. My name is Corin. Or Knowle."

"Mercedes calls you Knolly."

"Mademoiselle Lavalier has called me many things, but I didn't think you wanted to be quite as familiar as Mercedes," he said, knowing he'd get to see Lena's blush start at the lace tucked into the bodice of her gown. "But I'm willing if you are, Angel."

Instead of answering, Angelina turned away from Corin, to his disappointment, and threw a stick for Ajax. The big dog went bounding after the tree branch, then raced back, just as Angelina took a step forward. Ajax's momentum carried him forward, right into Angelina, who would have gone flying, except that Corin's strong arms were there to steady her.

"Oh, I'm sorry," she started to say, expecting him to release her and step back. He didn't. Her bonnet had slid back on her head, held only by the ribbons around her neck. Staring down into her eyes, Corin untied the bow and let the straw hat fall to the ground. Then he raised one hand and, with butterfly gentleness, brushed back the curls that had tumbled onto her forehead.

"Oh." That was all Angelina could think to say. Her wits had waltzed away while her pulse danced a Highland jig. He was going to kiss her, and she was going to let him.

Corin touched her hair again and her cheek, then he laid his fingers on her lips, her soft, pink, parted lips. He groaned, knowing he'd lost the battle of conscience without firing a shot. What conscience? What battle? "Ah, Angel."

Finally he kissed her, holding her so close that his waistcoat buttons would leave an impression on her skin, but not as deep an impression as his lips made on her soul. He groaned again, or she did. They kissed until there was no ground beneath them, nor air between them. Lilacs and lips and lingering touches, that's all there was, besides dogs barking.

Dogs barking? Oh, dear! Angelina pulled back, and Corin released her immediately.

"Lud," he said. "I am sorry, Angel. That is, I'm not sorry, but I do apologize for breaking my promise to behave like a gentleman. Some gentleman I turned out to be, by Jupiter."

Angelina was busy knotting her bonnet's ribbons with trembling fingers. "But I let you, Corin. I suppose I'm not much of a lady, either."

And Lady Hathaway was not much of a chaperon, waving gaily from the window when Angelina glanced back at the house. Countess Lillian had vowed to keep watch over Angelina Armstead just like a mother. Any mother with a pretty, dowerless daughter would have done the same.

161

Chapter Twenty-one

"One of my tenants mentioned losing his dog recently," Corin said, trying to fill the silence as they walked back toward the cottage. "I thought I'd bring him one of yours, on approval, naturally."

"Yes, that would be fine."

"One of the outdoor dogs, to help on the farm."

"Yes, of course."

They were almost to the door where Lady Hathaway was waiting, the Pekingese in her arms. "And I do wish you'd listen to me about venturing afield by yourself."

"Very well, I'll think about what you said."

If he'd known that a simple kiss could turn the persnickety female this amenable, Corin thought, he'd have kissed her before. No, dash it, he had kissed her before. He shouldn't have then, and he shouldn't have now, especially if a mere kiss was going to leave her speechless and shaken.

"Deuce take it, Angel, it was only a kiss."

She nodded, but they both knew that an embrace so earthshaking, so profound, wasn't a kiss, a simple kiss, a mere kiss. And they both knew nothing could come of it.

Corin had to marry well: a hostess, a polished ornament to his elegant life, a social equal to bear his sons. Angelina didn't have to marry at all, but if she did wed, it would be to a simple gentleman of modest means who cared more for her than for titles and wealth and ambition. He'd be in touch with nature and the land, she reflected, and he wouldn't need reminding that violets didn't grow in some London market barrow. He certainly wouldn't care so much about his silly old boots, she thought.

Lady Hathaway thought they were both gudgeons, but she greeted them warmly, then suggested that lemonade was just the thing after a walk in the garden. Angelina took the opportunity to escape to the kitchens, as they all knew she would, and Lady Hathaway took the opportunity to lecture his lordship, as they all knew he deserved.

The lady was too subtle to come out and call him a cad and a bounder, Corin thought later. She only mentioned what a fine lady Angel's mother had been, what a fine lady Lady Sophie had been. And, oh, yes, how did he find his lady mother when he visited last? Lady Hathaway would be sure to write her dear friend Lady Knowle on the instant. If the countess had said "lady" once more, Corin feared he might forget he was a gentleman for the second time that afternoon.

He knew what was owed a gentlewoman, by Jupiter, but this was not the Dark Ages, when a stolen kiss required a declaration of marriage. Besides, they weren't of the same worlds. They wouldn't suit.

They wouldn't suit, Angelina thought. Even if she didn't find the viscount prideful and pigheaded, she'd never let herself care for a so-called gentleman who went around kissing any available woman. Kissing was for married couples, affianced at least. If that was her puritanical upbringing speaking, it was saying the wiser thing.

Not that Angelina blamed Corin entirely. She admitted to finding Corin attractive, attractive enough that she hadn't protested, hadn't stopped the kiss. She'd stopped breathing, for goodness' sake, much less stopped thinking. He certainly knew how to do the thing properly, likely from his years of practice.

No, Angelina would never let herself fall in love with a man who would only break her heart with his affairs and infidelities. And love, she firmly believed, was the only reason for marrying. Let Viscount Knowle and his highborn circle make alliances of advancement, coalitions of lands and fortunes, not marriages of hearts and minds. Let him and his friends make vows they intended to break. Let the blasted rake fetch his own cursed lemonade.

The butler, not Angelina, brought the lemonade. Corin took a large swallow to soothe his dry throat, then gasped. Someone had forgotten to add the sugar; the kitchens also overlooked the rear gardens.

Angelina was obviously not returning, so Corin took his leave of Lady Hathaway, with a bad taste in both their mouths. He checked with Jed, the groom, before unpenning the sturdy black-and-white herd dog he'd seen in the side yard. The dog's long coat was shiny, his eyes were bright with intelligence, his tail was a wagging plume, and his name was Buttons. What could be more innocuous than Buttons?

Jed didn't answer, having been in the kitchen with Cook enjoying a glass of lemonade, one sweetened just right.

Corin saw the dog settled in the castle stables, away from his niece and nephew and his sister's diatribes on his lack of familial devotion. He'd take Buttons to Ligett, the sheepherder, in the morning, notching a major victory, in his own eyes at least, toward getting another dog out of Primrose Cottage. Unfortunately for his success rate, both his chef's dog, Molly, and the architect's setter had been banished back to Angel's place for the duration of Florrie's visit to the castle, which was already too long.

"Ugh," his loving sister said. "You stink of the stables, Knowle. Could you not have changed before entering a lady's parlor with all your dirt?"

Corin sank into a chair after ringing for tea. "No, make that lemonade, with lots of sugar." Then he looked at his sister, with her hair braided into some convoluted edifice atop her head, her hands so white they must never spend a night out of chicken-skin gloves, poor Talbot, and her rather long nose wrinkled in disgust. Angel had a sweet little nose, with the slightest tilt to it, and a band of freckles across the bridge. Then, too, he recalled her soft-ness against his chest, her gently swelling curves that fit so well. He looked at his sister again. Poor, poor Talbot.

"And your boots!" Florrie squawked. "Doddsworth would never send you out like that. Whatever happened to you?"

"Doddsworth is gone, you do not want to know what happened to my boots, trust me, and this is still my parlor, isn't it? I cannot be sure, with Talbot snoring in my library and one of your children creating mayhem in my billiards room, the other destroying the conservatory. I understand I have to replace my head gardener, in addi-tion to my valet. Unless, perhaps, I have been deposed from the viscountcy while I was visiting my tenants."

"Visiting your tenants? Since when do you take an interest in mangel-wurzels and milch cows? I saw you come back from Primrose Cottage and those women, Knolly. It simply won't do, do you hear me?"

"I always hear you, Florrie. Your voice is as shrill as Mama's. But you're right, for once. I cannot keep visiting there; you'll have to invite them to the castle for tea."

"Are your attics to let, Knolly? Lord Wyte sent a mes-senger to inform us that he and his daughter will be arriving tomorrow afternoon."

Somehow the news did not please Corin as much as he

thought it should. "Very well, you can wait a day or two before inviting the ladies from Primrose Cottage. That way they can meet everyone at once."

"Meet Midas Micah Wyte and his precious Melissa? Oh, all that lovely money will land in someone else's bank account," she wailed. "You know what a high stickler Wyte is since he returned from India. He'll be outraged if you introduce his darling Melissa to actresses and upper servants. A ball or a large gathering is one thing, Knolly," she pleaded, "where the Frenchwoman can be passed off as part of the entertainment and Lena will fade into the woodwork as usual, but tea? Here?"

He thought he'd like to see Angel here very well; he also thought he'd like to see Florrie's face when she glimpsed their aunt's former companion. Allergies to dogs were nothing compared to the apoplexy she'd suffer. "Where else would you serve tea but the parlor? Of course if you'd rather have them to dinner—"

"No! No dinner, no tea, or there will be no engagement! Wyte will be offended by the slightest hint of fastness, Knolly. You know what he's like."

"Do you know what Countess Hathaway is like, Florrie?"

"Why, of course. Everyone knows she's a veritable dragon. One word from her and a debutante's Season is rescheduled for Bath."

"Exactly. Well, see that you don't offend her, either, then, in case you'll be bringing what's-her-name to London for her come-out in the next ten years. Lady Hathaway is staying at Primrose Cottage."

Florrie snatched up her brother's glass of lemonade and drank it down in one swallow. "Countess Hathaway, here, oh my. Just imagine what she could do for Talbot's career!"

Nothing could be done for Talbot's government career except winning the lottery, Corin thought, but Lady

Hathaway must be used to toads and mushrooms; she'd know how to depress his sister's pretensions nicely.

Florrie was already thinking ahead to her seating arrangements. "If I ask the countess to dine, do you suppose I must invite her companion, too?"

"Angel? That is, Lena? Don't you ever listen, Florrie? Lena is Lady Hathaway's hostess, not her paid servant. The countess knew her mother."

"Who ran off to Gretna in a scandalous misalliance. Be assured Lady Hathaway would not countenance such conduct. Why, they say that she never looked at another man, not once, despite Hathaway's—Well, suffice it to say he was not the ideal husband. The countess is known to be even more high-principled now that she is widowed."

"Nevertheless, she is a guest at the cottage, at Miss Armstead's cottage."

Florrie sat back. "Well, I can see you are singing a different tune. Miss Armstead's cottage, is it?"

Corin simply nodded.

"With all those dogs? Oh, dear, and I was going to leave my card first thing in the morning. But you know how I am around that many animals."

Not a pretty sight, he acknowledged. "Then I'll carry your invitation for you. If you ask the ladies to make a morning call, you might even get lucky. Mrs. Gibb will be teaching, and Mercedes Lavalier never gets out of bed before noon."

"The French high flier? Now I know you're teasing, Knolly, and you are too old for this kind of prank, I swear. Lady Hathaway would never recognize the likes of your émigré jade."

"Luckily the countess recognizes great talent. I believe Lady Hathaway is even now playing the pianoforte so Mademoiselle Lavalier can rehearse. Perhaps you should practice your scales, too, Florrie. If I recall, you were as flat at the pianoforte as you were everywhere else."

* * *

Lady Hathaway and Mercedes Lavalier were indeed rehearsing, in between deciding the fate of the world and everyone in it, with Lord Knowle's name at the top of the list. Mercedes thought Knolly could make her *bonne amie* happy; the countess thought he could make the dear girl a good husband, a very different proposition.

Angelina was at loose ends for a change, with two of her guests closeted in the music room and Elizabeth upstairs putting her daughter to bed. She would read aloud, Angelina knew, then sit for hours simply watching her little girl sleep. At length she'd come thank Angelina all over again, as if Robinet's tentative smiles weren't reward enough.

Angelina decided this was a good time to go over the household accounts. She might dislike the job, but she disliked her own thoughts more tonight.

At the castle, Florrie was in a flutter, driving herself and the Belgian chef to distraction over the menus for her tea party. Corin was of the opinion that, after insisting Henri send his dog away, Florrie would be lucky to get Molly's leftover beef-broth, biscuits, and bones. But, of course, Florrie did not ask Corin's opinion. So what if he was the host? He was only her brother. He shrugged his broad shoulders. Chunks of raw meat would look lovely on the Wedgwood.

Talbot did want Corin's opinion—of his new waistcoat, all puce stripes and cabbage roses. Angel wouldn't dress her dogs in it.

Averill Browne wanted only to rhapsodize over Mrs. Gibb. Corin hired the clunch to renovate the schoolhouse, just to send him off to his drawing board.

Major McKennon was locked in the library with his codebook and Corin's finest cognac. The billiards table needed repair, and Florrie cheated at cards. The brats would still be terrorizing the nursery staff abovestairs, and the servants who hadn't given notice would be having their supper below. Now Corin remembered why he didn't spend much time in the country. He decided to take the dog Buttons down to the local tavern, to see if the sheep man Ligett stopped in for a drink after a hard day's work. Lud knew Corin could use one. Or six.

Chapter Twenty-two

"Deuce take it, woman, why didn't you tell me the blasted dog was a sheep killer?" Corin was on Angelina's doorstep before breakfast the next morning, not even wondering what she was doing opening the door herself. He had to return that miserable mutt and get home before his company arrived—his proper company, a lady who wouldn't think of sending him off to defend the worst criminal in the animal kingdom, according to the men at the Drovers' Inn. Now he had to go find Doddsworth, hoping the fellow hadn't left for London, hoping the valet was still greedy enough to accept a bribe, hoping he still knew how to use the hare's foot to cover bruises. Bruises, by George, a cut near his eye and a huge purple mark on his chin, with Melissa Wyte and her father arriving in just hours. Hell and damnation!

"Why couldn't you have named the cur Slasher or Gnasher? Medea? Anything that would have warned a fellow not to make a fool of himself in front of half the shepherds in the shire. Why not Wolfie! No, you had to call him Buttons, sweet little button nose, adorable little button eyes, great big bone-crunching teeth!"

Angelina was standing in the hallway, biting her lip. "I—"

"No, I don't want to hear it. The dog should have been destroyed! Would have been, too, if you hadn't interfered with Shep Cavanaugh, I understand. Did you think the others wouldn't recognize Buttons? Let me tell you, missy, sheepherders can recognize a killer dog no matter how many years and miles have passed. Those men were ready to murder the blasted beast right there!"

And heaven knew what Angelina would have done if Corin had let them. So he'd had to defend Buttons, first with words and smiles and buying several rounds for everyone. Not a good idea, he found out, as some of the shepherds lost a deal of their respect for the peerage with the loss of their sobriety. The men weren't Republicans, but they did hold grudges against the aristocracy, even if the aristocrat was paying their wages, paying for their ale. They particularly resented a nobleman who stayed away from his responsibilities so long, who brought a Frenchy spy into their neighborhood, and who was trifling with that sweet Miss Armstead, a proper lady if there ever was one, even if she was touched in the upper works when it came to dogs.

One word had led to another, one drink to another, and then fists were flying. Corin hadn't had so much fun in ages, but he wasn't about to admit that to the cockle-headed Miss Armstead. No, he'd return the rogue sheepdog and wash his hands—skinned knuckles and all—of Angel and the rest of her worthless waifs, plus the hundred or so she'd find to fill that hell-spawned dog hotel she was building. His lordship didn't want a dog, didn't need a dog, and didn't care if he never saw another dog in his life, especially not this one that was leaning against his leg in a misplaced gesture of canine affection. "Get away from me, you lamb chopper."

"Buttons didn't kill the lamb." Angelina was stroking the black-and-white head.

"What, Shep Cavanaugh was mistaken when he found the bones, and his dog with a mouthful of wool?"

"I didn't say he didn't eat the lamb, I simply said he didn't kill it. And the whole episode was Cavanaugh's fault in the first place. It was just easier to blame the dog for his own laziness. He left the sheep in the hills too long, during a terrible storm, never coming to check for early lambs, never coming to bring food for his dog. Buttons was starving, but he wouldn't leave the sheep. The lamb could have died naturally."

"The lamb could have put on ice skates and sung at the Frost Fair, too! Deuce take it, you'd make excuses for the cannibals that ate—I'm sorry. That was unforgivable. But you cannot know what happened up in the hills. Cavanaugh is an experienced man who knows sheep and sheepdogs."

Angelina just said "Watch." She whistled once and made a series of hand gestures. Buttons barked once, then herded the three yapping Yorkshire terriers, Pug, and the epileptic Pekingese into a corner of the hall. At another signal, Buttons nudged the half-blind Maltese into the corner, too, before lying down in front of his corralled flock as they yipped in his ear, made swipes at his wagging tail, and pawed at his thick fur.

"Buttons would not hurt anything, my lord. He deserves another chance." She waved her hand, and the big dog got up, releasing the others from the corner.

So they were back to "my lord." Fine. "No one will give a sheep killer a second chance, Miss Armstead. They cannot afford to when every lamb makes the difference between their own children going hungry. There are a lot of dogs."

"And there are a lot of competent, conscientious sheepherders. If that lamb meant so much to Shep Cavanaugh, he should have been the one out in that storm guarding it."

"Dash it, you *do* care more for the dogs than for people. You're sounding more like my aunt Sophie every day. If you're not careful, you'll end up like her, too, alone and lonely."

"She wasn't alone! She had her dogs and her friends and a staff that adored her. She had me, too, remember, her paid companion. Except she did not pay for my affection; I gave that freely and happily, unlike others who have to trade their titles and fortunes to—" Angelina bit back the words she was about to say concerning loveless marriages, like the one he was about to contract if rumors were true. "Excuse me."

"Touché. Now we are even for saying more than we should. I shall bid you good day, Miss—What the deuce cloth-headed thing are you doing now?"

He'd finally gotten around to taking stock of his nemesis. Angel was back in her shapeless black gown and drooping black mobcap. She was wearing sturdy boots and thick gloves, and an old-fashioned blunderbuss rested on the ground near her foot. He took a step back when she raised the ancient weapon. She couldn't be that offended, could she?

Angelina stepped around the little dogs and around the viscount. "Excuse me, I am going for a walk." When she followed his gaze to the firearm, she added, "You did warn me it might be dangerous, didn't you?"

"Bloody hell," Corin muttered, following her out of the door and down the path. He should have left the dog on her doorstep. He could feel trouble in his bones, especially his bad leg and the aching ribs from last night. He should turn his back and keep going, without asking one more question whose answer he wasn't going to like. Hell, he should shoot himself for interfering, if Angel didn't shoot him first. "Halt!" he shouted in his best military voice. "Halt, I say, or I'll march inside and ask Lady Hathaway if she knows where her proper young miss is going."

Angelina stopped, cursing the man for his meddling. "I am in a hurry, and Lady Hathaway is still abed."

"Too bad. To my everlasting regret, I must insist on knowing where you are going, my girl, and what you are going to do with that gun once you get there."

Angelina didn't have the heart to rip up at him for his overbearing ways or the familiarity, not now. "I am going to the woods to kill a dog, my lord."

"Well, that's a novel twist, I must admit. Is your victim any dog I've had the pleasure of encountering? How about Caesar, or the one who ate my gloves again yesterday?"

"Is making light of things all you can do? This is not a joking matter, my lord. Someone has shot a dog in the woods. One of the children reported hearing the shot and the animal's screams. He couldn't find it, so he came to me."

"To you? What can you do about it?"

"I can put the poor creature out of its misery, of course. Did you think I would let an animal lie there and bleed to death in agony?"

"Of course not. But why didn't you send for one of the soldiers at the gatehouse to take care of the problem?"

"Because the problem, as you call it, came from the gatehouse, where you have those ruffians quartered. That's what the boy Leroy said, anyway, and I believe him. None of our local people would shoot a dog."

"There are always poachers."

"With all the watchmen you have patrolling the grounds and woods? Not likely. Besides, the last thing a poacher would do is fire a gun where someone could hear it. And a dog? Not even the most desperate of thieves would shoot a dog."

But any number of herdsmen would shoot Buttons. Thank goodness the sheepdog was safely inside. He looked around to see if he could tell which of the others was missing. "Is it one of your dogs?"

"No, thank heaven, but that doesn't change anything except that I'd practice my aim at the gatehouse first."

"What would you do, shoot the whole contingent of soldiers? You have no proof." He eyed the wide-muzzled, unreliable gun skeptically. "You do know how to use that thing, I assume."

"I know the mechanics, thank you. Jed Groom taught me." Patting the pocket of her skirt, she confessed, "I am better with the pistol here. But I do not know how close the dog will let me come. Wounded creatures can be unpredictable and dangerous. I do not want the poor thing to run farther into the woods, either, where it will be harder to find."

"I can see where you'd be concerned—anyone would be—but why the deuce isn't Jed going with you, or in your stead?"

"It's market day; Jed has driven Cook into the village. I could ask one of the footmen, but none of them can handle a weapon, and this is not their province. Lady Sophie left me in charge here, so this is my responsibility. I can do what needs to be done."

She could if she could see between her tears.

Corin cursed to himself. "You're not even taking Ajax, your bodyguard?"

"He shouldn't have to see this."

Bloody hell, Corin thought, the widgeon was protecting the tender sensibilities of Attila the Hun. And looking more like Florrie's blotchy children with every tear she tried to hold back. Damn, damn, damn. He took the heavy blunderbuss from her and fell into step.

"Oh, but it's not your responsibility," Angelina started to say.

"No? In case you haven't noticed, we are on my land now. I sent for those soldiers, and I pay the gamekeepers, who should have seen to this. Furthermore, you might not think I am much of a gentleman, but the day I permit a lady to shoulder such a task is the day I shall be in my grave."

"Thank you. Do you know, the vicar must be right after all, that there is some good in all of us."

Except the military mawworms at the gatehouse.

*   *   *

They heard the dog before they saw it, a low wailing sound of death and fear and pain that would have brought tears to the hardest heart. Angelina and Corin crashed through the brush, following the sound and the trail of blood; then they had to pull apart a thicket of briers that the creature had crawled under, to die.

"Don't look," Corin told her, but Angelina didn't listen, as usual. The dog was medium-size, black and tan with a dash of white, with a thick, matted coat. There was a huge, gaping wound above the right hip, with blood slowly seeping onto the already sodden ground. The animal didn't raise its head when they came closer; it just kept up the rhythmic keening.

"Don't get any nearer," Angelina whispered, reaching into her pocket for the pistol. "An animal in such pain doesn't know what it's doing and can inflict a terrible bite."

But Corin had put the blunderbuss down and was kneeling on the muddy ground next to the dog. He moved his hand cautiously forward until the animal could smell him, and a tongue reached out to try to lick his fingers.

"Stand away, my lord," Angelina entreated him, her voice wavering as much as the pistol she held in both hands, trying to aim through tear-filled eyes.

"Don't shoot."

"I can do it, really I can."

"But don't. See, he's trying to move, to come to me. He's not dying, I know it."

"But all the blood, and the pain the poor dog must be suffering."

"Blast it, the dog deserves a chance!" he echoed her earlier words.

"I cannot believe this," Angelina said, lowering the gun and coming to his side. "You'd have me destroy Buttons for one suspected misdeed, and the other perfectly healthy dogs because they are not useful or they misbehave, yet you'd let this poor creature suffer because it licked your hand?"

He was petting the dog's head now, and the yowling had stopped. Angelina thought it was because the dog was too weak to cry anymore; Corin thought it was because the dog was reassured by his presence. "He likes me."

"He is a she, and it makes no difference. We cannot help her, Knolly, no matter how nice a dog. The only merciful deed we can do is end her misery."

"We can try, damn it." He had his neck cloth off and formed into a pad to hold to the wound.

Without a word Angelina turned, bent, and ripped the hem of her petticoat. She handed the length of fabric to the viscount and said, "I have a bottle of laudanum in my pocket that might help, if you can get some into her without getting bitten."

"She won't bite me, will you, girl?" The dog let him bind the wound and pour the opiate down her throat. A lot dribbled out of her mouth, so he tried again. "I don't know how much . . ."

Angelina shook her head. "It won't matter if you give her too much."

"I've seen men with worse wounds live to fight another day, Angel. She can make it, I know."

"Perhaps, if we get the bullet out, if there is no infection, and if she hasn't lost too much blood already, or caught a lung inflammation. But we are miles away from the cottage. She'll be dead by the time we can get back with a wagon, or even a horse if you could hold her, so what's the use?"

"I'll carry her. She's only skin and bones under all this fur. The poor mite must have been wandering for days without proper food. Look, her eyes are shutting. The laudanum must be working, so we can move her now."

Angelina thought the dog must be lapsing into blessed

unconsciousness. She'd let the viscount carry her toward the cottage, where someone could come dig a grave.

"No, we'll take her to the castle. It's closer." He took off his coat and handed it to Angelina, then slid his hands under the dog. "Come on, Sunshine."

"Sunshine?"

"The sun will rise again tomorrow."

So they carried the half-dead dog back to Knowle Castle, through the briers, through the woods. By the time they reached the drive to the castle, his lordship was damp with perspiration, covered with blood and grime, and limping badly. Angelina was looking as if she'd been dragged through a thicket backward, which she had been. Her skirts were trailing, her bodice was ripped, and her cheek had a large scratch down it, which matched the bruise on Lord Knowle's chin. He had an unconscious dog, she had a blunderbuss, and Miss Melissa Wyte, stepping out of her carriage, had a fainting spell.

Chapter Twenty-three

Thank goodness his cousin Nigel was there to catch the chit, Corin thought, since his own hands were full and filthy. Then he wondered what the deuce Nigel Truesdale was doing there in the first place.

It made no never mind, for there was nothing Corin could do at the moment about any of it: his screaming sister, the swooning miss, or her upset sire. He hadn't carried this pathetic bundle all the way home just to have it die on his doorstep. His sister could see to the guests when she was done having palpitations.

His bewigged butler came down the front steps, frowning his disapproval of such indecorous proceedings at a gentleman's residence. Bradshaw thought he would relieve his lordship of whatever noxious burden he carried, send the ramshackle female with him to the right-about, and restore Knowle Castle to its proper dignity for greeting guests. He took one look at his lordship's burden, then a better look at his draggle-tailed companion. Lady Sophie's protégée. Of course. Bradshaw shuddered, did an about-face, and marched back up the front steps.

Angelina wanted to giggle, right after she dug a hole to jump in.

"Don't you get missish on me now," Corin warned, thinking she was about to get hysterical finally, in reaction to the sights and sounds and smells. Lud knew every other female of his experience would have needed burned feathers and smelling salts hours ago. He doubted Angelina Armstead even possessed a vinaigrette.

"I am never missish, my lord," she confirmed, "but I don't think we should be standing here."

"Right, we'll go to the stables." He made a half bow toward the convoy of carriages in his drive, then turned his back on the woman who would be his bride—if she ever recovered from her swoon—and headed around the side of the castle.

Angelina ran ahead to warn the grooms that they'd need water and blankets and bandages. Most of the stable hands had gone to help with the guests' carriages, however, and the remaining three young lads were trying to get a fractious cream-colored horse into a stall. The Arabian was the most beautiful mare Angelina had ever seen, with long, dainty legs, a narrow, tapered head, and a flowing mane and tail. She was also biting, kicking, rearing, and making a dangerous nuisance of herself. The smell of blood around Angelina didn't help matters. Without stopping to think, Angelina tossed his lordship's coat, still in her hands, over the horse's head. The mare stilled instantly, long enough for the boys to drag her into the double stall reserved for her.

No, his Angel wasn't missish at all, Corin thought, coming through the stable doors with the dog in his arms. She was shouting to his lads, directing them to spread fresh hay and blankets. Corin placed the dog on the soft bed as gently as he could, then checked to make sure that the dog was still breathing.

"Send for Ben," he ordered one of the grooms, then told Angelina, "He knows everything there is to know about horses. He'll be able to help."

Ben shook his head when they'd unwrapped the

wound. "Horses don't go around getting shot, milord. You needs a doctor."

Angelina snorted. "That puff-guts won't leave his posh practice for a farmer's child; he surely won't bestir himself for a stray dog."

"We'll find one who will, I promise," Corin said, swearing to himself, Angelina, and the dog. "But that bullet has to come out now."

The woman and the head groom just looked at him. Angel's face had lost all color, and Ben was holding out his clumsy, arthritic fingers. Oh, lud.

The dog stayed asleep—unconscious or scratching on Death's door, Corin couldn't tell—during the operation. His own surgery on the Peninsula hadn't been this awful, he thought, wishing he were back in Spain.

Angelina was glad she hadn't stopped for breakfast this morning, but she didn't faint and her hands didn't tremble too badly to thread the needle or cut the matted hair away from the bullet hole.

"Good girl," Corin said, and she didn't feel so weak-kneed anymore. They spread basilicum powder on the wound, then put fresh bandages over it, just as Sunshine started to stir. "Good girl," he said again, this time for the dog. Angelina didn't feel quite so proud.

"It's early days, but I reckon how it's not only cats what has nine lives," Ben commented as the dog moaned, stopping as soon as Corin put his hand on her shaggy head. "Sure knows who saved her, too."

"She does like me, doesn't she?"

Angelina was biting her lip again. "I cannot carry her back to the cottage, my lord. I know your people are busy with all the extra horses and such"—she waved her hand at the bustle in the stables that they hadn't noticed before—"but do you think someone could drive us in a wagon?"

"What, and destroy all my handiwork at the first bump? No, Angel, the dog stays here, where my staff had better

181

not be too busy to look after her. Zeus knows there's enough of them, and you have enough in your dish without adding a sick dog that's going to need constant attention."

"That's very kind of you," she said, adding "my lord," for Ben's eager ears. "But she'll have to come to the cottage eventually, not that I mean to add her to the count of Lady Sophie's dogs, of course. She can be the first dog at the Remington place, the first dog offered for adoption once she has recovered."

"No. Sunshine stays here."

"But your sister, your guests—"

"Sunshine is my dog. That's final."

Angelina wasn't about to argue. If his lordship wanted this pitiful melange of mixed parentage, he was welcome to it. Angelina hated seeing the dogs sick or distressed. "Then I had better be going. Lady Hathaway will be wondering what became of me." She picked up the blunderbuss and bobbed a curtsy. "Thank you for your help, my lord. I could not have managed without you."

"*You* could have, Angel, it's the dog who couldn't have." He was wiping his arms and hands on a towel Ben had brought. "But no matter how intrepid you are, Miss Armstead, you are not going home without me. Until we find out who shot the dog, the woods are too dangerous. Besides, you've had an exhausting morning."

"But your sister, the guests—"

"Dash it all, I know who is staying at my house! For once, Angel, cease the argumentation and get in my curricle!"

"But one of the grooms could drive me, I'm sure."

"I'm sure he could, too, but I happen to have an errand at the gatehouse that won't keep, don't you know."

She handed him the blunderbuss.

Corin did not enter Primrose Cottage with Angelina, citing the state of his clothes and his mood. Eager to be gone, he did promise to send word of the dog's condition.

After a much-needed bath and a change of clothes, Angelina joined the older ladies—Lady Hathaway older in years, Mercedes Lavalier older in experience—in the morning room for luncheon. Elizabeth was taking her meal upstairs with Robinet.

Angelina hadn't thought she could eat after the harrowing morning, but discovered she was famished when Penn brought out Cook's steak and kidney pie. Between bites, Angelina related the day's events. She told how the viscount would not let her shoot the injured animal, after all his protestations that dogs were worthless creatures, every one.

"I would have returned an hour ago," Angelina told her guests, "except Lord Knowle insisted on driving me home, and he couldn't bear to part with the dog. He spent an age giving directions to the stable hands, making sure Sunshine had beef broth and chopped meat when she awoke, lanterns and warmed blankets, and a boy to sit by her side ready to fetch the viscount if the wound started bleeding again. It's a wonder Corin didn't decide to spend the day in that stall with the dog."

"But that's what you would have done, isn't it?" Lady Hathaway asked.

Angelina buttered a slice of fresh bread while she considered her next words. "But his lordship never seemed to care. This one dog, this bedraggled stray, changed everything with one lick of his hand." She smiled. "Now Corin will have to believe in love and loyalty, trust and responsibility."

Lady Hathaway smiled, too. "I think he always believed in love, he just didn't know he did."

Mercedes disagreed. "*Mon cher* Knolly always knew his duty, but it takes a good woman to teach a man how to love."

Or a good dog.

The soldiers at the gatehouse never saw a dog, never heard a dog, and certainly never shot a dog, they all swore. Corin swore he'd shoot them all if he found otherwise. Without proof, there was not much else he could do except make threats.

Dissatisfied, he was in an even worse temper when he drove home and found his cousin Nigel in the stable, inspecting the dog through his quizzing glass. "Leave her alone, she needs her rest."

"Just looking, cuz, to see what was so important you snubbed Midas Micah Wyte."

Corin walked past Nigel and knelt by the dog's side. She gave one feeble tail wag, which he took to be a good sign. The boy delegated to keep watch said she'd taken some broth, and Corin held the bowl so she could drink some more. The dog was going to live, by Jupiter! He'd done the right thing. Without looking up, he said, "I didn't exactly snub Wyte, and he arrived hours early, confound it."

"To find you in deshabille with the little lass down the path. My, my, how convenient, cuz, but how indiscreet! And Aunt Sophie's companion? You're a braver man than I, Knolly, or you don't believe in the hereafter. The old girl will have your head for washing, my friend."

"I don't believe in blood being thicker than water, Nigel, so be careful how you speak of Miss Armstead. She is a lady, and I would not hear otherwise from your lips."

"Sensitive subject, eh, cuz?"

Nigel was as sharp-tongued as ever, and as badly dressed. Corin might look a mess now, but Nigel wore yellow cossack trousers, a puce-striped waistcoat, a lavender frock coat, and periwinkle blue slippers. On purpose. Corin winced. The battered dog looked better.

Noticing his cousin's scrutiny, Nigel puffed out his chest. "In honor of spring, don't you know."

"What, you decided to look like a pouter pigeon in mating plumage?" Corin was positive the shoulders of Nigel's coat were stuffed with buckram wadding, and that creaking sound had to be a corset. "What the devil are you doing here anyway?"

"Why, Cousin Florencia invited me, of course, to even the numbers. It seemed courteous to offer my escort to Miss Wyte and her father."

"And cheaper than hiring your own rig." Corin knew his cousin never had the dibs in tune, and he was actually glad someone had been on hand to do the pretty for the Diamond.

"Besides," Nigel continued, "I had to consult with my client, Miss Armstead, and there was a note concerning Lady Hathaway possibly requiring my services."

"Do you ever actually find anyone for your poor gulls, or do you just take the flats' money?"

Nigel brushed a speck off his sleeve. "You wound me, cuz, honestly you do. I charge only for expenses unless and until I am able to solve the case."

"Well, I'll wound you worse if you upset Miss Armstead."

"So the wind really does sit in that corner. I'm surprised, cuz. I thought you more fastidious than to be interested in such a harum-scarum miss."

"I am and she's not. Angel—Miss Armstead is a lady. I feel somewhat responsible for her, thus I do not wish to see her upset. She really believes she is going to find that sister of hers."

"I do my best, you know, and I actually am quite good at it. Found Lord Cranshank's gold watch last week. My years of visiting the pawnshops are finally paying off, don't you know. Of course, Miss Armstead wants me to find something that was purposely hidden, and ages ago to boot, but I have a few leads."

"Just see that you don't get up to your usual tricks and lead her astray."

"Miss Armstead? I didn't think it was possible, if you couldn't."

"Dash it, I told you, she is a lady. If you're looking for

the sister, you ought to know she is Kirkbridge's grand-daughter. Leave her alone, Nigel, that's all."

"My, my, how vehement. But don't worry, Knolly, your little neighbor is safe from me. She's not rich enough, for one, and all those dog hairs, for another." He shuddered delicately. "I don't know how you stand it. Then again, judging from your current appearance, one more dog hair or two wouldn't matter." He polished his looking glass and used it to survey his cousin's ruined boots, filthy shirt, and torn coat. "My, my."

For once Corin agreed with his cousin. "If you are so good at finding things, I'll pay you fifty pounds to find me a valet before dinnertime."

"For fifty pounds you can have mine, Knolly. Excellent chap, has a way with a curling iron."

"No, I'd pay you the blunt to drown anyone responsible for your ensemble and hairstyle," Corin stated, pushing his own untrimmed hair back out of his eyes.

"Fine, but I am not the one trying to impress my future father-in-law. Is that a bruise I see on your chin, cuz?"

"Very well, I'll pay you twenty pounds to share your man, if you swear to take him with you when you go. But I'll double that if you can find me a physician."

"What? The bruise doesn't look that bad, Knolly. Or did you mean for the dog? You really have been rusti-cating too long, my dear fellow, if this pathetic lump of fur is of such importance to you."

"Leave the dog out of this. I want a doctor for the vil-lage, a permanent surgeon who's not too high in the instep to treat the blacksmith's boils and the cottagers' colicky infants. No drunks, no quacks, and no basket scramblers who are on the lookout for a wealthy patron."

"I'm not in the employment agency business, you know, but I'll see what I can do. Between you, Lady Hathaway, and a bit of investigation Lord Wyte is thinking of having me do, this could turn out to be a prof-itable sojourn in the country. My thanks, cuz."

"Fine, but remember what I said about Miss Armstead or you'll be on the first coach back to London."

"My, my, we are sensitive, aren't we?"

Corin didn't know what he was anymore. He knew only that he didn't want his foppish, fashionable cousin anywhere near his dog, or his Angel.

Chapter Twenty-four

$\mathscr{A}$ngelina wished the woman who came that afternoon were her sister. Charlotte Franklin was lively and levelheaded, with a large family of sun-browned children. She was blond and as pretty as Angelina thought Philomena would have turned out to be, except for the thickened waistline and double chin. The children were wonderful with the dogs, gentle with Robinet, and courteous to Lady Hathaway and Angelina. Charlotte's husband, Preston, was a soft-spoken man with twinkling eyes who won Angelina's admiration by not instantly fawning over Mercedes Lavalier.

She would have a whole family, Angelina thought, a big, noisy, happy family, if Charlotte were her sister. Charlotte wished it were so even more, she admitted, for Preston had just been discharged from the army, where he had served with distinction until contracting an ague and a weakness in the lungs. The army had sent them all home from the Peninsula, with a recommendation and one month's pay.

"And how they think we are to survive, I want to know, for my Preston's not skilled in anything but soldiering," Charlotte said when her husband went outside with the youngsters. "And not the bully-boy posturing of those pigs who tried to stop us at the gate, either. An insult to the uniform, those jackstraws. My Preston is a good man who would turn his hand to anything to provide for the children, but he hasn't got his strength back yet. And after all those years following the drum, we have no friends in England to call on, to see if they might know of an open position. We often talked of saving up to buy an inn when he retired from the military, but then there was always another mouth to feed."

Charlotte smiled fondly at the horde of children romping with the dogs. "Not that I'm regretting a one of the darlings, but the boys should go off to school to learn a trade, and the girls will be needing dowries. How we are to manage is anybody's guess. That's why, when I saw your advertisement, I said to Preston, 'This sounds like our luck has changed.' "

Unfortunately for everyone's hopes, Charlotte couldn't remember their father's pet name for her, which was Angelina's key to proving her sister's identity. Not only could Charlotte not recall a nickname, she could not recall a father. A beautiful, laughing mother dressed in silks and satins and diamonds and pearls, but no father. Charlotte and an older sister had been taken to the workhouse when their mother died during an influenza epidemic. No father had come to claim them there, either. "For two days I had myself convinced my mama was a real lady, a nobleman's daughter, instead of a whore."

"What happened to your sister?" Lady Hathaway wanted to know, dabbing at her eyes with a lace-edged cloth.

"And you?" Angelina asked.

"I was adopted by a nice couple, my sister wasn't. The workhouse burned down a year later. I never found out what happened to her." Charlotte looked at Angelina with regret. "It would have been a treat, Miss Armstead, if you could have been her."

While Lady Hathaway and Angelina were both planning on hiring Nigel Truesdale to track down yet another young woman, Mercedes Lavalier predictably inquired how Charlotte had met her *très charmant* lieutenant.

"Preston moved in next door. He never wanted to be anything but a soldier, and I never wanted to be anything but his wife. Now I suppose I might find a job in service and leave Preston at home to mind the children. He won't be happy, thinking it's the man's job to provide for his family, but what can we do?"

They could manage a soon-to-open shelter for stray dogs, that's what. If Angelina couldn't have Charlotte for a sister, she'd have her for a neighbor. As she told Corin when he called to tell her about Sunshine's progress, Charlotte Franklin was perfect for the job. "She is honest and loving and not given to hysterical agitations, not after raising six children, including one set of twins, at the war's front."

"What, six children? How old is she? I thought you said she was of an age with your missing sister?"

Angelina pursed her lips. "Yes, she is, but she and her husband are very much in love. I know that Lady Sophie would not approve of such prolific breeding, either, and Mercedes has agreed to explain to Charlotte how to—" Scarlet-faced, Angelina recalled her company. "Anyway, when the children get a little bigger, they'll be able to help, and now there is time for Preston to finish recuperating while the rest of the kennels are being built. They can move into the new living quarters at the old Remington place next week. They'll stay here, meantime, and send for their trunks from the posting inn."

"You've just met them, and yet you are so sure of their characters, Angel? Not only have you hired them, but you've invited them into your home? Lud, what if he was a deserter and she a purse snatcher? You can't know."

"I trust my instincts—but I asked Lady Hathaway and Mademoiselle Lavalier's opinions, too." Those ladies had tactfully if negligently gone to practice in the music room when his lordship arrived.

Angel hadn't waited to ask his opinion, Corin complained to himself, deciding not to inquire if she thought Sunshine would be happier in his dressing room or in the estate office. His sister had mentioned she'd be happy if he tossed the dog back in the woods, where it belonged. Lord Wyte was resting after the journey, and Miss Melissa was still recovering from her *crise de nerfs*, lying abed with rosewater-soaked cloths on her forehead. He couldn't help noting that Angel looked fit and fetching in her sprigged muslin, and she'd been the one to suffer through the ordeal.

"Furthermore," she was saying while his mind wandered over her various charms, "you'll be happy to know that the Franklins will be taking Buttons with them when they move to the new facility. He has adopted the children as his flock and keeps them from straying out of Charlotte's sight, especially the twins, who tend to be little imps. She is thrilled and, yes, I did tell her about the lamb. She says she'll make sure Buttons is the best-fed dog in Britain, if he keeps the infantry in line."

"I wish someone could do the same for my niece and nephew. The brats tore up one of my favorite atlases, looking for pictures to paste onto the nursery walls, which were too plain, according to my sister."

"Perhaps my next sister will be a competent nursemaid, Corin. You can always hope."

He'd hoped Lord Wyte would take dinner upstairs on a tray in his room, or with his ailing daughter. But Papa Wyte was not one to let his quarry escape so easily.

Corin was dressed to his own exacting standards, if not to Nigel's valet's taste, after much *tsk*ing and tongue clicking by the fussy little man over the viscount's severe style. Lord Knowle had tied his own cravat, preferring to ruin three neck cloths than to look like a Christmas-wrapped mummy..

More of the house party guests had arrived, so Corin was relieved that the dinner was excellent: turbot in oyster sauce, vol-au-vents of veal, and plain English beef, in case the India nabob missed traditional British cooking. Henri was back in prime twig, now that his dog, Molly, was back in the kitchen, and to hell with Florrie's brats. Let her keep those limbs of Satan in the nursery, where they belonged, Lord Knowle had decided after listening to his chef's request that the two hellions be kept out of his domain. Those weren't precisely Henri's words, which were more to the effect that he would boil the bastards in oil if they switched the sugar for salt one more time or put another toad in his stock pot.

After the meal the Duke of Fellstone excused himself. Most of the other guests speculated correctly from Florrie's thin-lipped smile that he was off to visit Mercedes Lavalier, which was no one else's business except his and the government's. Talbot, Nigel, and a few others were getting up a game of cards, and the ladies, *sans* Miss Wyte, were in the parlor with their needlework and nimble tongues.

Corin was cornered. Now he knew how the grilled salmon felt.

"My precious wasn't happy."

"No, and I hope you have conveyed my deepest apologies for the sorry welcome she received at Knowle Castle. My sister did say that Miss Wyte was recovering enough to join the company tomorrow."

Lord Wyte nodded, almost scraping his chin on the boulder-size diamond in his cravat. "Aye, she's not one of those sickly females who're always dosing themselves for some megrim or other. My gel's got bottom. She can't stand to see an animal suffer, is all."

Neither could Angel, but she didn't faint; she did something about the suffering. Still, Miss Wyte had been reared in cotton wool. Then again, there were all those stuffed creatures in Wyte's library. "I thought you said Miss Wyte had accompanied you on some of your hunts."

"Oh, she comes along, but she don't watch the kill. I thought a Corinthian like your lordship would appreciate a woman who's a bruising enough rider to keep up."

Miss Wyte would have to be an excellent horse-woman, if that mettlesome mare was any indication of her ability and not just her father's wealth.

Wyte was going on: "Aye, she's a real picture on a horse, my Missy. And she's right fond of her cats. Won't travel without a pair of the little rascals."

"Won't travel . . . ? Do you mean she has cats up-stairs?" No wonder Florrie was looking so feverish. Corin had thought she was still agitated over his leaving her to deal with the debacle in the carriage drive.

"Aye, two long-haired beauties. We had to chase one down the hall before dinner. Want to go exploring, don't you know."

Corin knew that the dog he had in his dressing room wasn't half dead anymore, and the footman assigned to watch wasn't the brightest. Oh, lud.

The bloody cat wasn't his biggest problem, just as seeing the bloody dog hadn't been Melissa's, which her papa finally got around to pointing out. "Missy couldn't help but notice the female with you."

She would have had to be blind to miss the grimy, gun-bearing woman tumbling out of the woods at his side. She'd had no hat, no chaperon, and no qualms about going beyond the pale. Corin didn't like Lord Wyte referring to Angel as a female, though. "That was Miss Armstead, who resides in Primrose Cottage at the edge of my property."

Lord Wyte nodded. He knew all about Miss Armstead, thanks to Nigel Truesdale. What he didn't know was what Miss Armstead was to the viscount. He waited expectantly.

"She was my aunt's companion, who has now become a woman of modest but independent means."

"Aye, but is she the kind of female you'd want at your dinner table?"

What he meant was, was Angel good enough to invite to meet Corin's sister and future bride, or was she a convenient to be visited at her own place? Corin resented the implication. "Miss Armstead is dining with us tomorrow, I believe. Or perhaps it is the next day. She is a lady, my lord. Her mother was daughter to the Duke of Kirkbridge."

"A duke, eh? What about the father?"

"Gentry."

"But the chit's been employed."

"Genteelly."

"Knows how to behave like a lady?"

Corin remembered the kiss. "Generally. Miss Armstead has a mind of her own and a generous nature that sometimes leads her toward rash behavior, but only in defense of her pets." And any other cause she happens to espouse, like finding a lost sister. Corin didn't mention that, though. "She would grace the finest drawing room in the land, my lord, if she chose to."

While the nabob seemed to weigh Corin's words, the viscount was hoping he hadn't been too vocal in his defense. Deuce take it, was he to be accused of dalliance with every female he spoke to? Or rescued dogs with? "We were in a great hurry, my lord. It was an emergency."

"Aye, I could see that. Still, don't look right, young female with no dragon in sight."

"I assure you, Miss Armstead has a resident *duenna* and any number of other friends and neighbors looking out for her welfare and her reputation. You'll meet many of them at the dinner also."

"Yes, well, I only want what's best for my girl, you know."

"Of course, what father would wish otherwise?"

"And I'd hate to discover after the fact that I gave my little minx to someone not worthy."

Corin nodded. He would hate to discover after the fact that his ideal bride wasn't so perfect a match for him, bruising rider or not. But, he pondered, what if a man married a Diamond of the First Water, a belle, a Toast, then lost all his money? Could Miss Wyte kill a chicken? Could she cook it and serve it and clean his house? His own sister Florrie couldn't even take care of her children without an army of inept nursemaids. Charlotte Franklin could manage, he knew. Angelina Armstead would learn, he thought. Melissa Wyte would faint, he feared, or sulk in her bedroom. He wasn't apt to find himself needing a helpmate, an unpaid housekeeper, a drudge. But did he need a rich man's pampered pearl-beyond-price?

And cats?

Mostly he was hating the discovery that his dog had fleas.

Chapter Twenty-five

"*P*ennyroyal and eucalyptus leaves, my lord, that's what Lady Sophie used." Angelina had taken Corin back to the stillroom at Primrose Cottage, and she was lifting jars down from the shelves. "You will have to sprinkle it on the dog's bedding until she is strong enough for a bath. Oh, and try some powdered garlic in her food. That might help."

Moving Sunshine back to the stables might help him get a good night's sleep as well, after a night spent half awake, listening for her whimpers from the dressing room. Deuce take it, an infant couldn't be more troublesome. Then again, Corin would trust a nanny to look after an infant. No, Ben in the stables would have to take charge of the recovering dog and let his underlings see to the guests' horses. The viscount drew the line at having his clothes smell of witches' brew and garlic. As it was, he had all he could do not to itch in front of Angel. Knowing that she was an early riser, he'd ridden over first thing in the morning, before any of his company would be stirring. Considering that he hadn't yet welcomed his future fiancée, Corin could only hope that Angel didn't recommend garlic for him, too.

She was searching through the shelves for other remedies. "It would be best if you cut all that matted hair off the dog. Cleaner, too. Perhaps you could have your valet do it."

Nigel's valet would sooner cut his own throat, and Ben's fingers were too stiff. "I suppose I could try," Corin said, but the very idea made him itch worse. What if he cut the dog, after all the sewing he'd done?

"Would you rather Mavis and I come up to the castle to see what we can do? We've had a deal more experience."

"Would you? I'd be relieved." He'd also be in deep trouble with Lord Wyte and his daughter if he permitted Angel anywhere near his bedroom, dog or no dog, maid or no maid. Sunshine was going back to the stables the minute Corin got home.

Angelina nodded. "I must admit I am eager to see this miracle dog you say is up and walking already."

"And eating like she hasn't seen food in a month," which was another reason to send her back to the stables. Corin was busy admiring how the thin fabric of Angel's muslin gown pulled across her chest when she reached for a bottle on a high shelf. Now *there* was a miracle of creation. Those shapeless black gowns of hers ought to be burned, he thought, starting to feel an altogether different sort of itch.

"I'm happy to admit that I was wrong about that dog from the beginning. I didn't think she was worth saving. I didn't think she *could* be saved. So you were right; my intuition isn't always to be trusted. Oh, did you hear that another woman claiming to be my sister arrived last night?"

Corin dragged his mind back from noticing how the sunlight through the stillroom's bottle-filled window made rainbows in her hair. "What was this one, a traveling actress?"

"A thief, can you believe that? Why, she was at least five years too old, had no background that was similar, and spoke with a cockney accent. Do you think my sister could have lost her aitches since she was four?"

How should he know when children developed dialects? He was more concerned that there had been a criminal in Angel's house. "What did she steal? Between Lady Hathaway and Mercedes Lavalier there must be a fortune in jewels here. I can only hope it was Mercedes Lavalier's overbred poodle that got snabbled and nothing you valued."

"Just the silver salver on the hall table where Penn puts the mail. I don't mind, except that I gave the jade ten pounds for her trouble. So you see, my intuition is failing me."

"Not your intuition, only human nature not meeting your high expectations."

"Well, thank goodness that woman wasn't Mena or one of Lady Hathaway's daughters, either."

Corin's mind must have been wandering again to those curls and curves. "Did you say that a petty cutpurse might have been related to the dowager countess?"

So Angelina told him about Lady Hathaway's missing children. The older woman had told Elizabeth, Charlotte, and Mercedes Lavalier, saying that she had nothing to be ashamed of. The more people who learned of the situation, she'd decided, the better were the chances of someone knowing the solution. "And she's giving Mr. Truesdale a retainer to search the magistrate's records and wherever else he can think to look."

"The bastard."

"Mr. Truesdale?"

"No, that cad Hathaway. I'm already turning my life upside down for a sweet little dog I found yesterday. How could that dirty dish not have moved heaven and earth to get his own daughters back? Unless, of course, they were like Florrie's children."

"I am sure your sister's children are lovely, Corin."

"You see? Your gentle nature wants to find good in

198

everyone." Corin reached out to touch the glimmers of color in her hair, but Angelina turned away.

Embarrassed at the unexpected compliment, suddenly realizing she was alone in this smallish room with a largish rake, Angelina busied herself packing the various powders, potions, and salves into a basket. "That reminds me, Corin. It was very kind of you to invite Charlotte and Preston Franklin to your entertainment tonight, but they've decided to stay home instead. Charlotte doesn't like to leave her children, and Preston's health is too fragile still for late nights. They'll keep Robinet company so Elizabeth can enjoy herself, though."

"And thus Averill Browne. I'm glad Mrs. Gibb will have a treat. I hear nothing but praise for her, and not merely from her smitten beau. I admit I am looking forward to seeing Mercedes dance again."

The "again" gave Angelina pause until she recalled that this time he'd be watching his former mistress dance while seated next to his future missus. Viscount Knowle had nothing whatsoever to do with Angelina Armstead, she told herself for the hundredth time that morning. And he had fleas.

Melissa Wyte did not usually arise so early in the morning. Then again, she did not usually spend her evenings resting in bed, either. The sun was out, she was totally refreshed, and it was time to hear his lordship's apology for her abysmal welcome. Besides, the only good thing about being in the country was that she could ride whenever she wanted, and as fast, unlike London, where a lady was restricted to the carriage paths at the fashionable hours.

Melissa rang for her maid and her riding habit, knowing she appeared to advantage atop Firefly. She wore her amber velvet ensemble because it matched the mare's coloring. It also made her own blond hair seem even more golden where it trailed in ringlets down her back, and her fair complexion appear more glowing. The little matching hat had a scrap of net veiling and a feather that curled along her cheek in an adorable manner, if she had to say so herself, which she didn't, for London gentlemen had been complimenting her throughout the Season. Bucks and beaux and Bond Street swells had been tossing praise and posies and proposals at her feet ever since she arrived in Town, where she'd be right now if not for her father's insistence.

Melissa gave her hair a final pat and went downstairs to see if his lordship could neglect her in favor of a mangled mongrel now. The smile on her perfect lips said she didn't think so, not at all. Unfortunately, the unbending butler informed her, his lordship was not at breakfast. He had already left the house. Something about a dog.

Something about that woman at Primrose Cottage more likely, Melissa thought. Papa had explained last night about the aunt's old maid companion, the will, and the waste of good money on a pack of mutts. He'd also mentioned a veritable houseful of other females of dubious birth or character, presided over by the Countess Hathaway, which made everything right. Not for Melissa, it didn't, not last night and even less this morning.

She was giving up her London Season to be ignored? Not by half, she wasn't. Shredding a sweet roll, Melissa sent a footman to ask her father to accompany her on a ride. He was the one wishing her to make a match with the viscount; let him come along to track Lord Knowle down. She could ride out with her groom, of course, but if there was anything havey-cavey about that cottage, Melissa wanted her father to see it, too. She'd be back in Town that much sooner.

It wasn't that she didn't want to marry Knowle, Melissa told herself. He was the most eligible *parti* on the Marriage Mart that Season, after all. He was handsome, she supposed, although not as good-looking as his exquisite cousin, Mr. Truesdale. Even that young architect person she'd caught a glimpse of last evening had more dash than the viscount. Of course, Lord Knowle had the title and wealth Papa considered necessary for her future happiness, and he was a good horseman, she conceded. Melissa wasn't sure that was enough if he didn't also worship her. What did Melissa want with a husband she couldn't wind around her dainty little diamond-ringed finger?

Nigel Truesdale wasn't one for early mornings. His acquaintance with the dawn, in fact, was usually noticing it as he went home to bed. At the castle, though, things were different. His valet, pleased with the extra income from serving the viscount, was happy to be on the lookout for just such an opportunity for Nigel to be of service to Lord Wyte or his daughter. The valet threw open the drapes and shook his master's shoulder. "Miss Wyte is calling for her horse," he said. "Lord Knowle rode out forty minutes ago, in the direction of Primrose Cottage."

Truesdale hadn't made such a hasty toilette since the time the bailiffs were at his front door. In no time at all he was in the breakfast parlor, pouring cream into his coffee and pouring the butter boat over the beautiful heiress.

Nigel didn't have much of a seat, but he made a more than creditable appearance on one of his cousin's high-bred hacks. At least the Wytes were pleased with his company; he could lead them to Primrose Cottage.

"Bit early for a morning call, don't you think?" He made a halfhearted attempt to alter their direction as Melissa brought her cavorting mare back under control. She'd dismissed the groom, and Nigel was eyeing that fidgety creature with a bit less enthusiasm. "Although the primroses should be worth seeing this morning. We can ride by to take a look, I suppose."

"A good look" was all Lord Wyte had to say, disgruntled at being roused so early, disgusted with the viscount's derelict wooing.

The primroses, not quite in full bloom, were magnificent. There were rows and rows of them, reds and yellows, pinks and oranges. Birds and bees and butterflies hovered around them, only momentarily disturbed by the horses' passing. The sight put even Melissa in a better mood, as did seeing his lordship walking alone toward the cottage's stable with a basket in his hand. He must have been fetching something for the injured dog after all, she thought.

She rode away from the others toward him, to make sure it was the viscount who handed her down off Firefly. So pleased was she by the appreciative smile he gave her that Melissa chirped down at him, "What a lovely cottage, my lord. We can use it for a retreat from the drafty old castle after we—Oh." She put one hand in its Limeric yellow gloves to her mouth.

At that moment Jed Groom came around the side of the cottage to return one of the dogs from its morning run. Jed looked up to see the sweetest little filly he'd seen in years. The Arabian mare was a prime article, too. So lost in admiration was the old groom that he relaxed his grip on the leather leash he was holding—the one with Domino at the other end.

That was all the black-and-white horse hater needed. Lord Wyte had been appraising the value of the cottage, and Nigel had been staying out of his cousin's sight. He was too far away to help anyway, Nigel was relieved to note, as the dog snapped at Miss Wyte's horse's feet.

The horse kicked, the dog barked, everyone shouted. Jed ran to grab the dog's collar. Corin tried to grab for the Arabian's reins. And Melissa, one hand still at her rosebud lips, tried to grab for air—and missed.

She landed on her seat in a bed of primroses, the feather on her bonnet broken and sticking in her eye. Everyone came running, asking if she was injured, including that female Melissa had seen yesterday. Only now Miss Armstead wasn't any dowdy spinster, she was elegant and willowy and well dressed, and she wore her hair in the most fashionable curls, à la Caro Lamb.

That was too much for Melissa, in her ignoble position. Her lip started quivering, and her eyes started filling with tears.

It was too much for Corin, too, and he committed the utterly unforgivable mistake of laughing as he reached a hand down to help her up.

Instead of accepting his hand, Melissa picked up his basket, which had landed near her during Corin's dive for the horse's head, and heaved it at the insufferable brute. Lord Knowle, that was, not her beloved Firefly or the dog that was being dragged away by the servant. If she'd had another basket, Melissa would have tossed it at the pretty female who was even now asking if the *dog* was all right.

The stuff in the basket went every which way, over Corin and over Melissa as well. He seemed to think that was even funnier, that now she smelled like garlic, too! Melissa drummed her feet on the ground and sobbed.

All the attention from all the females at Primrose Cottage restored Miss Wyte's equilibrium. Lady Hathaway managed to soothe Lord Wyte's agitated nerves, while Mavis, Mrs. Franklin, Mrs. Gibb, who hadn't left for school yet, and Miss Armstead took turns at brushing and wiping and smoothing Melissa's offended dignity. Her habit was ruined, but Miss Armstead offered to purchase another one for her.

At last Melissa felt ready to join the others in the parlor for a calming cup of tea. Her father, Lady Hathaway, and Mr. Truesdale ended their discussion to make much of her entrance. The viscount had gone home to change his clothes, thank goodness. The architect fellow didn't seem eager to leave, and two uniformed officers calling too early on Mademoiselle Lavalier were inclined to linger in Miss Wyte's presence. This was more like it;

Melissa preened. She sipped her tea, batted her eyelashes, and smiled at everyone, including Miss Armstead, who was really too old, too thin, and too poor to be of competition.

The old dragon Lady Hathaway could make or break a young lady's social Season, so Melissa decided to curry her favor by petting her dog, the tawny Pekingese who matched Miss Wyte's ruined habit.

"Don't pet Tippy!" came from at least three voices, three pats too late.

She'd killed Lady Hathaway's pet. Miss Wyte sank gracefully to the floor, next to the twitching dog, whilst out in the hall, Sadie ate her Limeric yellow leather gloves.

Chapter Twenty-six

*D*inner was canceled. That is, dinner was held at Knowle Castle for the viscount and his houseguests, and dinner was also served at Primrose Cottage for Miss Armstead and the other residents thereof. Florrie was in despair, Henri was in high dudgeon, and Miss Wyte, according to the physician, was in a temporary decline.

The doctor had driven out from Ashford, posthaste, when informed his patient was the Wyte heiress, the distance from here to there growing considerably shorter with a larger fee. He declared the young lady in excellent health except worn to a frazzle from trotting too hard at social London's frenetic pace. Nothing a quiet stay in the country couldn't cure, he declared: fresh air, healthful exercise, regular meals, and no parties lasting all night, every night. Which regimen sounded so dull to Melissa that she would have had the megrims anyway, even if she weren't still furious with the viscount.

Her frantic papa was relieved. His little puss wasn't vaporish, he repeated to everyone, especially Lord Knowle; she was simply exhausted from her Season as reigning Toast. It was a good thing he'd taken the chit out of Town when he did.

It was also a good thing that handsome Mr. Truesdale and an array of undersecretaries and military aides were parading through the castle or Melissa wouldn't have left her room until it was time to return to London, with its balls and breakfasts and Bond Street shops. She did like to ride, though, and there was no denying that his lordship was an excellent horseman.

Corin escorted Miss Wyte about the countryside whenever he could in atonement for his many sins. He also had flowers sent to fill her room, her favorite dishes prepared in the kitchens, and he let her win at croquet, charades, and the nightly card games. Compliments had Melissa smiling, gifts had her cooing, he quickly realized, so he emptied the local stores of everything suitable for a suitor to present—everything except the family engagement ring.

She was beautiful, Corin couldn't deny that. And, when things were going her way, she was charming company, with tinkling laughter and fluttering lashes. She was a deuced fine horsewoman, too, even if Corin privately thought the high-strung Arabian a bit too much horse for her diminutive strength to handle. A regular pocket Venus, was Miss Wyte. Melissa would make some man a delightfully decorative wife, even more delectable when one considered her father's fortune. Corin simply hadn't gotten around to making Lord Wyte a formal offer for his daughter's hand.

He had spoken to Nigel again, however. The fellow was actually turning out to be helpful, agreeing to escort Miss Wyte on afternoon calls to the neighbors, sightseeing in the vicinity, shopping in the nearby towns, so Corin could get some work done. With all the rides he'd taken, the viscount could see improvements that needed to be made on his lands—cottages that needed repairs, fields that needed draining. He had to confer with his steward and his tenants, so he couldn't dance attendance on Melissa as much as he thought he should. Nigel was decent enough to take up the slack.

His cousin was more of a detective than Corin had given him credit for, as well. He'd found Doddsworth by sending notes around to the employment agencies, and he'd found a doctor, the brother of an old crony of his, who was just finishing his studies at Edinburgh. The chap and his wife would arrive in a month if Corin would pay their coach fare. The viscount would send his own carriage, by George.

Nigel had feelers out in the dives and dens in London about Lady Hathaway's daughters, but he wasn't holding out much hope. Old crimes were hard to uncover; old criminals were rarer, their way of life not being conducive to longevity. Nigel reported that he wasn't moving any closer to finding Angel's sister, either, but he did hint about a quick success in the confidential search he was conducting for Lord Wyte. Corin couldn't imagine what the mogul had lost that he couldn't just go buy another of. The viscount found that he was too busy to care, what with entertaining Miss Wyte, running his estates, and conferring with the chaps who came down from Whitehall to see the Scribe. And looking after his dog.

Sunshine was improving daily, hobbling about now and gaining weight. She looked much improved with the filthy hair trimmed away, although he feared she'd never win a beauty contest with her straggly whiskers and shaggy eyebrows. No matter, she barked when he came to the stables and whined when he left. She didn't like the stable hands changing her bandages and wouldn't take food from anyone else's hand. No one in the world had ever held the viscount in such esteem, not his mother, none of his lovers, and certainly not the woman he was thinking of making his wife.

That other woman, the one he was determinedly *not* thinking about, the one whose company he was avoiding with all his ditch-digging and diversions, thought he was an ass half the time. The devil knew what Angel was thinking the other half of the time. Corin knew only that he couldn't be near her. It wasn't fair to be courting Miss Wyte while craving another woman in his arms. His thoughts were as dishonorable as his intentions toward Angel. 'Twould be best to stay away.

Angelina had nothing to do. Elizabeth was teaching the children, Preston Franklin was helping with the dogs, and Lady Hathaway was accompanying Mercedes during her practice sessions. Mr. Browne had plans for the kennels in train and wanted to consult with Elizabeth when he called, not Angelina. Her wardrobe was complete, her accounts were up-to-date, and her library books were boring.

Sisters came and sisters went, with Mr. Truesdale or on their own. None stayed. The Duke of Fellstone came with his assistants and associates to see Mercedes. Then His Grace came alone to see the Frenchwoman, who had remarkably little of her memoirs to show for all her time in her sitting room. Florrie Talbot called once to invite them to tea, but she left after the third sneeze. Even Lord Wyte visited to pay his respects to Lady Hathaway, and he stayed for what would turn into a daily afternoon chess match. Everyone came, in fact, except Knolly and his china doll heiress.

So that was all Angelina could think about, two of the most beautiful people in the world traipsing across the countryside on their magnificent mounts, looking like bookends for an atlas of social consequence. Angelina had never even learned to ride.

It was a good thing he didn't come, she told herself. She'd get over this silly green sickness all the sooner, drat the paperskulled, pride-filled, priggish man and his perfect peagoose of a riding partner.

He was spoiling his dog anyway. And the primroses were starting to fade.

Then it was time for his lordship's ball. The evening wasn't to be a ball, precisely, nor a musicale. A *divertissement*, the invitation read. Mademoiselle Mercedes Lavalier was to perform in the ballroom, followed by an informal supper during which the servants would remove the chairs and makeshift stage, so the entire company could later dance to the hired orchestra. Florrie Talbot, on Lord Knowle's direction, had invited every family of note in the neighborhood, and some not quite as notable, such as the proprietress of Primrose Cottage.

He couldn't not invite her, Angelina understood, not with her houseguest providing the entertainment; but he didn't have to invite all of them, the Franklins and Mrs. Gibb included, to the small dinner held beforehand. Only Elizabeth accepted, for Mercedes never ate before a performance, and Lady Hathaway, who was to accompany the ballerina on the pianoforte, declared herself too nervous to eat. Angelina was, too. The ball would be the perfect place to announce an engagement. The entire village was speculating about nothing else. Miss Armstead would gladly have declined the invitation altogether.

Instead she was all rigged out in a new dress, compliments of Lady Hathaway, to repay her hospitality, the older lady said. The gown was a blue-green watered silk that shifted colors as Angelina moved. It reminded her of the ocean, she thought, pleased with the gown's simple lines and the feel of the gossamer silk, until she glimpsed Miss Wyte in ivory satin with blush-dyed lace at the scalloped hem and the low bodice.

Elizabeth also had a new gown—the rose silk ball gown Mavis had been fashioning for Lena—and Elizabeth's dance card was already half filled by the time the Primrose Cottage contingent arrived at Knowle Castle. So what if Averill Browne's name was scrawled across half the dances? Elizabeth was glowing with excitement. Angelina tucked her own blank card into her reticule.

Then Mercedes was dancing and nothing else mattered. Not even playing for the ballerina's practice had prepared Angelina for the actual event. Like everyone else in the audience, she sat spellbound by mademoiselle's grace and fluidity, entranced by the intensity of Mercedes's performance. If Lady Hathaway faltered, no one noticed, so engrossed were they by La Lavalier in her feathery ensemble and fluttering gauze drapery.

So what if her limbs showed a bit more than was decent or her lips were too red, her eyelids too dark? She was an *artiste*, the *première danseuse* in all of Europe, including Britain, and the thunderous, standing ovation in the ballroom proved it. Angelina was as gratified by her guest's success as if she could take credit, like Harry Elkins learning his letters, or Charlotte Franklin's baby taking his first steps. Her heart swelled with pride.

Angelina was more pleased when Lord Wyte immediately claimed Lady Hathaway for his dinner partner, and the Duke of Fellstone raced General Cathcart to the Frenchwoman's side. There would be no slight to her friends for performing in public.

Lord Knowle was escorting Miss Wyte, naturally, and Averill was bowing to Elizabeth. Angelina stood uncertainly. Should she trail after them or trip on her hem so she could escape to the retiring room, claiming to make repairs? For once she did not have Lady Sophie's wheeled chair to hide behind, to pretend that she didn't mind being ignored.

Then Mr. Truesdale made an elegant leg and offered his arm. Nigel was stunning in burnt-orange satin, with saffron knee smalls, and hummingbirds embroidered on his green waistcoat. "Inspired by your primroses, don't you know?" he drawled when Angelina was struck dumb by his magnificence. How lowering to be overshadowed by one's supper partner, she thought, besides every other female at the table.

Nigel was pleasant and polite, even if his eyes did keep

straying to Mercedes—along with all the other men's stares—or to Miss Wyte. Angelina couldn't blame him. She herself thought Melissa looked like a princess in her lace-trimmed gown, with a ruby pendant at her low décolletage and a diamond tiara in her honey gold hair.

"It's too much for such a young girl," Elizabeth whispered in Angelina's ear, noting the direction of her gaze and comprehending the direction of her thoughts. "They may as well put a price tag on the chit."

Elizabeth's sympathy was no consolation. Angelina was sorry she'd refused the countess's offer of a necklace or Mercedes's offer of a brooch. She had the cameo Lady Sophie had given her last Christmas. That was enough, she'd thought—earlier.

She gave herself a mental shake. Rubies and sapphires and emeralds wouldn't have made a difference. Lord Knowle was standing up and asking everyone for quiet. The lobster patty Angelina was eating tasted like sawdust in her mouth. She only hoped she wouldn't disgrace herself when Corin made his announcement.

Instead of a public declaration, however, Corin proposed a toast—to Mercedes Lavalier for her great talent she'd shared with them, and her great service to the country. Corin was making sure everyone knew that Mercedes was a heroine in addition to being a famed performer, as well as an infamous courtesan. Everyone raised their glasses, and tears came to Angelina's eyes.

And to Miss Wyte's, she was pleased to note, although she did not think their reasons were the same. Melissa's beautiful face was disfigured by a scowl, now that she wasn't the center of his lordship's attention.

Of course, opening the ball on the arm of the host, a viscount to boot, went far toward mollifying Miss Wyte. It made Angelina wish she hadn't had that second lobster patty.

Chapter Twenty-seven

$\mathscr{A}$t least Angelina had a partner of her own. It seemed, at an affair such as this, that everyone kept their supper partners for the first set, the minuet and promenade, thank goodness.

Angelina stood up with Averill Browne for the next set, happy that the figures of the country-dance kept separating them, sparing her a continuous litany of Elizabeth's charms. Then Florrie Talbot introduced her to a series of weak-chinned youths—Talbot's relations, Angelina inferred—as suitable partners. For her pittance of an inheritance, Angelina also inferred, but she was happy to dance with the stuttering, spotted ninnyhammers anyway, rather than hold up the wall.

Later she danced with His Grace of Fellstone, likely at Mercedes Lavalier's urging; he had been a frequent visitor at Primrose Cottage. If nothing else, Angelina could remember this night as the one she danced with a real duke. She smiled at His Grace gratefully, and didn't even mind when he took a coughing fit during the quadrille, causing them to sit out the rest.

Mercedes was holding court near the terrace, surrounded by scarlet regimental jackets and black formal swallowtails. She chose not to dance again after her exertions. How else could she have so many gentlemen at her feet at once?

Lady Hathaway wasn't dancing, either. She was sitting to the side of the room with a group of older ladies, Florrie Talbot's mother-in-law and Squire Hardwick's wife among them, with Lord Wyte hovering over her shoulder. The nabob had on almost as much sparkling jewelry as the countess.

Angelina thought of joining Lady Hathaway after the next intermission, so she wouldn't be so obviously without another dance partner. And then he was bowing before her. "May I have this dance, Angel?"

Angelina thought she'd never seen a gentleman so handsome, so perfectly formed, as Lord Knowle in his evening attire. "Thank you, my lord. But you don't need to—that is, if you'd rather—"

"There is nothing I would rather do, Angel."

The contra dance kept them apart, except for matching smiles. Melissa was in the same set, scowling again, this time at one of the spotty Talbot sprigs.

Instead of returning Angelina to her place by the wall after the set ended, Corin kept her hand tucked into the crook of his arm. "To prove that the last wasn't any duty dance, I am claiming the next one also. It's not spoken for, is it?"

If the Prince Regent himself had his name scrawled on her card, Angelina would have said no. But the orchestra started playing a waltz. Angelina bit her lip.

"What, the intrepid Miss Armstead nervous over the latest dance craze? It's accepted at Almack's nowadays, don't you know, so it's perfectly proper for the mistress of Primrose Cottage."

Melissa Wyte was already on the floor in Nigel Truesdale's arms, swirling and gliding as gracefully as a butterfly. Angelina looked at her slippers, scuffed from her last Talbot partner. "I only practiced once, my lord."

He was already leading her toward the dance floor. Corin was not going to miss holding this female in his embrace, not when he had a perfectly legitimate excuse for doing so. "It's a simple dance, really. Once is enough. It's like horseback riding, you don't forget."

Angelina had to laugh. "But I don't ride, either."

"What? I cannot believe you don't like horses, so you must not have learned how. The devil, is that why you didn't accept the invitations to ride out with me and my guests?"

No, that wasn't why. She didn't need to see him making sheep's eyes at Melissa Wyte, thank you. Angelina could have driven Dumpling in the donkey cart if she wanted to torture herself that much. She just nodded.

"Well, you'll learn," he said.

It wasn't a question or a request, only the arrogant aristocrat's typical assumption of authority. Angelina started to bristle, but he added, "I'll teach you. I know you've got backbone beneath that fragile beauty, so you'll do."

Angelina almost tripped.

Holding her steady, Corin went on: "I need you to come with me around the estate. I'm thinking of staying on here instead of seeking a government position, and there are some improvements that I'd like to make. I want your advice first."

Suddenly Miss Angelina Armstead was the best dancer in all of Kent. How could she not be graceful and gliding when her feet never touched the ground? She'd learn to ride an elephant if that's what Corin asked.

The temperature in the room must have risen by five degrees. Either that or Angelina's flushed cheeks and fevered brow must be due to Corin's hand at her waist, the hard strength of his shoulder under her own fingers, the occasional brush of his thigh against hers in the turns of the dance. She could hardly breathe by the end of the music.

Corin was likewise affected, she was happy to note. It

must be the closeness of the room, then, not the closeness of their bodies. "Come," he said. "Let's get some champagne."

"I think I've had more than my tolerance of champagne, thank you." The room was already spinning.

"Then I have a better idea." He started to lead her toward the terrace, where Mercedes Lavalier was still surrounded by gentlemen. "Let's take a walk. There are any number of people strolling in the gardens so you don't have to worry about your reputation."

"Oh, but they are your guests. You cannot leave."

"Why not? I've wined them and dined them and provided entertainment for them. Now it's my turn to enjoy myself."

Hadn't he enjoyed taking supper with Melissa or having the first dance with her? Not even the night air could cool the spark that glowed somewhere in Angelina's midsection.

Corin didn't stop when they reached the last of the Chinese lanterns in the garden. He kept walking, around the house and toward the stables. He was taking her to see his dog, Angelina realized, suddenly chilled. That's what he meant by enjoying himself, not spending time in her company. The dastard most likely wanted to know what to do about the dog's worms! And she could have been dancing with Squire Hardwick's nephew or the new curate. The devil fly away with all men.

The devil had already stolen Corin's good intentions. And worms were perhaps the farthest thing from his mind that night as he watched Angel bend to get a better look at the dog.

Sunshine was looking fine, Angelina decided, carrying her plumed tail jauntily over her shiny black back. She'd always have a limp, but that didn't seem to matter to Sunshine or to his lordship, who was grinning like a proud papa over his progeny. And she was right, he was spoiling the dog, likely overfeeding her the way the dog was growing so rounded. Why—

"Did I tell you yet how beautiful you look tonight?"

Angelina had to turn around to make sure he was speaking to her, not the dog. She laughed. "What, after seeing Mercedes Lavalier and Miss Wyte in the same room? Hardly, my lord."

"They are not half so beautiful in my eyes."

Still smiling, Angelina said, "Perhaps you should wear spectacles, then, sir, for you think this sorry little dog is beautiful, too."

"Isn't she?" he asked, stepping closer. He told himself that he had to shorten the distance so she was in his lantern's light, so he could make sure she wasn't cold. No, he couldn't detect any goose bumps. Angel seemed to shiver under his scrutiny, so obviously Corin had to take her into his arms, which was what he'd been wanting to do since she stepped through the door of his home tonight. And the whole week before, at least.

Corin had fully intended to make his comfortable marriage of convenience with the nabob's daughter. But he was so deuced uncomfortable with wanting another woman that he couldn't bring himself to the sticking point. He thought that if he held Angel, if he kissed her, then he could get the craving out of his mind, get the lilac scent of her out of his nostrils. Which proved how foolish men's fancies were when they were in rut.

Holding her didn't help, of course, and kissing Angel just made Corin want to kiss her more, and kiss more of her.

Angelina's knees were trembling, but she didn't resist, didn't pull back. In fact, she participated fully, reaching, stretching, pressing herself to him in an effort to deepen the embrace. Corin wasn't engaged. And he thought she was beautiful. So what if he must have had too much champagne also, Angelina was going to have this one night of magic to cherish for the rest of her life.

The guests, the party, the grooms checking the stalls, nothing mattered. The dog blankets on the hay-strewn stable floor were looking better and better. And then they heard the shot.

There was a scream, a shout, another shot, then a moment of silence before everyone at the party, guests and servants alike, was yelling, running, crying out. Corin grabbed Angelina's hand and started racing for the terrace.

Before they reached the ballroom, they found the Duke of Fellstone on the ground near one of the lantern-lit pathways. He was coughing and clutching his shoulder. "Mercedes," he gasped. "The blackguard got Mercedes."

Corin tore off his neck cloth and wadded it up to press against His Grace's shoulder. Angelina was loosening the duke's collar so he could breathe more easily. Others came running now, so Corin shouted to someone to ride for that blasted too-faraway doctor, and someone else to find pistols and saddle horses for any man able to ride with him.

"Damnation!" Corin swore while he waited for others to help carry the duke inside. "I thought she'd be safe here with the soldiers all around." He didn't mention how foolish he thought the duke was, taking Mercedes off the lighted paths, away from the company. Then again, he understood such driving forces, indiscreet or not. "I'll throttle that clunch Fredricks for letting this happen."

The duke grasped his hand. "Save a piece of the traitor for me, lad, what? Fredricks is the bastard who shot me and dragged Miss Lavalier off."

Florrie was shrieking, Lady Hathaway was quietly weeping with Elizabeth at her side, and Melissa was passed out, in Nigel's ready arms. The rest of the neighboring guests were dithering whether it was safer to stay where the madman had attacked one of the company, or leave to face the dangers on the road.

"There is no danger to anyone else," Corin advised while he marshaled his forces. "The man has taken Miss

Lavalier with him when he could have shot her, so he has to be on his way to France. I'll find him. Who's coming?"

Not Nigel, who was not relinquishing the languishing heiress, even into her father's arms. And not Averill Browne, who was turning green at the sight of the duke's blue blood. There were enough officers and adjutants ready to ride that Corin told the architect, "You take the ladies back to Primrose Cottage in Lady Hathaway's carriage, with a squad of my armed grooms as outriders. Keep them there until you hear otherwise."

Angelina stepped to his side. "I'm coming."

He was tucking a pistol in his waistband. "You can't even ride a horse, you said."

"And you said I could learn. I'll come in the cart if you don't take me with you. Mercedes needs me."

"She doesn't need you in the way of a bullet! The scum would have killed her if this was about revenge, so Fredricks is in this for the money. He has to take Mercedes Lavalier back to France to collect if he doesn't have a contact here. He's not going to hand his prize over to you, Angel, no matter how nicely you ask. And I'm not going to let you get caught in the middle."

Angelina stood her ground, her hand on his arm. "Mercedes needs me, and you need me because the dogs will find her a lot sooner than you will, going off in every direction at once. Fredricks could have carried Mercedes to any rocky shore or he could keep her somewhere until the French come for her. You can't know, but her own dog Juliette can. Ajax is a tireless tracker, and Spooky's got a good nose."

"What, no bloodhound?" he asked sarcastically.

"That's Cyrano, but he's asthmatic. He'd be as useful as Miss Wyte after the first mile, unless he can ride in your carriage and catch the scent from there."

Deuce take it, Corin realized, she had a point. His plan was to call out the militia, blanket the roads with searchers. But if Angel came now with the dogs, while the scent was strong, they had a better chance. He called for his curricle instead. It would be slower than horseback but more effective. Fredricks must have Mercedes in some kind of carriage, or riding double with him, so the gallows bait wouldn't be making good time, either.

He sent some of the other men on ahead to spread out and ask questions while the horses were hitched. He paced furiously in front of the stable, wondering if he could handle both the horses and the dogs himself, or if Jed Groom could come with him in Angel's stead. She might let him take her dogs after a paid mercenary who had to know he'd hang if caught—when hell froze over. Lud, Corin thought, he'd be driving this woman into the path of danger when he should be locking her in a fortress to keep her safe.

"But you can't bring the blunderbuss. And don't bring the dog that hates horses. Or the one that chases rabbits. Or the little yippy ones in case we have to sneak up on the muckworm. And not the one who . . ."

Chapter Twenty-eight

$\mathcal{I}$n the end Corin took Angelina up with him on his gelding. Major McKennon could follow with the curricle. They'd get to Primrose Cottage faster on horseback, to gather the dogs. That's what Corin half convinced himself anyway. The other half was delighted with another opportunity to hold Angel close.

Lord Wyte was leading another contingent of riders toward the road to Ashton and on to the coast. Corin could almost feel sorry for Fredricks if the India Company nabob caught up to him first; the traitor should hang, not be made into a rug.

The dash to Primrose Cottage through the Knoll's home woods at night was too fast, too dark, and too bumpy for Angelina to feel anything but glad that Corin's strong arms were around her. She considered that perhaps she didn't want to learn to ride after all.

Then they were at the cottage, and all other thoughts fled. Something was dreadfully wrong. The dogs were in a frenzy, for one, and the door was open, for another. Preston and Charlotte Franklin had moved to the Remington place and were keeping Robinet with them this evening, and the servants had the night off—those who weren't in attendance at the castle, that is. But Penn would never have left the place unlocked and unattended. Jed Groom would never have gone off leaving the dogs loose to roam. Most were outside, from what Angelina could see through the confusion in the yard: the little dogs, the old dogs, even half-blind Diamond wandering in circles through the primrose beds.

And yes, there was Juliette, in love again or still, accepting Homer's carte blanche. No wonder the other dogs were in an uproar. But where was everyone else, and where was Ajax?

"Quiet," Corin whispered when he lifted her down from the gelding, for she was about to speak. "Be quiet and stay here. I'll go see what's happening."

He hadn't needed to whisper; the dogs were making such a racket that he couldn't even hear Angelina creeping behind him. Closer to the house he felt a presence, though, and spun around, his pistol drawn. "Hell and damnation, Angel, I could have shot you!" But he took her hand in his left one, the hand that wasn't holding the gun. "At least stay behind me, dash it."

They edged through the open door—and almost tripped over Ajax, where the big dog was spread across the foyer. Corin threw his hand over Angelina's mouth so she wouldn't scream, then he bent down. "He's breathing," he whispered.

She was already running her hands over the dog's sides and legs. "I don't feel any blood or broken bones, but there's a lump on his head."

"That bastard Fredricks has a lot to answer for. But I'd like to know why—"

Then they heard the shouting. It was definitely Mercedes Lavalier's voice, and it was coming from above, from her suite of rooms.

"I told you, *bâtard*, I have not had the time to write my memoirs. You waste your time and your stupid life trying to find what does not exist, *non*? *Quel bêtise*, thinking you will make your fortune selling what does not belong to you, *chien*. Go, and I shall try to forgive you for shooting *mon cher le duc*. I do not want your filthy blood on my carpet."

They heard a slap and a scream. "Stay here, damn it," Corin ordered, heading for the stairs at a run. Angelina was right behind him, grabbing up the silver candelabrum from the hall table. Some of the dogs followed after her, to see what new game she was playing.

The viscount paused at the top of the stairs to listen. He felt a tug at his jacket and heard a whispered, "To the right, fourth door down." Muttering foul and dire curses, he headed in that direction. At the fourth door he pressed his ear against the wood. He could hear Mercedes weeping—the bastard was going to hang twice for this night's work—and drawers being slammed. He stepped back and then lunged forward, crashing his shoulder into the door. Which hadn't been latched, so he went tumbling into the room to land at the renegade soldier's feet.

Fredricks shifted the aim of his pistol from Mercedes Lavalier to the fallen viscount. "Now what have we here? His high and mighty lordship's not looking so fancified tonight." He brought back his boot to kick Corin in the head.

"No!" shrieked Angelina from the doorway, which stopped six dogs in their tracks, and Fredricks.

"And the uppity companion, too," he said, moving the pistol again.

That was all Corin needed. He rolled and aimed, but missed intentionally because Pug was suddenly in his line of fire, trying to lick his nose. "Blast!"

But the blast was all Spooky needed. The gun-shy gun dog was going back to his house in the yard, where no one shot at him, no matter who was in the way. Which happened to be Fredricks. Spooky tore right between the soldier's legs, upending him almost at Angelina's feet. She raised the candelabrum and brought it down on his head.

She missed, too, but then Ajax was there, roused by his mistress's earlier scream. The huge dog was on Fredricks in a flash, with a debt of his own to pay and wolf-long teeth to do it.

"Get him off me!" Fredricks screamed. "Help me!" Which Corin was in no hurry to do. He got to his own feet, checked to make sure that Angelina was unharmed—she was untying Mercedes from the chair—then politely asked Ajax to desist. He wasn't putting his own hands anywhere near those ivory hedge clippers. Not when Ajax had a headache.

Fredricks was still screaming, the three little terriers were yipping, Mercedes was crying, and Sadie was attacking the soldier's boots. Corin was reloading his pistol. "Uh, Angel, do you think you might tell Ajax to leave enough of the dastard to hang?"

Then Major McKennon arrived, pistols drawn. He'd seen signs of trouble, so he'd gone around the back, where he'd found the servants locked in the kitchen. They were right behind him, armed with frying pans and meat cleavers. If a few of the former happened to fall on Fredricks's head while the footmen bound the villain, no one seemed to notice, except Fredricks, of course.

And everyone seemed to be looking the other way when the viscount tucked his pistol away and then took Angelina by the shoulders and shook her. "Don't you ever listen to orders, you impossible female? I told you to stay downstairs, by George!"

Ajax noticed and started growling again, so Corin just folded his arms around Angelina and held her against him, where she fit perfectly. "My God, you could have been killed," he spoke into the curls on the top of her head. "I've never been so frightened as when I saw the bastard turn his gun on you, Angel. If you ever do such a corkbrained thing again, I swear I will shoot you myself."

"Me, I am happy *mon ange* is not one of your soldiers, Knolly, to obey orders." Mercedes was repinning her hair as if she'd just finished a nap, instead of being abducted. "She saves my life again, no?"

Blushing, Angelina stepped away from Corin. "No, Mercedes, I did nothing. Thank Lord Knowle if you must, for riding with the wind to get us here, but it is Ajax who is the real hero."

So Mercedes hugged all of them, Angelina, Corin, and the great dog. Then she wanted to go back to the castle to see how her dear duke was faring.

With McKennon and two armed grooms escorting Fredricks to the army post via horseback, Mercedes and her rescuers squeezed onto the bench of Corin's curricle. Having refused to be left behind, Ajax rode on the tiger's bench behind them, drooling on Corin's shoulder. The viscount didn't even mind, not with Angelina pressed against him.

Despite the absence of Florrie and her husband, who had taken to their beds, the threesome's welcome—four if one counted Ajax, who was determined not to let Angelina out of his sight—was heartfelt and tearful, with much hugging between the ladies of Primrose Cottage. While Mercedes went to check on Fellstone, Angelina was enfolded by Lady Hathaway and Elizabeth. The viscount received his share of back-slapping congratulations, too, from Browne and Nigel and Lord Wyte, who had given up the chase when he recalled his daughter was alone and unprotected.

But Melissa hadn't been, it seemed. Nigel still had his arm around her, as if the fragile miss couldn't lift her teacup without his assistance. Corin raised his brow, and Nigel, speaking low, said, "I hope you don't mind, old chap."

"Not at all, Nigel, but Papa Wyte might object."

Truesdale smiled. "Actually, he doesn't. He rather fancies a son-in-law in the ton, not the country gentleman you're turning out to be. Besides, I think I found a shabster who owed him a bundle, so he believes I'm a handy fellow to have around. And, unlike other sons-in-law he could have settled for, I'll watch out for Lord Wyte's interests, instead of being more concerned over my own estates and investments."

"You *have* no estates or investments."

Melissa spoke up from Nigel's other side. "He does now, my lord."

"Then I assume congratulations are in order. I wish you both much happiness. You'll certainly be the prettiest couple in London."

"Thank you, cuz. We'll be leaving in the morning to insert the notices in Town. We've missed enough of the Season, and I'm sure everyone will want to throw balls in our honor, that sort of thing, don't you know."

"Oh, I do indeed." And Corin wouldn't mind missing any of it.

"I hope you don't mind something else, cuz. Lady Hathaway is coming along with us to help plan the wedding. Lord Wyte wants a big affair, of course."

"Of course. But whose wedding?" Corin couldn't help noticing that Lord Wyte was standing behind Lady Hathaway's chair, his hand on her shoulder. 'Twould be a good match: the countess would gain the family she missed, and the nabob would gain the polish he lacked. Corin had no doubt those stuffed trophies would be in the attic before the countess was in London for a week. Good.

Confident that Angelina was being comforted and cosseted, Corin went upstairs to check on His Grace. The duke was lying in his bed, one arm in a sling. The other was around Mercedes.

"Good job, my boy," the duke said. "Saved one of our national treasures, what?" He coughed, then went on: "I think we'll toddle up to Town in the morning. Recuperate better in my own home, what? And the lady will be safe there, once we give out that she's not publishing her memoirs. Greedy bastard, what? Can't trust anyone, my boy, can't trust anyone. Except you, lad. Good show. And I'll be sure to put in a good word at the War Office for you. In fact, make you an undersecretary if you'll keep the poodle here, what?"

"No, thank you, Your Grace. I've had my fill of the spy business. There's too much to be done right here and too many people dependent on me."

And one who wasn't dependent upon him at all. Corin returned to the drawing room where the others, weary but reluctant to part, were having tea. He sat beside Angel on the sofa.

Nigel was saying, "I'm sorry I wasn't more help in locating your sister, Lena."

"It was a goosish notion to start with," Lord Wyte stated. "Let the past stay past, I say."

Lady Hathaway started to object, but Melissa agreed. "I don't see how you hoped to identify the girl anyway, Lena. I don't remember much from when I was so young."

So Angelina explained how she'd hoped her sister would retain the strongest memory there could be, of the nickname their parents had used. "Even if she was renamed, even if she could not recall Philomena, she might have remembered Papa's pet name for her. No one else would know it."

"How can you be so certain of that? Why, Papa used to call me Tootsie. I'm sure there must be thousands of little girls with the same memory."

The teacup slid out of Angelina's fingers onto the floor. "Tootsie?" she whispered, just as Lord Wyte blustered, "Nonsense, I always called you Missy."

Melissa was remembering more: "And I had a sister, Popsie, but they said she died."

Tears were running down Angelina's cheeks. "I didn't die, Mena. I didn't die."

"You mean . . . ?" Melissa looked at Angelina, then she looked at her father, whose face was red and whose eyes wouldn't meet hers. "But that can't be! Why, you don't even know how to ride!"

"And you don't like dogs," Angelina blubbered into Corin's handkerchief until he took her onto his lap altogether. Then she wept into his shirtfront.

Lord Wyte called for a brandy. "Blister it, they never said a word about another chit. Never let on Missy was the granddaughter of any duke, either. The solicitor never gave us names and we didn't ask; my wife wanted a chick of her own very badly. She couldn't have any, and it was eating her up. We were on our way to India, so there was no one to say the little moppet wasn't ours. We never told her she was adopted because we never wanted her to feel like an outsider. And we loved her as much as if she was our own blood, I swear."

Melissa was crying in *his* arms now. There was hardly a dry eye in the parlor, in fact. "You did, Papa, you did love me better than any girl was ever loved. That must be why I never remembered anything else."

Lord Wyte cleared his throat, still patting Melissa's back. "We would have taken you, too, Miss Arm— Angelina. I only wish we could have."

How different her life would have been if her four grandparents hadn't been so cruel and unforgiving of their own children, Angelina thought. She could have been raised by loving parents with every luxury and a sister of her own. She would have had a London Season, with a dowry that might make her as attractive on the Marriage Mart as Melissa.

But she wouldn't have been the same person. She wouldn't have had the schooling, and she wouldn't have

227

known Lady Sophie. She might never have met Viscount Knowle.

Angelina went over and kissed Lord Wyte's cheek. "I would have been proud to call you father, my lord. Thank you for being there for Mena."

Lady Hathaway was dabbing at her eyes. "Does that mean I'll have two daughters now? And Elizabeth, too, and darling Robinet?"

"You can have as many chits as you want, my dear," Lord Wyte told her, "but only the one dog." He turned to Corin. "Does it have to be the stupid mutt that takes seizures?"

When Corin nodded, the older man shrugged. "Oh, well, it looks like Truesdale will be there to catch Missy when she swoons. I suppose I can deal with a passing-out Pekingese."

Eventually they were all too tired to talk anymore. Lady Hathaway's carriage was called for, but Corin declared he would see Miss Armstead home in his curricle with Ajax to chaperon. No one argued with him, least of all Angelina, who rested her head on his shoulder. Which was better than dog drool, Corin reasoned, a great deal better.

It was almost dawn when they reached the cottage, but instead of seeing her inside, Corin lifted Angelina down and led her along the path to the gardens. There was the faintest tinge of pink on the horizon, and the dogs in the yard barely made a whimper. Ajax padded over to the front door and lay down.

When they reached the primroses, the rows upon rows of flowers that bloomed every spring, Corin raised Angelina's hand to his mouth and asked, "Will you make me the happiest of men, Angel? Will you marry me?"

Angelina took her hand back. Reluctantly. "You don't want me, my lord."

So he kissed her until she couldn't breathe. "That's

how much I want you, Angel. No, that's not even half as much."

"But you don't want to marry me."

"Can I have you any other way?" he teased. "No, I'm too much the gentleman to offer you a slip on the shoulder, Miss Armstead, but if you go around kissing every man that way, people will begin to doubt your morals, you know."

"I don't—Oh." She could see his grin. "Well, you only want the cottage anyway."

Now he laughed out loud. "My dearest peagoose, this cottage comes with twenty-five mongrels. No, thank you."

"But what about the dogs, then?"

He didn't mistake her concern. "They will be welcome at Knowle Castle, every last useless one of them. But I think Mrs. Gibb and your architect will be needing a place to set up housekeeping in the near future. Perhaps they'd be interested in staying here, with a few of the dogs. Fifteen? Twenty? Not Ajax, of course. Not the hero."

"Oh, I forgot—"

"Enough, sweetheart. Enough talking. You have to know that I love you more dearly than life, that I want to spend the rest of eternity making you happy."

"Even if I'm not a real lady and have no dowry?"

"You're the only lady I want, and what do you call those twenty-five dogs, if not a dowry?"

"In that case, I cannot think of anything I'd rather do than marry you, Corin, for I do love you with all my heart, you know. Even when I thought you arrogant and stuffy, I couldn't help falling in love with you. But I have to tell you—"

She didn't get to say much of anything else for a while except "ah." Or perhaps "hm." Corin was arrogantly making sure his love no longer thought him stuffy. He was sealing their engagement with every fiber of his being, with the promise of forever in his kiss.

It was much later when Corin brushed the tumbled curls off her forehead and asked, "What was it you wanted to say, Angel?"

"Say? Did I? Oh, yes, now I remember, Knolly. I love you. And your dog is going to have puppies."